The Bible promises that God will not suffer us to be tempted above what we are able to bear, but tonight I wonder. I quoted that passage to myself so often in my flight from captivity, especially the part about God providing a way of escape. But yesterday, the temptation to hate was so strong it nearly swallowed me up, until fear took its place, looming so large in my mind I thought surely I would faint. We're told to love our enemies, so I did what seemed right at the time, but now, as I listen to the labored breathing of a man who wears the uniform of my enemy, here in this place where we once hid those escaping oppression, I have to wonder. Did God send a smidgen of love as my escape from hate, or was this all my own misguided choice?

Heavenly Father, what have I done?

Prudence Willard
July 1863

SECRETS OF WAYFARERS INN

SECRETS OF
WAYFARERS INN

Moonlit Shadows

BECKY MELBY

New York

SECRETS OF
WAYFARERS INN

Moonlit Shadows

CHAPTER ONE

July 19, 1863
Near Buffington Island, Ohio

The deck of the steamboat *Katie Isabella* was slick with the blood of wounded men. Blue or gray, they bled and died the same.

Prudence Willard ducked behind a stack of feed sacks and removed her petticoat from beneath her dress. Methodically ripping the muslin into strips gave her a moment of distraction, precious seconds to shut out the chilling chorus of moans that engulfed her.

Stepping over bodies, she walked back to the stern and the man she'd left moments ago with a promise to return with bandages for the arm she knew he would lose.

Too late. All she could do for him now was close his powder-blackened eyelids and pocket the name he'd scribbled with charcoal on a scrap of paper. Lenora Alexander. The girl he'd told her about in weak but urgent words. The blue-eyed girl from Cooperstown, Pennsylvania, who waited for her Robert to return.

If ever she got home to ink and pen and clean paper, Prudence would write the letter.

"Water." The raspy voice came from behind her and became an echoed chant.

It was the one request she could fulfill.

She and seven others had answered the cry—"Nurses. We need nurses"—brought by a bedraggled young man on horseback, after Union gunboats and a thousand Union soldiers rose out of a thick dawn fog and surprised Brigadier General John Hunt Morgan and his band of Confederates. The boy told them about the *Katie Isabella*, now a makeshift hospital. "If you can dress a wound, please come."

Prudence could dress a wound. How many bruised and blistered feet had she bathed and bandaged? Feet that had traveled miles over dirt roads and frozen rivers…feet fleeing to freedom.

But this…This was different.

There weren't enough doctors or bandages or shots of whiskey in all of Ohio to kill the pain. There weren't enough mothers and wives and sisters willing to hold hands, wipe brows, and whisper prayers. There wasn't even enough room on the slippery deck of the *Katie Isabella* to hold more groaning, dying men.

She gave drink to five men, then stood and stretched out the spasm in her back. Fingers reached out and grasped the hem of her blood-stained skirt. "Water."

She looked down at the man in the filthy Confederate uniform. One bloody hand gripped the wide strap of a battered leather satchel. With a deep breath, she dropped back to her knees, slid her hand beneath the man's head, and held the tin cup to his blistered lips. *Love thy enemies.* "God is with thee. His love surrounds thee. He is ever pres—"

The words shriveled in her mouth. Her tongue refused to form the words. Her heart ceased its rapid beating and slammed against her ribs with a force that threatened to collapse her.

That scar. A perfectly straight line above his right brow. A neat scar…thanks to her mother's expert stitches.

Water sloshed from the cup and dropped to the deck. Her hand flew to her mouth to stifle the gasp.

Hatred blazed deep in her chest, spilling like liquid fire into her veins.

Dull eyes stared up at her.

He didn't know her. Didn't recognize her as a grown woman.

She was no longer the little girl whose back he'd flayed with his father's whip.

Janice Eastman set the phone on the polished surface of the front desk. To her credit, she did not slam the phone, nor did she scream at the top of her lungs or fall to the floor sobbing. With dry eyes, and only a teensy bit of panic fraying the edges of her voice, she simply looked up at her two best friends and business partners and said, "The caterer has gone bankrupt. We are ruined."

The expressions on the faces of the two other co-owners of Wayfarers Inn did not reflect any of the dread that was rising in Janice like last year's Ohio River flood.

"We'll find someone else." LuAnn Sherrill, the trio's official list-maker, pulled her phone out of the pocket of her cobbler's apron. "Let's look at our options."

Tess Wallace nodded, spikey auburn curls bobbing along with her optimism. "We still have just over a week to find someone, after all."

Janice looked around the space. The lobby side glowed red from tiny heart lights festooning pots of tall white branches. Red candles in silver holders decorated the fireplace mantel. On the café side, white tablecloths dotted with red hearts covered each table. Small antique bowls, some glass, some china, filled with candy conversation hearts, sat in the middle of each one, along with a tented card advertising the banquet.

They'd decided against a traditional red-themed sweetheart banquet. By a week from Saturday, the trees would sparkle with tiny white lights. The room would be awash in navy blue and white, hopefully giving the illusion of a moonlit night.

"Marietta Moonlight is scheduled for the Saturday after Valentine's Day. Do you know how many other sweetheart banquets, not to mention weddings, are scheduled for this week? How in the world are we going to—"

"We'll do it ourselves." The voice, filled with twice the conviction of the other two, came from the kitchen doorway.

"Winnie. No." Tears stung Janice's eyes as she watched Wayfarers Inn's head cook winding around small café tables to reach them. "You are not going to miss your niece's wedding, and we can't do it without you, and..."

"Nonsense. I can make a whole lot of the food ahead, and you three can cook better than pert near anybody I know. Now where's your faith, Miss Janice?"

Gone. Disappeared. Evaporated. Janice stared out at dark clouds spitting sleet onto the pewter surface of the river. Usually, the view from the front windows of the inn brought calm and an overwhelming sense of gratitude. How was it possible that less than two years since losing her husband and life purpose, she now belonged to what they'd dubbed the Inn Crowd, part owner of a beautiful historic B&B, in business with the two people who had been her closest friends for more than forty years? She took a deep breath. "You're right. We've gotten through worse. We'll figure this out."

Just as she felt the muscles at the corners of her mouth twitch into something resembling a smile, the front door opened and her son walked in. As always, the sight of her oldest chased the blues away. "Stuart! What are you doing here in the middle of the afternoon?"

Stuart hugged his two honorary aunts, giving them each a peck on the cheek. "Had a break between a hernia and an ear infection. Stacy said I should stop by and see if you need sandbags."

Stacy. Her daughter ran the medical clinic reception desk. Janice's heart warmed at the thought of Stacy looking out for her like this. They'd weathered a few stormy patches in their relationship, but the mother-daughter dance had been much more in sync lately.

Stuart held out a plastic grocery bag. "This was hanging on the door handle."

Janice walked over, took the bag, and pulled out a large heart-shaped candy box wrapped in clear plastic. A square yellow sticky note written in elegant backhand cursive on the top read, "Johnny, meet me at Austyn's at six." A hand-drawn heart dotted the *i* in six.

Tess peered over Janice's shoulder. "Do we have a reservation for a Johnny?"

"No. We have five guests arriving today, and not one of them is a Johnny." Janice looked closer at the box. *Putnam Chocolates.* She pictured the decadent assortment of chocolate-covered deliciousness inside as she set the box on the front desk.

"There's serious talk of flooding?" Tess rubbed her arms as she turned toward the window.

"Depends on how much rain they get upriver." Stuart took off his hat. It was dotted with melting blobs of icy snow. "I'm stocking up on sandbags for the clinic, and the inn is lower than we are."

A bright thought struck Janice, lifting her out of the gloomy mood filling the inn. "We can cancel the banquet because of the flood warnings!" No need to hunt for a caterer. They could simply reschedule the inn's first-ever sweetheart banquet to another time.

Tess didn't appear to share her enthusiasm. "We need the revenue from the event. We've sunk a lot of money into—"

The desk phone rang. LuAnn answered it. She listened for a moment without speaking, silver hair falling across her face as she slowly lowered her head.

Janice held her breath. Whatever it was, it wasn't good.

Finally, LuAnn spoke. "I'm so very sorry, Valerie. No, of course. Don't you worry about us. We'll have no trouble finding a replacement. You just take care of yourself."

"What? She's backing out? A week before Marietta Moonlight, and our keynote speaker is bailing on us?"

"She slipped on the ice and broke her femur."

"But...We can't..." Stuart's arm wrapped around her, and she leaned into him. "Couldn't she come in a wheelchair? No. I'm sorry. I know that's selfish, it's just that...First the caterer goes bankrupt and now this?"

Janice closed her eyes. What would Lawrence have told her to do? Have faith. Trust God to provide a way. How she missed his calming spirit.

"Ma. It'll be okay." Stuart eased her into a café chair.

Her boy. As steady as his father. So confident. It was what made him good at what he did. Doctor. Teacher. Speaker.

Speaker. "Stuart! You can do it!"

"I can do what?"

"You can be our speaker. You'll be perfect. You have such a gift."

"Ma. Nobody wants to listen to a coroner speak at a Valentine banquet. Though maybe I could rework some of my archived talks. I can see it now..." He arced his hand across an imaginary marquis. "'How to Find Love at a Crime Scene Investigation.' Or 'Keeping Romance Alive While Determining Time of Death.'"

Tess, LuAnn, and Winnie giggled. Janice wasn't feeling the humor. "You can talk about young love. Inspire people." *Drop down on one knee and propose to someone*. Okay, maybe that was a bit over the top.

Did her favorite son just roll his eyes at her?

"Seriously, Ma, you know I would, but I've got a deposition on the Monday after the banquet and—"

"Oh! That's right. Forget I asked." Though Stuart hadn't talked about it, other people had. Stuart would be testifying on behalf of a young father who'd been injured on the job. The Moore family desperately needed the compensation due him. Stuart hated these things. So much pressure. She couldn't ask him to do anything that would interfere with his preparation and focus.

The front door opened, ushering in snow-laced February air and a tall man. As he took off his hat and gloves, he smiled at each of them in turn. A wide, bright smile on a handsomely chiseled face.

Tess grinned back. "Welcome to Wayfarers Inn. Do you have a reservation?"

"Sure do. RJ Dulak." He set a leather bag on the floor, shrugged out of a backpack, and shed his water-spotted coat.

Janice looked away from the man as Stuart patted her shoulder. "Gotta run. We'll talk." He dropped a quick kiss on top of her head and left.

Back to work. Janice rose to her feet and squared her shoulders. It was her turn to man the front desk. One of her mother's favorite sayings popped into her head. *Do the thing at hand.* She smiled at the man as she stepped behind the desk. "You're with the Love Is conference, right?" She'd looked at the conference schedule online. Geared toward college-age and older singles, the conference name came from 1 Corinthians 13:4-5. "We're so happy you chose Marietta." Though she had no clue why several of the conference organizers had chosen to stay at the inn rather than the Oakshire Hotel, the Love Is venue. She introduced herself and told him a bit about the history of the inn. "Will all of the rooms be on the same card?"

"No. Someday, I hope. This is our fourth year, and we don't have the funds yet. Our people volunteer their time and cover their own expenses."

"Sacrificial serving." Janice hoped he heard the admiration in her voice. She swiped his credit card and got his signature. "Dulak. That's French for 'of the lake,' right? Like Lancelot Dulak in *Camelot*?" She imagined him clunking across the wood floor in full medieval armor.

RJ smiled a slightly strained smile. "Not quite the same spelling. Dulak is Polish. It means 'lives by a quince tree.'"

"Oh." What else could one say?

He tapped the box of chocolates. "Someone's lucky."

"If only we knew who that someone was."

He arched his right brow.

"We don't have a Johnny staying here. The only Johnny I know is a three-year-old boy who comes into the café with his grandma. We've got ourselves a bit of a romantic mystery."

"Interesting."

She held out his room key.

He stared down at the skeleton key with the metal tag dangling from the end. "Quaint."

"Our doors and keys are all original to the inn."

His jaw unhinged, then slowly closed.

"We keep them in a locked drawer."

He nodded slowly. "I design online security systems, but I have connections with people who could offer some on-site suggestions." He pulled a business card from the nicked-up leather bag.

Sekureco. Interesting company name. "Se-*cure*-e-ko. Did I pronounce it right?"

"Almost. Se-cu-*ray*-so. It's Esperanto for 'security.'"

"Very international."

"I thought a Polish name would be cool. Turns out 'security' in Polish is *bezpieczeństwo*."

Janice laughed. "Not so user friendly."

RJ nodded. "Hey, are there safes in the rooms?"

"No, but you have the only key to your room, and I assure you, the locks and the doors are very solid and secure. We have a safe in the office, if you'd like us to lock something up for you."

He considered this. "I'll keep that in mind. Thank you."

The phone rang and she picked it up, saying to RJ, "Excuse me for a moment, please."

"Wayfarers Inn, this is Janice speaking. How may I help you?"

"This is Maybelline Rector."

A deep inhale shored her up for whatever was to follow. Never could be sure that a call from the director of the Marietta Underground Railroad Museum, the woman who'd once thought the Wayfarers Inn building should be hers, would go smoothly. "What can I do for you, Maybelline?"

"I was just wondering if you'd added anything new to your collection of things you've found at the inn. I'm always referring people to you, and artifacts are always a draw."

Strange little lady. Other than the lantern next to the front door and a few pieces of chipped china, most of the historical treasures they'd uncovered during renovations were on display at the Historical Society or the Campus Martius Museum. "Nothing new, Maybelline."

"Well, then, you'll let me know if you find anything, won't you?"

"Of course." She said goodbye and turned her focus back to their guest. She gave him a quick tour of the main floor and led him to the elevator. Whoever had made the reservations for the Love Is board of directors had specifically requested Woodsmoke and Pine on the third floor for RJ. It was the inn's only blatantly masculine room.

Watching guests' reactions when they first opened the door to their room was one of Janice's favorite parts of owning a B&B. RJ did not disappoint. "Very nice."

The king four-poster bed with its plaid comforter, the old-English hunting scenes framed on the wall, and the low fire in the brick fireplace offered a warm welcome. Janice pointed at a basket of fruit and bottled water, then handed him a list of local restaurants. "I imagine your group already has a plan, but if not, you shouldn't need a reservation tonight."

RJ ran his finger down the list. "Thank you." A wistful smile touched his lips. "I think I know exactly where I'm having dinner tonight."

"Enjoy." She stepped out of the room, closing the door behind her, satisfied that the first of their weekend guests was well taken care of.

Finished with their kitchen cleanup, Tess and LuAnn headed upstairs to relax, and Winnie left for home. Their second guest arrived about five thirty, just as the sun was setting, fingers of orange clawing at the dark clouds as if closing the shades on Marietta. A man wearing a shin-length camel coat stepped in, shaking wet snow from his short blond hair. Like RJ, he appeared to be in his late twenties or early thirties.

Before she had time to greet him, RJ bounded down the steps. "Cam!" Their back-slaps resounded off the pressed-tin ceiling.

Cameron Truman. His name had sounded familiar when the reservation was made, so she'd looked him up online. Their most recent guest was a psychologist with a popular blog.

"Have any trouble?" RJ asked. "Heard there were some flooded roads up by you."

"I came into town last night. Stayed with a friend."

Janice took Cameron's credit card. "We have you in Moonlight and Snowflakes."

"Interesting name." Cameron's broad smile glinted with amusement.

"I'm afraid the room names were created by three women who just weren't thinking of their male guests at the time. We are careful who we put in Lily and Lace, however."

RJ gave him an elbow jab. "Good test of your masculinity. If a guy can handle telling his buddies he's staying in Lily and Lace, he must be secure in his manhood."

The edge of a white gauze bandage showed beneath the cuff of Cameron's coat as he picked up a pen. He tugged his sleeve down before signing the charge slip.

Cameron and RJ wandered over to the coffeepots Janice pointed out.

Moments later, a pale, thin man with bangs nearly covering his eyes held an umbrella and the door for a woman in a short black coat and over-the-knee black boots. Janice checked them in. Without making eye contact, Noah Nichols introduced himself as the person in charge of sound and lighting for Love Is.

Everything about the woman, Natalie Hemmingway, exuded polished perfection, from her runway-straight posture to bright red lacquered nails with fanciful swirls of gold.

RJ stood and strode toward them. "Hey, Noah." He glanced at the woman. "Natalie?"

"RJ?"

"We finally meet in person." RJ extended his hand. They chatted for a moment, and then he told them he was on his way out to dinner, and he'd see them when he got back. "We're still waiting on Franny," he added.

Janice took one of Natalie's bags. "You're on the second floor."

Natalie touched the newel post at the base of the stairs. "I've driven past before but never been inside."

"You're a local?"

"I live in Columbus, but I have family here. They recommended the inn. I thought it would be nice for some of us to stay off-site. Change of scenery, you know."

"I fully understand." Janice pointed toward the stairs. "My two co-owners and I live on the fourth floor."

"Then you do get it. Does one of you have to be here at all times?"

"If not us, then one of our staff. The café opens for breakfast at eight and closes at two after lunch. In the evening, as long as someone is here to answer the phone and take care of anything that might come up, the rest of us are free."

They stopped at Lily and Lace. Natalie turned the key, then gave the expected "Ohhhhh" as she walked ahead of

Janice into the room and took in the watercolor of a bouquet of lilies of the valley matted with antique lace hanging above the four-poster bed. Her gaze traveled to the pale green and cream bedspread. "Is there a safe?"

Popular question. "There's one in our office."

Natalie walked to the window and parted the drapes, nodding more to herself than Janice. "This will...be fine." Her voice trailed off to almost a whisper. "Thank you."

Janice went back downstairs and settled into the antique swivel chair in the tiny office behind the front desk. She whispered a short but desperate prayer before beginning an internet search for a local caterer.

She was on the phone to Max's Catering when she heard a floorboard creak outside the office door. After hanging up, she opened the door, looking for an excuse to get out of making the calls. "Tess? Lu?" If one of them had come down in search of ice cream, it would only be polite for her to join them. She walked into the kitchen. No one in sight. Lawrence had always chided her for her overactive imagination. Shaking her head, she went back to the office. Two more calls and two more "I'm sorries" later, the front door opened.

Janice stepped out of the office. Their final guest for the evening stood at the door.

"You must be Franny Simon." Janice rushed to the door to take a heavily dripping umbrella.

"What service." The young woman, who couldn't be far past her teens, slid her hood back, releasing a jumbled mass of auburn curls. "But I'm not Franny." She held out her hand. "Brin

McLoughlin. I'm from Boston. I'm just here to look around. I don't need a room." She turned her head slowly from right to left, then up to the ceiling. "Can't believe I'm actually here."

It wasn't unusual for tourists to stop by just to see the inn, though it was a little odd for someone to show up alone, after dark, in such inclement weather. "Have a look around. We have a few empty guest rooms I can show you after you've seen the main floor. Would you like some coffee or hot chocolate while you look?"

"I'd love some hot chocolate. Thank you."

Janice walked over to the coffee bar in the café and added two hot chocolate packets to a cup of hot water, then stirred them in. She carried the cup to Brin, who stood in the corner of the lobby they called the library, looking at a stack of games. Janice handed her the cup. "What brings you to Marietta?"

"I'm going to a conference for singles at the Oakshire Hotel, but to be honest, I came because of this place. And a time capsule."

Janice narrowed her eyes. "A time—" The door chime announced RJ's return. He strode past them, his face a thundercloud. Maybe he had a bad experience at dinner? Janice shrugged and turned back to Brin. "You were saying something about a time capsule?"

Brin gave a nervous laugh. "Oh, I-I just meant in a place like this, surely there's all kinds of old things to look at—you know, antiques, old newspaper articles, that kind—"

She was interrupted by the sound of rapid footsteps coming down the stairs. RJ burst off the bottom step, wild-eyed. "Someone's been in my room, and my bag is missing!"

CHAPTER TWO

J anice stared at RJ. She couldn't get her brain to work.
"You're sure? You didn't just misplace it in the room?"

RJ looked at her like she had two heads. "Do you think I
accidentally put it in the bathtub or something? Of course I'm
sure. The question is, who took it?"

The door opened. A young woman, blonde hair plastered
against her head, pulling two wheeled cases behind her. Janice
couldn't tell for sure from across the room, but she looked like
she was upset.

RJ hurried to her. "Fran. What happened?"

"Flat tire up by Caldwell."

He put his hands on his hips. "Why didn't you call?"

Janice studied body language. The woman shrugged, then
looked beyond RJ to Tess and LuAnn, who were coming down
the stairs.

Tess introduced herself and LuAnn. "Let's get you checked
in as quickly as possible, so you can get to your room and
change."

Franny Simon. Their final guest for the day. Watching RJ
gave more clues than watching her. The two had a history, for
sure, but their greeting seemed chillier than the icy rain assail-
ing the windows.

RJ turned from Franny back to Janice. "What are you going to do about my missing bag? Even if you call the police, whoever took it could be long gone by now."

LuAnn gasped. "Your bag is missing? Janice, did you see anyone besides our guests come in the inn?"

Janice shook her head. "I didn't see anyone, but I heard a noise about thirty minutes ago. I thought it must have been you or Tess."

Franny put up her hand to get their attention. "I don't know if this has anything to do with RJ's missing bag, but I saw a guy hanging around across the road from the inn when I came in. He was behind a tree, smoking. Looked like he was waiting for something or someone."

RJ ran to the door and yanked it open.

"You'll freeze to death out—" Tess's voice was swallowed by the wind as RJ ran out.

Then he yelled, "Hey, you!"

LuAnn grabbed something from behind the front desk. "Here. Put this on." She shoved a folded rain poncho at Janice. LuAnn slipped one over her head and went to the front door, reaching for the handle.

"Lu! Stop!" Janice frantically put her poncho on. "This is crazy. I would have heard if someone had come in. There's no way—"

"It's happened before," LuAnn called over her shoulder as she ran out. Brin was right behind her.

"LuAnn, come on. What if the person has a gun?" What if it wasn't just one person but a whole gang? In spite of her misgivings, Janice followed the two women out the door, across slippery cobblestones, and down the grassy bank to the sidewalk and then the river.

The sound of a boat motor grew fainter as the outline of a fishing boat disappeared into the darkness. Janice could barely make out the white ripples of the wake.

RJ was yelling and waving his arms, making himself a perfect target. "Stop! We'll find you! The police are on their way!"

"Are they?" Janice scrambled to a stop next to him.

"No."

"Did you see anything?"

"Guy in black. He had his back to me the whole time." RJ stepped to the edge of the water.

"What are you doing? That water is deeper than you think. See the boats?" Janice gestured toward two more fishing vessels docked about fifty yards away. "And it's cold enough to stop your heart. Once hypothermia sets in it's only a matter of time before—"

"Something fell out of the boat. When the guy got in." He lunged at what appeared to be a branch floating in the water, but the current swept it away from his grasp. Janice ran ahead of him down the riverbank. Grabbing onto a sapling, she shoved one foot out and stopped the branch. RJ caught up with her just as the sapling cracked. Her feet went out from under her, and she slid up to her waist into the frigid water, hanging desperately onto the broken sapling now above her head.

RJ swooped down. In one fluid motion he scooped up the stick and her.

"You saved the day, ma'am." RJ laughed nervously.

"I th-think you're the h-hero here." Janice breathed fast and loud through clenched teeth.

"We've got her." LuAnn and Brin grabbed her arms. "Let's get you inside. Fast." LuAnn almost lifted her off her feet as they propelled her to the inn.

RJ led the way, clutching what he was probably sure was evidence.

Janice wasn't going to argue that they wouldn't be able to retrieve fingerprints from a wet branch. Let him carry the silly stick. Let him do whatever he wanted. He'd just saved her from a cold, watery grave.

"Wow. Talk about adventure." Brin fairly vibrated with excitement.

Tess held the door open. "By the fire. Put her by the fire."

Janice stopped, pulling away from her *paracletes*. It was one of Lawrence's favorite words. In Greek, it meant "helper" or, the longer version Lawrence preferred, "one who comes alongside." "I'm fine. Thank you." She appreciated their assistance, but she didn't need to be *put* by the fire like a stack of kindling.

She took a step. And winced. Her feet felt like ice blocks. How could that happen so quickly? Her *comealongsiders* eased her into a wingback chair. Tess grabbed a blanket and threw it around Janice's shoulders, then dropped to her knees and pulled off Janice's shoes and socks. For some unexplained reason, tears stung Janice's eyes. "Very Jesus-like," she whispered.

Tess smiled. "Like you putting ice packs on my ankle every hour when I twisted it, right? It's what we do."

It's what we do. How could she have survived the past two years without these women?

"It's part of a fishing pole." RJ sat in the chair across from Janice. LuAnn covered his legs with a blanket and ordered him to remove his wet shoes.

"What's the weird thing on the end? Can I move this lamp?" Not waiting for an answer, Brin picked up a floor lamp and positioned it next to RJ. "It's a fish! A dead, petrified fish!"

RJ put his hand under the thing that dangled from the end of the broken pole. "It's a wooden lure." He looked around. "Hey, where did Franny go?"

Tess looked up from drying Janice's feet. "I got her checked in and up to her room. She needed a hot shower ASAP."

Janice tried to get up, but Tess pressed her down again. "Did one of you come down after everyone left tonight?" Janice looked from LuAnn to Tess. "I heard one of the floorboards creak when I was in the office, but there was no one around when I looked."

"Nope."

"Not me."

Brin's eyebrows shot above heavy-rimmed square glasses. "Creepy."

RJ broke the uneasy silence that followed by lifting the lure to the light again and saying, "I think it's hand carved." He pulled a jackknife out of his pocket and used minuscule scissors to snip the tangled fishing line. He set the pole on the floor and lifted the lure to the light. From Janice's vantage point, it did indeed look like a petrified fish about as long as RJ's hand.

Brin leaned closer. "Kind of sloppy carving."

RJ nodded. "My guess is somebody made it to be functional, not pretty." He turned it over slowly. "A little red paint on the top fin. Can't tell if that's all there was or if the whole thing was painted originally."

"Well, that gives us something to go on as we open the investigation." Tess bent the top of the gooseneck lamp.

"Investigation? You're cops?" RJ's face contorted in an expression of incredulity.

"No. We're..." Janice hesitated, partly because of the shock of the warm water LuAnn was pouring around her feet, partly because she didn't really have an answer. What were they? They'd solved eight mysteries in the same number of months. What did that make them? "We're... good at this."

Tess took a chair. "Was there anything valuable in the bag?"

Janice cringed, not wanting to hear the answer. Of course there was. He wouldn't have been concerned about security if it contained his clean socks for the week.

RJ's shoulders slumped. "A money bag. Change for our merchandise table, among other things. About eight hundred dollars."

Janice sighed. "We need to call the police."

"Could we... wait a bit before we involve them?" The pleading in RJ's eyes didn't make sense. He seemed more afraid than angry. Afraid of what? "And, could we not tell the others?"

Janice looked at Tess and LuAnn. After a moment, both nodded. "I guess that's your call," Tess said.

"Thank you." RJ sighed in relief. "I just don't want to spoil the conference before it even starts."

They sat in silence. Janice imagined they were all processing what had just happened. She'd started her day by joyfully thanking God for plans falling perfectly in place. Marietta Moonlight had been her idea. Their first annual sweetheart banquet, a way to showcase the inn, raise a bit of needed money, and bless their guests. She saw it as a way to live out their mission statement, to preach the Gospel in a way that wasn't at all preachy. Tess and LuAnn had resisted. They didn't have the extra cash to put into it. They'd never done anything on this scale before. What if it failed? What if no one came? But they'd finally given in when Janice said she'd shoulder the majority of the responsibility. As a pastor's wife for almost forty years, she'd planned, cooked for, and served at more dinners than she could count on fingers, toes, and eyelashes. She could do this.

And all had gone well. Until today. They'd sold all of the tickets to Marietta Moonlight. Decorations had arrived yesterday—shimmering glitter stars they would hang from invisible thread. Silver candles and silver holders. Little crystal stars and moons to scatter across dark blue tablecloths. Guests were swooning over their menu and eager to hear their guest speaker. Well-known relationship author Valerie Gibson had been born and raised in Marietta, baptized and married by Pastor Lawrence Eastman.

This morning, God had been in His heaven, and all was right with the world.

Now, God was still in His heaven and Janice knew, from years of trusting in the dark, all was still right with His big plan for the world.

But it sure didn't feel like it at the moment.

She bent down and picked up the fishing pole. Near the broken end, two letters were carved into the wood. *WW.* "Hey people, I think I found a clue."

Tess pulled out a café chair for Janice, and LuAnn tucked a blanket around her shoulders. Janice had taken a hot shower and put on fleece-lined jeans and a cable-knit sweater. She was warm and dry and no longer in need of hovering handmaids.

RJ walked down the stairs, showered and changed, but still as distraught-looking as when he'd trudged up to his room an hour ago.

"Where is everyone? I heard the door." Janice ran her fingers through hair she'd blow-dried but nothing else. "Where did Brin go?"

Tess took three cups from behind the café counter. "She left. Said she'd be back tomorrow. I saw the others leave about six."

RJ lowered himself into a chair. "Cameron told me earlier he'd ask whoever got here in time to go out for supper with him and then for coffee afterwards."

"Did Brin say anything more?" Janice ran her finger along the curved handle of a red stoneware mug. "Does anyone have any ideas about the fishing pole and lure?"

"No clue." LuAnn set a pot of hot tea and two additional mugs on the table. "I called Brad."

"Of course you did," Tess said sweetly, winking at Janice.

LuAnn rolled her eyes. "Stop. It's not...I...Brad and I are—"

"Just friends." Janice singsonged in harmony with Tess and laughed again.

The friendship between LuAnn and Bradley Grimes, the Realtor who had first shown them the inn, seemed to be on the verge of progressing to something deeper. She had, after all, accepted his invitation to accompany him to Marietta Moonlight. The urge to tease was nearly irresistible.

LuAnn pretended to ignore them. "Irene knows all the fishermen. He's on his way over, and he's bringing her along."

It didn't surprise Janice to learn Bradley's elderly relative, the diminutive eighty-eight-year-old woman with the silvery hair and glasses too large for her face, was friends with fishermen. Irene Bickerton Martin was as spunky as they came. "Wouldn't shock any of us if we found out Aunt Irene had captained a sternwheeler back in her day."

RJ took a chair in front of the mug of coffee Winnie had poured for him and set the wooden lure on the table. "I washed it and examined every inch under good light. Can't see any identifying marks." He rubbed the back of his neck and sighed.

Brad opened the door and held it as Irene, all four-foot-eight of her, stepped under his arm.

"We've only got a few minutes," she said. "I have to get home to help Thelma get ready for bed. She could do so much more than she thinks she can if she'd just stop thinking of herself as an old lady. Ninety-four is nothing these days. I just read an article saying that in 2040 the average life expectancy could be a hundred and twenty."

"Chamomile tea, Irene?" LuAnn filled a mug and pointed to a chair. They'd all learned from watching Winnie, who'd worked for the Bickerton sisters for decades and knew the exact balance of patience and firmness to use with each.

Irene eased into a chair. "Fishermen, huh? Tell me what you know and what you want to know."

RJ introduced himself and handed the lure to Irene. LuAnn set the pole, initials showing, next to the lure.

"Oh, that's an easy one. I was hoping I could be part of solving a big mystery. You ladies have all the luck, chasing one perp after another."

"Easy?" Janice hugged her teacup and attempted Winnie's tone of voice to end the rabbit trail.

"Sure. Albert Frankenmeyer. Everyone called him Franky. Funny old guy. He could spin a yarn longer than a Texas mile, they used to say. Made all his own lures. 'Don't trust anything store-bought,' he said. I can still hear him saying, 'What's some city kid workin' in a factory know about jiggin' for walleye or haulin' in a forty-pound muskie?'"

Tess wrinkled her nose. "That all sounds very past tense, Irene."

"Franky passed away about three weeks ago. Made it to eighty-four. He was still fishing last year when he had his stroke."

Janice sighed in unison with the three others in the room. "Did he sell his lures, or give them away?"

"No. Not even to friends. Except one. Stingy old guy."

"What happened to the lures then? Who would have them now? Kids, grandkids?"

"Franky never married. He was close once. Wilma Westlake." She tapped the *WW* on the fishing pole with the tip of her finger. "Wilma loved him something fierce, but she couldn't stand the smell."

Brad laughed. "Of the fish?"

"Of Franky. Didn't believe in bathing much. Soap smell scared the fish away, he said."

"So... the lures," Janice prompted. "What would have happened to them?"

"Can't imagine there would have been many of them. He'd carve one when he lost one. Never cared much about getting them perfect. 'Fish cain't see more'n a few inches in that murky water,' he said. He did like pretty colors, though. He painted a red and silver one just for Wilma. She's still got that thing. Took it with her to the nursing home. Now that's true love, don't you think?"

"Aunt Irene." Brad put his hand on her shoulder. "Do you know any way we could find out who this one belonged to?"

"Your best chance would be Axel Barrett. Grisly old guy. Knows everything about everybody, but I wouldn't trust him any farther than I could throw him."

"Why's that?"

"That man will do anything for a buck. Always just one wrong move ahead of the law. I've heard rumor he's changed, had a come-to-Jesus moment some say, but I'm not sure I believe it. He's not the guy you want to talk to."

"Actually..." Tess tapped a fingertip on her chin. "He's exactly the guy we want to talk to."

July 19, 1863

Tabitha Post leaned against a railing on the port side of the boiler deck, wiping perspiration from her face with a dirty handkerchief. "Did thee hear? The boat's moving upriver at dusk."

Prudence closed her eyes. The metal railing bit into her back as she pressed against it. She'd thought she'd have longer to make her decision.

"Is thee staying on or going home, Pru?"

Home. Oh, how she longed to fall into Jason's arms, to bury her face in Moses's curls and smell nothing but her son's sweet scent. To wake in the morning to a peach-tinged dawn and fresh-cooked coffee.

"Tabitha?" Prudence said the name with caution. What she was about to ask could cost her life.

"Yes?"

"I have watched thee over the years." She turned to face the woman, whom she'd known since she was twelve, since a kind Quaker family took in a young Melungeon runaway named Euphemia Collins and renamed her Prudence to protect her, and gave her their last name to let her know she belonged. Tabitha, daughter of a bishop and newly widowed, was two years older and had always treated Prudence with nothing but kindness. She could be trusted, couldn't she? "Thee is a woman of wisdom."

"I sense this is leading to a question. What troubles thee, Pru, in particular?"

"The forty-fourth verse of the fifth chapter of the book of Matthew."

Tabitha nodded, slow and thoughtful. "Thee is wondering how to love and pray for the men who caused this."

"M-more specific." Prudence knit her hands together. "One. One man."

Turning to give her full attention, Tabitha touched Prudence's sleeve. "Go on."

"The son of the man who…" She wrung her hands and struggled to breathe through the tightness in her throat. "Bought my parents and me at auction in Fredricksburg when I was eight. He's here."

Tabitha's gray eyes widened. "Here on the boat?" she whispered.

Prudence nodded. "I don't know how badly injured. His uniform is so dirty and tattered the color is…camouflaged. If they find out he's a—"

"Shh." Tabitha glanced toward the officer who passed them. "They will imprison him. Or worse."

"Yes."

Tabitha nodded. "Like hundreds of other men taken captive."

"Yes." Prudence hardly recognized her voice, hoarse and tight and barely above a whisper.

"But this is different because thee knows his name."

Prudence unclasped her hands and gripped the top rail. "He was just a boy when I knew him, sixteen, maybe, when I left. A conflicted soul. Kind to us one moment..." She thought back to the charcoal pictures Ira Fitzhugh had drawn to entertain the slave children. "But as soon as his father or mother walked into sight he—" She winced, feeling the lash tearing her skin all over again.

"Did what he had to do," Tabitha finished.

"What?"

"He may have had no more choice than thee."

CHAPTER THREE

Even before she opened her eyes, a strange mixture of dread and anticipation filled Janice. She'd gone to bed wondering what kind of liability the inn had for a guest's stolen property and hadn't dreamed about any answers. She replayed RJ's response when they'd wanted to call the police. The only reason she could come up with was that he suspected someone he knew—someone he wanted to protect. Unless...there was something other than money in the bag, something he didn't want anyone to know about.

Brad and Irene had left with a promise to meet them in the morning at the Busy Bee, a small café in the Harmar district. Situated on the west side of the Muskingum River, the café had been in operation since before Janice was born. Irene was sure they would find the infamous Axel there. "Used to be they'd be there by five," she'd said, "but old bones, including mine, don't get out of bed as early. And they won't be fishing in this weather. He'll probably hang out at the Bee all morning."

Irene had only reluctantly agreed to go with them. Though it was true they needed her to identify the man, it had also seemed apparent Brad wanted her along as security. Who would hurt a sweet little old lady? But that didn't exempt the people with her from danger.

Maybe it was that hint of danger that caused the tingle of excited anticipation. Janice had led a nice, safe, but relatively dull life until the past eight months. Life at Wayfarers Inn was anything but dull.

Janice swung her feet out of bed and headed for the bathroom. How necessary was it to shower before meeting with men who gutted fish for a living? She glanced out the window. From her side of the inn, she couldn't see the sunrise, but this morning the underside of heavy, rain-laden clouds appeared to have been spray-painted gold.

She savored the beauty, knowing the rain would start again before noon. A year ago, Marietta had battled flooding. There were signs, before the renovation, of water in the basement of the inn. It was a risk they knew they were taking when they bought a place on the river.

Half an hour later, showered and dressed, she sat in a chair by the window and opened her daily devotional book. "I know You've got this all figured out, Lord, but I could use a little encouragement here." For almost four decades she'd depended on Lawrence for almost everything. Learning a measure of independence at this stage of life, along with daily waves of grief that came without warning, was taxing. She looked down at the verse on the top of the page and smiled as she read, "Weeping may stay for the night, but rejoicing comes in the morning."

Still smiling, she began to pray…for family, friends, guests…and fishermen. And then she went downstairs to her favorite part of owning a B&B—serving breakfast to their guests and customers.

Winnie was already taking a pan of her famous orange rolls out of the oven when Janice walked into the kitchen. "Smells scrumptious." She took a bowl out of the cupboard to start making the frosting. She loved how they'd all so naturally fallen into different roles. Sauces, gravies, and frostings were her specialty, though none of them did any of the cooking quite as well as Winnie. Janice took an orange from the fruit bowl and began zesting it. "Did you hear what happened last night?"

"Haven't talked to anyone since I got here. Did you find Johnny?"

The heart box. With all that had happened last night, she hadn't given it another thought. She filled Winnie in on the evening's excitement.

"Oh my." Winnie took off her oven mitts and rested her hands on her hips. "What'd the police say?"

"RJ didn't want us to call them." Janice opened the powdered sugar canister.

"You think he knows who took his bag?"

"I think he's afraid he knows." Janice looked up as Tess walked in.

"RJ wants to talk to us," Tess said. "Sorry, Winnie. We'll make it short."

Winnie waved her off with a wooden spoon. "I do love sharing the kitchen with you three, but I can handle things until the café opens. Go catch the bad guy."

LuAnn was already in the office. Janice, Tess, and RJ wedged in and closed the door.

RJ played with a key fob, shifting it from one hand to the other. "I should have said something yesterday when I read the note on that candy box..." He slid the fob into his shirt pocket. "My full name is Reginald Jonasz Dulak. Polish, of course. For obvious reasons, I went by Johnny until after college. Only one person here knows me by Johnny."

Janice resisted a maternal pat on his shoulder. "Franny?"

RJ nodded. "We were almost engaged."

"What happened?" Tess's voice was soft, inviting but not pressing.

"We met when we were both coming out of a dark place in our lives. She and I started Love Is, kind of as therapy for ourselves while wanting to reach out to others. Franny makes jewelry. She has a whole line based on the love chapter in First Corinthians. And she's a gifted speaker. It all just dovetailed. We were great partners, business and otherwise. All went well until I proposed. I realize now she was scared for a lot of other reasons, but she said she wasn't ready to settle down. She wanted to travel and experience adventure.

"I tried to convince her that the two things don't have to be mutually exclusive. Life doesn't end with marriage, right?" He searched the faces in the room. Of course, he had no way of knowing that none of the women, for various reasons, were currently married.

Janice glanced at Tess. They'd had many long talks about the life-changing impact of becoming a widow. Had they been honest, they would each have given RJ a different answer to his question. For Tess, the color drained out of her life when Jeffrey died. For Janice, though she grieved the loss of Lawrence's solid presence, she couldn't ignore the fact that her first taste of a life of adventure had come last year in June—the day they peered through the dusty windows of the abandoned inn.

"Absolutely not." Oddly, it was LuAnn who answered RJ. LuAnn, who hadn't yet had the chance to say "I do."

"Anyway, I was sure the message on the candy box was for me. This is the first time we've seen each other since we broke up. We're trying to stay business partners. As you can imagine, it's been tough. I had this silly hope she'd changed her mind, but she never showed. When I saw her last night…she looked so sad. It makes me afraid she…" He left the statement unfinished.

LuAnn touched his sleeve. "Franny wasn't here when your bag went missing."

"I know, but…what if she…"

"Wanted to get you away from here so someone could take your bag?" Janice surprised herself for saying out loud what had only been floating around the edges of her consciousness.

"Yes." RJ closed his eyes for a moment. The sound of his sigh echoed off the walls.

"Was it her handwriting?" LuAnn asked.

"I don't think so. We mostly just text or message each other, and she usually prints if she has to write something, but she's artsy. That little heart on the *i* looked like something she would do. Maybe she could write like that if she wanted to disguise her handwriting. I don't know."

Tess shook her head. "Innocent until proven guilty. It seems clear someone wanted to distract you, but there's no need to put Franny ahead of anyone else until if and when we have some concrete evidence. She wasn't even here. And what motivation would she have for stealing your bag? It wasn't all that much money. Would she do it to get back at you?"

"No. But she might…" Again, he stopped before expressing whatever was on his mind.

Janice felt RJ's angst as if it were a separate entity in the room. "It might be awkward for you, but it seems like the easiest thing would be to just ask her if she left the box for you."

"I know. I rehearsed it so many times during the night, but she seems so fragile right now. If she had someone deliver it and then changed her mind, wouldn't it be better for her if I just pretend I never got it?"

"Well…" Janice softened her voice to soften the message, "I've learned from past experience that honesty is the only course of action that doesn't lead to regret."

Janice had suggested a few weeks ago that they reserve the long harvest table in the center of the café for their paying guests at breakfast. The Love Is board held hands as RJ prayed over the food, the inn staff, and the conference setup they would tackle today. They raved over Winnie's orange rolls and andouille sausage egg bake between talk of microphones, merchandise arrangements, seating, and boxed lunches. And the Inn Crowd watched.

Franny seemed more energized this morning. Her hair, much lighter than it had looked when it was wet, hung in a long braid down the middle of her back. She wore black pants and a teal sweater with a cowl neck. Minimal makeup allowed the freckles that speckled her nose to show. In shiny silver cursive, the word *PEACE* hung from a silver chain around her neck. Janice filled Franny's coffee cup and bent to admire the necklace. "One of your own creations?"

"Yes. How did you know?"

"RJ mentioned you had a jewelry line."

Franny's cheeks pinked. "Yes." She picked up a roll. "These are so good."

"Thank you. We'll bring out our secret weapon so you can all meet her." Janice turned to fill Cameron's cup, giving Franny time to let her face cool to a normal color.

"Hope you three had a good time in our fair city last night. Not a whole lot to do on a weeknight in the middle of winter." Janice set the sugar packets closer to Cameron, having noticed his liberal use of them with his first cup.

"We had fun." Cameron tugged on his right sleeve. "Had some massive burgers at the Boat House, then Noah and I drove around a while, getting to know the town. Ended up at the Galley for cheesecake."

Natalie lifted her cup. "I spent half my evening getting to know your Walmart. You'd think I'd never traveled before, considering everything I forgot."

Janice smiled. "I always forget something." Though she found it hard to believe the woman who looked so completely put-together in skinny jeans, gray suede boots, and a black smock-topped blouse wasn't a meticulous packer.

Noah held his hand over his cup without looking up at her. But he wasn't looking down. His gaze was glued on Natalie. Janice tried to read his expression. A crush, maybe.

Whether clueless or deliberate, Natalie Hemmingway appeared oblivious to the attention.

CHAPTER FOUR

Y ep. Franky was somethin'."
This observation was made by a weathered man with white-streaked hair pulled back in a ponytail, fastened with a strip of leather decorated with what appeared to Janice to be a salmon fishing fly, hopefully without the hook. Bright orange feathers, tipped with purple. It was hard to determine Axel Barrett's age, but Janice guessed he had to be in his late seventies. How had she lived here all her life and missed *this* character?

Brad, Irene, RJ, and Janice sat at a dark wood table drinking coffee from heavy white mugs with the infamous Axel Barrett. In front of Axel sat a cinnamon roll the size of a Frisbee. Three other men, decades younger than Axel, sat on swivel stools with their backs against the counter. They'd introduced themselves as Stick, Raven, and Bobber. Evidently nicknames were a prerequisite to successful fishing.

Janice took in the feel, and smell, of the Busy Bee. She hadn't been here in years. The words circling the bee logo on the front window read "Fresh ingredients from local farms. Since 1944." Mint-green walls were crowded with framed photographs of men, women, and fish, some dating back a century or more. Square green and gold tiles gave the feel of stepping back in time.

She could easily picture it decades ago, when the men in front of her fished for a living rather than a pastime—a haze of pipe smoke hovering around their heads, the clamor of braggadocious men nearing a crescendo with each can-you-top-this story. It was the kind of place a regular could walk into and say, "I'll have the usual."

The ambiance brought Janice back to memories of fishing with her father when she was young. Sitting in their rowboat early on a Friday evening, they'd watch the bigger boats returning from a day on the river. The fishermen's laughter floated across the river, and Janice and her father would catch bits and pieces of their stories. Her father, who spent five days a week behind a desk, always had a wistful look in his eyes as he listened. On one such night, after reading *Moby Dick*, she'd asked him if he'd rather be a ship's captain on the ocean than be a dad. His laugh had carried like the fishermen's. "Not in my wildest dreams, Peaches. Raising you is all the adventure I've ever wanted."

The man with the unkempt ponytail didn't remind her at all of the men her father chatted easily with as they docked their little boat and carried their catch onto shore.

RJ handed the wooden lure and the piece of pole to Axel.

Broom reached out with a long, skinny arm and took the pole. As he ran his finger across the *WW* carved into it, Janice was sure she saw a flash of panic. He glanced at Axel, who answered with an almost imperceptible shake of his head.

"That's his work, all right," Axel said. Not a trace of concern edged his voice. "Know how you can tell?" He turned the fish on its left side. "See these Xs?" He placed a stained fingernail on a row of slash marks. "Look close."

Janice blinked to sharpen her vision. But it was Irene, with her weak-looking eyes behind giant glasses, who let out a hoot before the others caught on.

"*WW*. Wilma Westlake. That's just plain sweet."

Janice still couldn't see it. Unlike the letters on the fishing pole, the marks on the lure still just looked like crisscrossed lines.

Axel nodded. "He sure did love that woman. Till the day he died." He looked up, a bit misty-eyed, Janice thought. "So where'd you find the lure?"

They'd agreed not to give away any details. RJ shrugged. "In the water by Wayfarers Inn."

"Huh. What else can I do for you all?"

"Who would be likely to have one of these?" Janice chewed on the corner of her lip.

"Anybody," Bobber said. "Franky handed 'em out like candy."

Exactly the opposite of what Irene had said.

Stick pointed in the vague direction of the front door. "That lady from his building prob'ly got rid of all his junk."

Axel ran a finger through his ponytail. "Franky was a simple guy. Don't imagine there was much of anything to give away after his demise."

Demise? Janice hugged her arms across her middle. This guy gave her the creeps. "Where did he live?"

"I can show you." Irene raised her pale, petite hand. "Not far from here. Let's go." She rose out of her chair quicker than an eighty-eight-year-old should be able to.

RJ shook his head. "I have a few more questions. Do you fish at night?"

"Sometimes." Axel stared into RJ's eyes, not blinking. "If the moon's full."

"Were you out last night?"

"In that wind? Person'd have to be crazy to go out on a night like that."

RJ leaned in. "Know anyone crazy enough to be out on a night like that?"

One of the men at the counter laughed. "I do."

"Who's that?"

"Some new guy. I was out walking the dog last night, around seven maybe. Maybe earlier. He was trollin' back in, nice and slow, actin' like he's just out for a joyride even though the wind was practically capsizin' him."

"Was he alone?" RJ asked.

"Couldn't rightly tell in the dark. Mighta been someone with him."

"Who is he?"

"I don't know. George somebody."

RJ was looking frustrated. "George? No nickname? What's he look like?"

"Oh, I don't know. Old guy." Stick looked at Bobber.

"White hair," Bobber said. "Curly hair. And he walks with a limp."

"Peg leg, I think," Raven added with a smirk.

Right. Janice stared from Raven to Axel, sure the men were having a good time at their expense.

Axel nodded. "Yep. Peg leg for sure." He handed the lure back to RJ. "What are you askin' all these questions for? Somethin' go down?"

RJ opened his mouth but closed it again when Irene put her hand on his shoulder.

"I think we better get going," she said.

Janice stood up. "I think you're right, Irene." She turned to Axel. "Thank you for your time. All we needed was to be sure Franky made this lure. I have a friend who's a retired history teacher, and she's studying Marietta history. I'm sure she'd love to hear stories about the locals."

"You want stories?" Axel laughed, showing two gaps where he'd once had teeth. "Come back anytime. Have we got stories for you!"

Janice had no doubt the four of them could hold their own in a tall tales contest.

She laid a twenty-dollar bill on the table. As they walked out the door, Axel and the men at the counter burst out laughing. "That was one of the best, Axel," Bobber said. "One of the best."

Once outside, they paused to get their bearings.

"We can walk." Irene pointed toward the river. "Franky's place is right over there." She pointed to a redbrick apartment building across the communal parking lot for the nearby businesses. Janice looked where she was pointing, and spotted an old pickup wrapped bumper to bumper in scenes of hooked fish—bluegill, bass, walleye, and others. As they passed it she could see that there was even a flailing catfish mural on the top of the cab. She said, to no one in particular, "Someone takes their fishing very seriously."

Irene snorted. "That's Axel's. The man would fish in his sleep if he could."

RJ laughed and offered his arm to Irene. The height difference was at least eighteen inches. Comical, but sweet. Janice and Brad walked behind them.

Janice glanced back at the Busy Bee, half expecting Axel and his nicknamed buddies to be following them. With guns drawn. "What was all that about George and a peg leg?"

"That was all about us getting hoodwinked, that's what." Irene shrugged. "So all we know now is that some or all of what they said was a big fat lie."

"Do you think the new guy they were talking about was real? Minus the peg leg, of course," RJ asked.

"I have no idea. Fishermen like their yarns, but most of them are honest folk. Those four... no idea."

"How do you know all these guys, Mrs. Martin?" RJ leaned down and spoke loudly, the way people often do around the elderly, something Irene wasn't going to put up with for long. Irene was not hard of hearing and wouldn't tolerate being treated like an old lady. Some women aged gracefully, but she was aging defiantly, something Janice admired and intended to emulate. Irene Martin wasn't one to pull the age card... unless it involved a fifteen-percent discount. "Was your father a fisherman?"

Irene sputtered. "My father put a worm on a hook? Not a chance. It was our groundskeeper, Hezekiah Arnold, Winnie's great-grandpa, who got me hooked." She looked up at him and laughed. "Get it?"

"Hooked. Yep, I get it."

"Back in the thirties and forties, children kind of ran wild. Guess they'd call us free-range kids today. We had a nanny and a housekeeper, but neither one of them cared to keep a close eye, so Thelma and I just did as we pleased. She mostly played with dolls and made up plays with her friends, and I went fishing with Hezekiah. Must have looked funny, now that I think about it. He was about as tall as you. Can't you just see this tiny white girl sitting on the dock with a great big black man? Anyway, Hezekiah introduced me to all his friends, and I kept fishing with them long after he was gone. Never told my parents. As long as I managed to sneak upstairs to change and wash up before supper, they didn't ask."

They turned onto the sidewalk leading to Franky's building. The door opened before RJ reached for the handle. A middle-aged woman with a single long braid walked out with a Chihuahua on a leash. "Irene!"

"Maria! We were just coming to talk to you."

Maria appeared confused. "Me? All of you?"

Irene made quick introductions. "We're wondering what happened to all of Franky's things. Especially his fishing gear. Do you know?"

"Sure do. We boxed it all up and gave it to Axel Barrett."

"What?" Janice stepped closer. "What was in the box?"

Maria stepped back. "Why do you want to know? Axel done something stupid again? He didn't hurt anyone, did he?"

"No," Janice answered. *Not that we know of.* "Irene has told us a lot about Franky. We just wondered what he left behind, what was important to him."

Maria leaned against the iron railing behind her. "I knew Franky since I was a kid. My daddy was one of his good buddies. Used to love to listen to all their fish stories when a bunch of their friends got together."

"Was Axel one of them?" Tess asked.

"Sure was. But Axel took a bad turn. Daddy said it was unrequited love that did it. He took to taking things that weren't his, if you know what I mean. Spent some time locked up. Not sure he was ever the same after that."

"Franky must have cared enough about Axel to leave some of his favorite things to him," RJ said.

"Nah. There just wasn't anybody else to give it to. I tossed most of Franky's things and gave his fishing gear to Axel. He's the only one left in that generation."

"Was Axel happy to receive it?" LuAnn asked.

"I don't know. Didn't talk to him. Just dumped it all in the *Wave Whisperer*."

"What's that?" LuAnn asked. "A tavern?"

"Ha. Sometimes." Maria laughed. "Nah. It's the name of Axel's boat."

Rain had kept the lunch crowd smaller than usual, but the cleanup seemed to take longer than most days. *Maybe it's just me.* Janice picked up a basket of damp towels and dirty aprons from breakfast and lunch, intent on taking them downstairs to the laundry room and then heading up to her room for a nap.

LuAnn hung her still-clean apron on a hook and took her "Kitchen Stuff" spiral notebook out of a drawer. "Clues and Suspects List time, people." She set the notebook on the table and pulled her favorite silver pen out of her back pocket.

"Just a minute." Tess held up one finger. "I need to gather some evidence." The door to the café swung back and forth after she walked out.

"Do you ladies need some sleuthing snacks?" Winnie opened a sealed plastic container and set it in front of LuAnn. "I always think better with a snickerdoodle in my hand."

Janice gave her a quick hug. "You're a gem, Winnie."

Tess walked in, candy box in hand. "I just noticed something." She set the heart-shaped box upside-down on the table and pointed at what remained of a price label.

Janice leaned in. She squinted at the perfect reddish-brown half-thumbprint. "It's chocolate, right?"

"I don't think so."

LuAnn got up and dug a magnifying glass out of a drawer. She handed it to Janice.

The enlarged swirls she saw through the lens did not look like dark chocolate or milk chocolate or anything in between.

"There's a Swiss company, Barry Callebaut, that makes red chocolate using 'ruby' cocoa beans. It's possible..."

Tess took the box and the magnifying glass. After a moment of studying the fingerprint, she said, "I think we need a field trip to Putnam." She turned to Winnie, who'd put on her jacket and was drawing her gloves out of her pockets. "Any chance you could stay a while and watch the front desk? We'll pay double time." Tess aimed a sweetly pleading smile at Winnie.

"Love to. I've been prayin' for a little extra to help out Mrs. Moore and those poor little kids. Money's mighty tight since the accident, I hear."

"Thank you. You're the best." Tess turned to Janice and LuAnn. "Let's go."

"Clues and Suspects first." LuAnn tapped the notebook like a no-nonsense schoolmarm and pointed to the chairs surrounding the table. Like dutiful school children, Tess and Janice sat.

"Clues: Heart-shaped candy box with a note, and what looks like a bloody fingerprint. Was the box of chocolates a romantic gesture by Franny? If so, how did it get here, and why didn't she show? Did she really have a flat tire thirty miles from here? Or was the note a way to get RJ to leave the inn so someone could steal his bag? Or was it something else?"

Janice waited while LuAnn wrote the questions and then said, "Don't forget the floorboards creaking."

LuAnn wrote, then looked up. "And the guy...or person...in the boat," Tess added.

"The fishing lure," Janice said. "And do the letters on the fishing pole really stand for Wilma Westlake, or could it be for the *Wave Whisperer*?"

The tip of the silver pen wove across the page. "On to suspects. Obvious ones first. The bag could have been taken any time between about three fifteen, when RJ checked in, and about seven thirty, when he discovered it was missing."

"Let's start with Brin McLoughlin," Janice said. "She came in just before RJ got home from dinner and said she wanted to look around. Could she have come to the inn earlier and taken the bag and then come back, acting like she'd just arrived, to throw us off?"

"That hardly seems likely," LuAnn said. "What, exactly, did she say?"

Janice strained to remember. Last night seemed far more than eighteen hours ago. "She said she came to town for Love Is, but it was really the inn she wanted to see. She said she came because of a time capsule, or something like that. She acted like she'd stepped onto the set of a famous movie or one of the seven wonders of the world, like she couldn't believe she was actually seeing it in person."

LuAnn laughed. "Maybe we're more famous than we think."

"I wish." Balancing the books was Tess's area of expertise, and she dwelled on the financial worry more than the other two.

"If Brin doesn't come back like she said she was going to, we need to go looking for her." LuAnn wrote *Brin McLoughlin*, then put seven more names on the list.

Cameron Truman

Natalie Hemmingway

Noah Nichols

Axel Barrett

Stick

Bobber

Raven

With a heavy sigh, she added *Franny Simon*. "There's something about her RJ's not telling us. Some reason he doesn't just flat-out ask her about the candy box."

Janice nodded. "I sure hope for his sake it's not her."

CHAPTER FIVE

Tess opened the door to a brick storefront with *Putnam Chocolate* spelled out in gold letters on the front window.

Bonita Nelson greeted them with a laugh. "This looks like trouble. Are you ladies in need of a chocolate fix, or are you investigating a real death by chocolate?"

An eerie question, considering the bloody fingerprint. "Just a couple of questions." Janice eyed the glass display case filled with mounds of chocolates identified by white placards. Coconut Haystacks. Chocolate-covered Caramels. Turtles. Raspberry Truffles. Dark Chocolate English Toffee. "But I don't think we'll be leaving empty-handed."

"Here, put these on and follow me." Bonita handed them each a hairnet. "I was just ready to dip some pretzels."

They entered the kitchen and, for a moment, Janice forgot why she was there. So much spotless stainless steel. So many state-of-the-art tools. A line of shiny silver chocolate melters. A mint-green and brown handheld chocolate sprayer. Scales, slicers, dippers, thermometers. After thirty-plus years teaching domestic arts, she couldn't help but get a bit weak in the knees at the sight.

"…bought this?" LuAnn was saying as she held out the heart-shaped box.

"We've sold at least three dozen of those so far." Bonita pointed to a corner where a tower of heart boxes rose from the counter.

Hopeless. Even if Bonita gave them the names of every single heart box buyer in Marietta, it would take them forever to check each one out. By then, the Valentine Villain, assuming it wasn't Franny Simon, could easily have crossed the state line.

"But you have records, right?" Tess looked toward the door leading to the front of the store. "The bar code is different for each item, right?"

"Yes. But I wouldn't have access to any of that."

Janice watched Tess's and LuAnn's shoulders fall in unison.

"We're investigating a theft." LuAnn reached into her purse and pulled out a zipper bag with the note in it. "This was on the candy box we think the thief sent as bait."

Janice cringed. Were they giving too much away? Rumors could spread like floodwaters.

"Oh! I remember that. A woman—long red hair, very pretty, late twenties, I'd guess, wearing a plaid coat with huge gold buttons. Vintage, from the sixties, maybe. Came in with three little kids. She went straight to the heart boxes without looking around, bought one, then went over to another counter and slapped a sticky note on it, then left. It struck me as weird all the way around. She knew exactly what she was after, and why a sticky note and not a card? These boxes aren't exactly cheap. Seems like if you're going to shell out for a quality gift you'd want a nice card to go with it, right? Weird all the way around, I say."

⚬⚭⚬

"Weird all the way around." Tess laughed as they walked down the sidewalk. "That's going to be our new catch phrase for this case."

Janice nodded, only half hearing what Tess had just said. Something niggled in the back of her brain. "Vintage. She said the coat was from the sixties. We need to—"

"Head over to Antoinette's Closet," LuAnn finished.

They walked to the end of the block and entered the resale store. Emma Carpenter stood behind the front counter, long dark hair tied up in a red bandana, Rosy the Riveter style. She wore faded jeans and a red-and-white checked shirt tied at the waist. The girl could have stepped right out of an *Uncle Sam Needs You* poster.

"Uh-oh. This must mean trouble." Emma stepped out from behind the counter and greeted them.

"Why does everyone use that word when referring to us?" Tess feigned genuine perplexity.

"Well, let's see...there was the incident with the fire department, the skeleton in the tunnel, the lost manuscript, the emerald bracelet heist..."

LuAnn laughed and held up a hand to stop the recounting of the Inn Crowd's escapades. "We're looking for a coat."

"Well..." Emma gestured toward a rack along one side of the store.

54

"Oh. No." Tess jumped in. "We're not shopping."

Emma chewed on her bottom lip, clearly waiting for an explanation.

Like with so many other tag-team conversations in the forty years the women had been best friends, Janice jumped in. "We're looking for a woman with long red hair who wears a plaid coat with big gold buttons. Maybe from the sixties. She has three young children and—"

"I know that coat!"

"You do?" Janice hugged the heart-shaped box to her chest. This was going to be an easy one to solve. Not that she didn't love a good mystery challenge, but this one couldn't have arrived at a worse time.

"I saw it just a week or so ago. At the skating rink. I took my nephew, and we left at the same time as a woman with red hair in a ponytail wearing a red plaid coat. The buttons were beautiful. Gold, concave. Unusual. I have an eye for things like that. I remember wishing I had the guts to ask if she wanted to sell it."

Not much of a lead. Janice rubbed her temple. The tension that started when she'd walked into the Busy Bee was on the verge of becoming an annoying headache. "Did you talk to her?"

"A little. Her son is the same age as my nephew."

Tess's eyes brightened. "Did they know each other? Do they go to school together?"

"No. My nephew's in private school." Emma straightened a row of pearl earrings in a velvet-lined tray. "Can I ask why you want to find her? I love hearing stories about you three. Sure you don't need some outrageous costumes for this caper?"

The women laughed. They'd first met Emma back in June when they were shopping for disguises to evade the stalker trying to keep them from buying the inn. The stalker who turned out to be a four-foot-eight octogenarian. Janice still had the sparkly blue gown she'd picked out. No place to wear it, but it made her smile every time she opened the closet.

LuAnn fingered a gold necklace hanging on a rack next to the jewelry counter. "Can you keep a secret?"

"Of course."

"We've had another theft at the inn."

Emma's eyes grew as wide as the hoop earrings LuAnn picked up. "And you think the woman in the plaid coat is the thief?"

Janice cringed. This was how rumors got started. "We have reason to believe she may know something. We need to keep this quiet, but anything you can tell us would be helpful. Any little detail."

"Okay, sure, any way I can help."

The women turned toward the door. Tess opened it. "Thanks, Emma."

"You're wel— Wait! I just thought of something. She had a stamp on her hand. Like a re-entry stamp you get at a concert. Red. Kind of faded."

The familiar clue-rush tingled in Janice's veins. "What did it say?"

"It was a star. No words."

Tess pressed her gloved hands together. "You're sure it was a stamp? Not a kid's tattoo?"

"I'm sure. She was putting on her gloves. I guess that's another detail. If someone's wearing one vintage piece, I'm always curious to see how far they take it. She had these buttery-soft-looking tan suede gloves. Hand-stitched, maybe from the thirties. That's what caught my attention, so I was looking closely at her hands. Close enough to see how the ink had kind of spread into the lines of her hand. Tattoos don't do that, right?"

"Good eye." LuAnn patted Emma on the shoulder. Her other hand slid into her purse. Janice knew she was itching to pull out her notebook while the clues were fresh.

"Any idea what the stamp was from?"

"No. I'm trying to think what day we went to the skating rink." Emma twisted her mouth to one side. "Last Saturday. Had to be."

"Perfect." Janice took another step toward the door. "You're an honorary Wayfarers Inn Private Investigator, Emma."

"I like that. I'll be on the lookout."

After they'd finished a supper of Winnie's beef barley soup, the Inn Crowd sat in the inn kitchen playing Ticket to Ride. When the door chime dinged, LuAnn got up. "That would be the Porters, I imagine."

Tess smiled. "Our favorite guests. Everything ready for them?"

Janice nodded. "Mints on the pillows, votive candles all over the room."

This would be Sam and Sammy Porter's fourth visit, but this one was special. This time they would be occupying the Honeymoon Suite, celebrating their second anniversary. Sam was seventy-four. Sammy was seventy-one.

"They are just the cutest." Tess got up to refill the bowl of mixed nuts they'd been munching on.

Sam was a police officer. After forty years of active duty, he now taught at the Kent State Police Academy and had no plans of quitting "until they haul me feet first out of the classroom." Sammy was a retired police dispatcher. They'd known each other professionally and, with their respective spouses, had been friends for decades. After they were both widowed, it seemed only natural they'd get married.

"Have you thought lately if you'll..." Janice stared at the tree shadows flickering on the curtains.

"Yes." Tess finished the question Janice hadn't actually asked. "I'm not ready yet, but someday maybe." She set the bowl of nuts on the table with a laugh. "I sound like I've got years and years of somedays left. But if God has another man in my future, He'll make it happen."

Janice nodded. Neither of them tried to fill the reflective silence.

Deep in thought, Janice jumped when the door swung open and LuAnn walked in. "The Sams are all settled. Sammy was just cute as a button. She thanked me about a dozen times for all the little extra touches and told me to give you both hugs." She sat down, drew two cards from the pile, and picked up her phone. "Where was I?"

Tess set a row of four plastic trains on the board. "You were about to tell us everything happening in Marietta the last couple of weeks, so we can track down the lady with the plaid coat."

LuAnn scrolled for several minutes, then shook her head. "Nothing in Marietta on that Saturday." She continued to scroll on her phone between turns. "No concerts. What else could it be?"

"Basketball game? Wrestling? Where would she go with kids?"

"How about a water park or bouncy house place?" Janice asked as she placed two red plastic trains between Las Vegas and Los Angeles and asked Tess to give her two points.

Tess moved the little red marker, then stretched her neck. "Can we table this discussion? Too much stress for one day."

Janice sighed. "No stress in my life. I'm going to get up in the morning and find a caterer for one of the biggest wedding and banquet weekends of the year and then convince Stuart to be our guest speaker and someday soon get married so I can stop losing hours and hours of sleep wondering who will make Dutch apple pie for him after I'm gone. Easy-peasy. I've got this." She stood. "Anyone else want some chamomile tea?"

No takers. Evidently no one else had so much on her mind that sleep wouldn't come without a little help from the soothing beverage. She walked through the swinging doors and into the café. She'd just filled a cup with water from the hot pot when the door opened.

Brin McLoughlin walked in, backpack slung over one shoulder, grin on her face. "Hi! Hey, do you guys have any vacancies? Can I book a room for six nights? I'm sharing a room at the Oakshire with this girl I never met, and she's way, way, way more of a talker than I am. She's nice and all, but she didn't stop talking until two o'clock this morning, and I'm an only child, so I just can't handle it. My mom sent me some spending money, so I can afford it now." She finally stopped, grin never wavering.

There is really a person who talks more than you do? Janice repressed a laugh before remembering Brin was on their list of suspects. Was she returning to the scene of the crime? Did she intend to steal more? "We have a room." She set her cup down and walked over to the front desk. "I can give you Lilac and Sage. It has a view of the river."

"Lilac and Sage. That's seriously the coolest name ever." Brin pulled a credit card from her back pocket.

"You mentioned something about a time capsule." Janice hoped to prime the chatty pump as she checked her in.

"Before we were so rudely interrupted, huh? What a crazy night. Did the cops find the guy in the boat? Did he steal that guy's bag? Things like that happen all the time where I live, but it sure seems weird here."

Was her curiosity genuine or just well-acted? Janice slid the charge slip across the desk and watched as Brin printed her name. Closely spaced letters slanting forward. "Follow me and tell me about the time capsule on the way." She pointed across the café. "The elevator is this way."

"Can we take the stairs? I just don't want to miss anything."

"Sure. Is this all you have?" Janice gestured toward the backpack.

"My mom taught me to travel light. She's a traveling singer/ songwriter. She's on tour in Europe this summer."

"Wow. What an opportunity."

"Yeah. She's always been a wanderer. I guess I inherited that. I love to travel. My mom was here twenty years ago, playing with a worship band at something like Love Is. She stayed for the whole summer. And what a summer it was. I've never had a summer romance, have you?"

Janice had. But it wasn't something she'd talked about in over forty years. Not that she didn't think about Sean on occasion. There was always something about your first crush. She paused at the second-floor landing. "Your mother had a summer romance here in Marietta?"

"Yep. Right here in this building."

She hated to ruin the romantic fantasy, but that just wasn't a possibility. "You said your mother was here twenty years ago?"

"Yep."

"I'm afraid you might have the facts mixed up a bit. Wayfarers Inn was empty back then. It's been many things over years. A dry goods store and a car repair shop, an antique store, but twenty years ago it would have been empty."

"Yep." Brin slid her glasses up. "That's what she said."

"What?"

"She and this guy would sneak in here and have picnics. She described the fireplace and the mirror and the bar, though I pictured the bar being right under the mirror."

It was until we moved it. Was that proof the girl was telling the truth?

"They'd buy bread and cheese and chocolate and spread a red-checkered tablecloth down on the floor and pretend they were sitting along the River Seine or in Venice, watching the gondolas float past."

"Interesting." Could be true, could be a story her mother had made up. "So you're here to find her old boyfriend? What about your—"

"My father? I've never met him. My mom doesn't know I'm here. I just wanted to get pictures. I'm not looking to stir up any problems. He's probably married with like a gazillion kids or something. My mom never told me his name, probably because she figured I'd do something stupid like come looking for him. I don't want to do that. She's happy, but every time she talks about him, I get the feeling she needs closure, you know? All she has is this one picture, and it's not very clear. I scanned it." Brin pulled a phone out of her pocket. "They found this old bag and put stuff in it for a time capsule. Here." She held out the phone. "Wait, that's my mom."

A girl that could have been Brin, except for the retro bangs, leaned against the bar that was now their reception desk. "You look just like her."

"Yeah. People say that all the time. Even now. She's in her thirties, but lots of people think we're sisters." Brin swiped to another picture. "This is the boy."

Janice blinked. Twice, then again, but the slightly distorted picture of a picture didn't change. A teenager, sitting on a plaid tablecloth in front of the fireplace that was now fifteen feet behind Brin. A young, handsome boy...wearing a shirt hand-embroidered by Janice.

It couldn't be...But it was.

Stuart.

Janice's hand shook as she slid the key into the lock for Lilac and Sage. She stepped back, letting Brin walk in first.

"This is incredible! I love, love, love the colors. Did you decorate this? I wish I had that talent. My mom is really good at decorating." Brin ran into the bathroom. "It's so...historical! It's like stepping back in time. Do you know anything about the people who used to run this place back in the day?"

"We do, actually." Janice stared at Brin's animated gestures, feeling dazed and disoriented. Who was this person? "We have a journal written by a woman who was a conductor on the Underground Railroad. She got a job here as her cover. She would row her boat across the river to bring runaway slaves to safety."

"Here? In this building?"

"Yes. There are secret rooms in the basement and hidden passages."

Brin's brows leaped over the rim of her glasses. "Can I see them?"

"Probably. Maybe we'll arrange a tour for all of our guests this week."

Brin twirled. "I wish I had a hoopskirt." She stepped in front of the mirror. "I think I'll put my hair up like they did back then." She gathered the mass of curls onto the top of her head. "What do you think?"

"I think..." *I think my head is spinning.* Stuart had been in the building twenty years ago with Brin's mom? Did that mean... "How old are you?"

"Nineteen."

She'd heard the expression "her blood ran cold," but never, until this moment, had she ever experienced the sensation.

Stop. This was not a time to let her imagination run off, leaving common sense behind. "Around the time the inn was built, women would often divide their hair into three braids, then weave them together, making a chignon at the back of the neck. You have enough hair for that, and it would look lovely on you."

"Really? Could you do that with mine? Tomorrow, maybe?"

Janice steadied herself with a firm grip on the door handle. "I could do that." She handed Brin the restaurant list, WiFi password, and told her how to get in touch with staff. "Do you need anything?"

"Not a thing." Brin flopped back on the bed. "This is way beyond perfect."

Janice had the strangest sensation of wanting to run and wanting to stay right here learning more about this girl. "Um... could we maybe keep all this quiet for a day or two?"

"All what?" Brin sat up, crossing her legs beneath her.

"The time capsule and the picture and everything you said about your mom and...the boy. We've got so much going on right now and..."

"Sure. I get it."

As Janice was closing the door, Brin called, "We can talk about the other mystery later, right?"

July 19, 1863

"Does he know thee?" Tabitha asked, staring down at Ira's still form.

Prudence shook her head. "I was only twelve when I left."

"For the best. Has thee told him thee wants to help him?"

"No." Because she still hadn't heard a clear word from God. Tabitha was right. Hundreds of Confederate soldiers were being ferried to Camp Chase or one of the other prison camps around the state, or into Indiana. Their treatment would be poor, she'd heard enough to know that to be true. Little food or medicine to be wasted on the enemy. But this one she could help. Should she?

What she was contemplating wasn't simply Good Samaritan kindness. It was treason.

Ira Fitzhugh opened his eyes. "Where am I?"

"On board a hospital boat."

Pained eyes narrowed. "Yankee?"

"Yes."

His eyes closed. His lips began to move. Prudence bent close.

"...over my children and my mother. Forgive me for my trespasses and..."

Without a word, she nodded to Tabitha. Prudence's skiff was tied at the edge of the river, about a quarter mile away.

Rubbing the chill from her arms, Prudence turned back to this man she wanted to hate. "Can thee walk?"

"I think so."

"Then if thee wants to live, keep thy mouth shut, and do exactly what we tell thee."

CHAPTER SIX

J anice stared into the darkness as the red numbers on her clock changed from 6:22 to 6:23 to 6:24. She hadn't slept more than an hour at a stretch all night. Had she made it clear enough to Brin that she needed to keep the picture a secret?

Brin probably wouldn't recognize Stuart even if they came face-to-face. Stuart had added considerable muscle since his gangly teens.

But "Aunt" Tess and "Aunt" LuAnn would recognize the skinny boy in the picture immediately. And Brin looked so much like her mother. If Stuart saw her, he couldn't help but make the connection.

Hadn't she learned her lesson about keeping secrets from her friends? Apparently not. But it was only for a few days. Just until after the banquet. And Stuart's deposition. This was not the time to rock the boat. She almost laughed at her choice of clichés. Almost.

Pressing the palms of her hands against her eyes, she thought back, picturing Stuart at sixteen. Wasn't that the summer he'd gone to Haiti on a mission trip? Wasn't that the year he'd served as president of the youth group and been asked to sing a solo at a rally for more than a thousand Christian teens from all over the Midwest?

Had he ever mentioned a girl he'd met at that rally? Had she been too busy to pay attention? She'd been teaching full time, playing piano for church, leading a women's study, running Vacation Bible School, planning the annual church picnic...

Lawrence, why aren't you here to help me? Did you know about this?

She imagined her pastor husband in heaven, engrossed in conversation with Moses, Peter, and the apostle Paul. If she could just butt in and tap him on the shoulder...

Lawrence was always the one with the level head, the cool composure. A perfect counterpoint to her runaway imagination.

Janice massaged a sore spot on the top of her head, feeling the pain radiate down into her temples. *We might have another grandchild, Lawrence.* Tears filled her eyes. *She's beautiful. A little quirky, maybe, and she talks incessantly. She has my curly hair, poor girl. And I wasn't there to give her tips on how to take care of it all these years. Curly hair isn't as easy as people think. Wonder what kind of conditioner—*

Janice, does this story have a beginning, middle, and end? She could hear the smile in Lawrence's voice as his chiding cut into her worried reverie.

Does Stuart know about Brin? If not, should he? And should I be the one to tell him?

"Stay in the moment," she chastised. "'Do not worry about tomorrow, for tomorrow will worry about itself. Each day has enough trouble of its own.'" The verse from the book of Matthew, which often brought clarity when fears overwhelmed her, didn't bring much peace this time since all she could focus on was the last sentence. What troubles would today bring?

She groped for her phone. She had to talk to Stuart. Glancing again at the clock, she decided it wasn't too early. She typed out a text, inviting him to dinner at six. It wasn't until after she'd pushed Send that she realized it was Valentine's Day.

A strange tension took over as she stared at the screen, waiting for an answer. Part of her wanted to talk to him, the other part hoped he'd answer that he had a date. She couldn't bear thinking about her son spending Valentine's Day alone. Or even sadder...with his mother.

Less than a minute passed until her phone vibrated.

I'll be there at six. And, yes, I will speak. Preparing a talk will actually be a welcome diversion. Thinking maybe something about love from a medical perspective... since I have so little real-life experience to draw from!

"Ha!" Twenty-four hours ago she would have believed that statement. What else didn't she know about her son? Did Stacy know? Did her big brother share the secrets of his past with her? They'd kept other things from their mother over the years. She decided she needed to talk to Stacy before she tackled Stuart. Then she remembered it was her turn to stay at the inn after church and let the others have the afternoon off. She sent a text to Tess asking her if she would like to switch shifts with her—go to church this morning, and be at the inn this afternoon. Tess answered immediately with *Sure, no problem.* Janice hated to miss church, but what choice did she have? She texted her daughter.

Happy Valentine's Day! Free for lunch today? My treat. Meet you at that tearoom near the Sassy Seamstress? She wouldn't ask about

Stuart outright, but mothers have ways of finding out what they need to know.

The reply came immediately. *Sounds fun. See you then.*

What to do about Stuart and dinner? Or Brin and dinner? She had to keep them apart. Before she came up with a solution, her alarm jarred the silence.

And her nerves.

Half an hour later, she was still in a mental fog as she helped prepare breakfast for their guests. It being Sunday, the café was closed, so Winnie had the day off.

"Hey, Happy Valentine's Day!" LuAnn waved a hand in front of Janice's face, causing her to blink. "You look like me. Where were you?"

Leaning against the kitchen counter, Janice shook her head. "Just lost in thought. Feeling a little *LuAnnish* this morning." She and Tess had always teased LuAnn about getting lost in daydreams like the main character in *The Secret Life of Walter Mitty*. "Maybe Walter Mittyism is contagious." She picked up a plate of cranberry-orange muffins and walked toward the kitchen door.

Most of their guests had assembled for breakfast. Brin had apparently chosen sleep over food, Natalie was just coming down the stairs, and Noah, RJ said, was a slow mover in the morning. The Love Is crowd gathered at the one long harvest table, leaving the honeymoon suite occupants sitting by themselves at a table for two by the windows, but Sam and Sammy seemed so lost in each other they probably hadn't noticed. This was more than a union of convenience. This was chemistry.

Janice watched them, holding hands across the table, with a touch of envy. Finding love again at this age seemed so improbable, and definitely not something she even wanted to consider yet, but... Like Tess had said, if it was in God's plan for her life, it would happen in His time.

"We need to be out here studying every move this morning." LuAnn pulled her from another LuAnnish moment.

"Right." Janice reached for a coffeepot. "Perfect opportunity."

"I'm going to plant myself at the front desk," Tess said. "I can't hear anything from there, but I can watch interactions and get a general feel for things."

"Good idea." Janice studied the seating arrangement. Interestingly, RJ had positioned himself at one end of the long table, and Franny sat at the other. Way more space than they needed to have between them with only five people, though it did guarantee a direct line of sight and mandatory eye contact. "I thought of something else. The handwriting on the sticky note is back-slanted and looks like someone who's left-handed wrote it."

LuAnn's eyes opened wide. "Why didn't we think of that before? Are any of them left-handed?"

Janice nodded toward the table and lowered her voice. "Cameron is."

"Oh." Tess gave a slow nod. "Wow."

Janice stared at Cameron's wide shoulders. "He sure doesn't look like the kind to dot his *i*'s with little hearts though."

LuAnn brought out two trays of Winnie's famous pecan caramel rolls, and Janice put a toothpick topped with red paper hearts in each one. Tess filled juice glasses while Janice passed trays of individual cheese-and-bacon quiches in adorable white ramekins, and fruit compote served in champagne glasses. Like a well-oiled machine, they moved from right to left, serving their guests.

"While we're waiting for Noah, I'd like to take a moment to thank our hosts for this incredible Valentine spread." RJ nodded to each of them in turn. "Thank you for providing a quiet place for us to regroup at the end of what will be fruitful but likely stressful days."

"Hear, hear." Cameron lifted his juice glass. "The atmosphere of this place is unsurpassed."

Noah clambered down the stairs, toting three black bags, one on his back and one on each shoulder. "Sorry I'm late." His pale face flushed as he glanced at the empty chair across from Natalie and then at Natalie. With more noise than Janice would have guessed a meek-looking man like Noah could make, he arranged his bags on an empty table. One bag slid off and he caught it, almost dropped it again, then held on. "Sorry." He grabbed the back of his chair, tipping it back too far, righted it, and finally managed to sit. "Sorry," he mumbled again, with a furtive look at Natalie.

"Let's pray." Cameron led them in giving thanks for the food and then moved to an impassioned plea for safety for all attending the conference, for no glitches in technology, and for all attending to hear and understand God's definition of love.

RJ opened the discussion. "This is it." He extended his arm and looked at his watch. "Registration begins in five hours and thirty-two minutes. We've had a few cancellations, which brings us to four hundred and twenty-three in attendance. Bigger than last year. Cam and I met with all the workshop leaders yesterday. So far, no issues we couldn't iron out. Vendors seem happy. Right, Fran?" He looked up at LuAnn, who was setting a jar of Winnie's apple butter on the table. "As well as being one of our amazing speakers, Franny is in charge of our vendors. We have twenty-one this year."

"All related to being single?" Janice interjected. "Sorry. I'm just curious. They didn't have events like this when I was younger."

Franny smiled sweetly. "We have a wide range of vendors. Colleges, organizations that sponsor mission trips, authors, relationship counselors, a world-renowned psychologist"—she nodded toward Cameron—"fashion, makeup, dating etiquette. We also have a bookstore this year."

"Well, I think it's wonderful," Janice told her. "I hope we have time to chat with each of you this week and learn about your roles in the conference. The three of us have been praying for all of you since we first heard about Love Is."

"Thank you." Franny smiled. "That means so much."

The talk slowed as they all began to eat. RJ took a bite, then lifted his plate, apparently searching for something he'd misplaced. Jumping up, he grumbled, "Forgot my phone."

Several minutes later, he returned, confusion digging deep lines between his eyes. "Janice?" His voice was hushed. "I need to show you something."

"What—"

"Come with me."

She followed him to his room. A large overstuffed white envelope lay on the bed. A single pink conversation heart balanced on top. Janice moved closer and stared at the red letters stamped into the heart. Clearly, some of the letters had been scraped off. It now read simply *Sorry*.

Janice was intrigued. "What in the world? What's in the envelope?" She had a feeling she knew.

"The money." RJ picked it up and showed her the contents. "All of it."

Relief coursed through Janice. But then, just as quickly, apprehension. "Did you lock your door when you came to breakfast?"

"Of course," RJ said. "Whoever returned this got in the same way they did last time, but I don't have a clue how they did it."

Janice shook her head, even though she did have a clue. Or two. She glanced toward the closet, where a locked panel concealed a secret.

"Are you sure this is enough for you?" Janice pointed at the bagel with cream cheese on Stacy's plate.

"Yep. This is perfect. I've been hungry for one of these. It's a perfect quick lunch."

"How's work?" A nice, easy step toward questions she hoped to get answers to without actually asking. "Busy?"

"Yep. Flu season. We had—"

"Stacy. Janice." The unsmiling woman with the unnatural red tint to her hair who stopped by their table gave a cursory nod to Stacy and lasered in on Janice.

"Maybelline. How are you?"

"Irritated. That's how I am. Did you hear there's talk of putting in another hotel and conference center out by the country club? Why do people always want to make things bigger? You grew up here. You remember what it was like back in the day when everybody knew everybody. It's not right. The historic part of town is going to get swallowed up in the name of progress. Pretty soon no one will remember the things that happened here. I think we need to protest. Are you in?"

The Inn Crowd had been on the receiving end of protest when environmentalists had tried to stop them from opening the inn. She wanted no part in it. "Sorry, Maybelline. I did love the way things were 'back in the day,' but progress is inevitable."

Maybelline huffed. "So, find anything new yet?"

Since yesterday? "Maybelline, is there something specific you're hoping we find?"

With a sigh, and without invitation, Maybelline pulled out a chair. "As a matter of fact, there is. A leather bag. Legend has it the thing went missing—"

"Legend?" Janice tried to keep her tone from sounding like she was finding humor at Maybelline's expense, but "legend" was a bit extreme. And then the rest of her sentence registered. "Leather bag? Who told you about the bag?"

"Can't say." Maybelline looked down, picking at her thumbnail.

"Well, I'd appreciate it if you'd help squelch any rumors. We're on top of it."

"So you have it?" Relief softened the lines around Maybelline's eyes.

Janice folded and refolded the edge of the napkin on her lap. "There's nothing to worry about." She offered her best pastor's-wife smile. The one that covered every trace of impatience. "I'm sorry, Maybelline, Stacy and I have just a few more minutes to catch up with each other. Maybe we could talk about this another time?"

Maybelline rose from her seat. "Change your locks, Janice. Lock up that bag and don't let it out of your sight."

"Sure, Maybelline. We will." As she watched Maybelline walk away, she couldn't calm the chills skittering up and down her spine. Why would Maybelline want them to lock up RJ's bag?

"Whew." Stacy slathered more cream cheese on what was left of her bagel. "She's intense. What was that all about?"

"Not sure." Janice bit into her sandwich to avoid answering. After chewing much longer than the bite required, she said, "Tell me the latest Larryism."

Stacy picked up her phone and started scrolling, then turned it around for Janice to see a picture of her grandson. Face covered in spaghetti sauce, he was grinning. A piece of spaghetti dangled from each nostril.

"Eeeww. Tell him Nana says he's a silly goose."

Think. Stacy would be ready to leave before she learned anything. "Larry reminds me so much of Stu when he was that age." She took a slow drink of coffee to keep from plunging into an inquiry. "Stu will also have adorable kids, don't you think?"

"If he ever gets around to it."

"I know. I just want to see him head over heels. I can't recall him being twitterpated by anyone, can you?" Janice held her breath and studied Stacy's face, watching for the slightest twitch.

All she got in answer was a shrug. "Hey, can I drop off Larry this afternoon? My singles Sunday school class is having a Valentine's party, and I'd like to go."

"Of course."

"Thanks. It's a potluck supper, and Stu said he's having dinner with you, so he'll just bring him to my place after."

Dinner. They'd be done eating by the time Brin came back from the conference. RJ had told her they would be registering people right up till nine o'clock that evening. But it would be much less stressful if she and Stuart just went out, and she didn't have to worry about it. She needed to text him and suggest a restaurant. The topic of dinner gave her just the springboard she needed. "Speaking of dinner, I gave Stuart a gift card for da Vinci's." The upscale Italian restaurant, across the river in Williamstown, had been in business for forty years. Great food, great atmosphere. A perfect place for a romantic evening. "I never heard if he used it. Do you know if he took anyone?"

"Mom." Stacy smiled. A patient smile, but not condescending. They were definitely on better footing than just a few months earlier. "You keep telling me God's going to bring someone special into my life when the time is right. Can't you trust He's going to do the same for Stu?"

Janice looked down at what was left of her sandwich. "You're right. You know what it is? I pray for both of you daily. I hate that you've been hurt, and I want you to find love again, but you have Larry. You're not alone. Stuart is."

Stacy slid her hand over her mom's. "I know. I've tried introducing him to a couple of my friends. I always hear glowing reports from them, but he...I don't know, he says he's going to know when the right one comes along." She crumpled her napkin on the table and reached for her purse. "We have to trust, Mom."

"You're right. We have to trust." And hope that her son would know that it's okay to fall in love again.

CHAPTER SEVEN

Thunder rumbled over the river as Janice placed two logs on top of a nest of glowing coals in the fireplace, then sat at the piano as she watched the first flames lick at the bark. Larry, finally worn out after an hour of running around with the inn's two furry mascots, was sound asleep on the love seat. Tom, their black-and-white tuxedo kitten, slept curled in a ball in Larry's arms. Huck, the stray dog who'd befriended Tom, slept at his feet. Cherubic, all three of them.

Janice hoped the late nap wouldn't interfere with Larry's bedtime, but he needed this if he was going to be on his best behavior at supper. They'd made plans to meet Stuart at Over the Moon for pizza. Larry was ecstatic about the promise of his own bacon-and-ground-beef Mini Moon.

Setting aside a stack of word search books Larry had pulled from the game table in the library, she found the music she was looking for and began to play, singing the comforting words softly. "'Great is Thy faithfulness, O God my Father. There is no shadow of turning with Thee. Thou changest not, Thy compassions they fail not. As Thou hast been, Thou forever will be.'"

LuAnn sank into a chair with her ever-present notebook and joined Janice in the last stanza. Tess, carrying a giant mug, chimed in. They were quiet for several minutes after the hymn ended.

"Perfect song for a perfect Valentine's Day." Tess propped her feet on the coffee table. "I still can't believe the money was returned. Did someone just need a short-term loan? Crazy. At least now we can focus on the banquet."

"I'm not so sure about that." Janice moved to a chair and kicked off her shoes. "I ran into Maybelline today. She knows about RJ's bag." She repeated what Maybelline had said.

"Legend?" Tess asked. "What did she mean by that?"

Janice stared at Larry, wishing for a moment of the deep and carefree sleep of youth. "I don't know. She never mentioned the money, just the bag, and she was so insistent that we keep it locked up."

LuAnn opened her notebook. "And we have a new prime suspect, now that we know Cameron is left-handed." She looked at Janice. "You said Cameron got into town the night before he checked in. He said he stayed with a friend, right? I think we need to check out his alibi. Did you guys see the bandage on his arm?"

Tess nodded. "There's something about him. I can't quite put my finger on it."

"Finger...I knew I'd forgotten something!" LuAnn tapped her temple as she joined them, stretching out on the love seat. "I was going to tell everyone to set the juice glasses aside after breakfast so we could dust for prints. I found instructions on the internet about how to use candle soot. We can get the fingerprints off the juice glasses and compare them to the one on the box of candy."

Janice checked her watch and put her shoes back on. "That sounds really interesting. I'd like to try that."

"Candle soot?" Tess tipped her head to one side. "That might have been easy for Prudence, but—"

LuAnn held up her hand to stop her. "You just hold a lit candle up to the bottom of a heat-proof glass and then scrape the blackened residue off, over and over until you get a teaspoonful."

Tess arched an eyebrow. "Or we go to Walmart and pick up a kids' detective kit."

"What fun is that? Tomorrow morning we save the glasses and—"

The timer on Janice's phone went off. Time to wake her grandson and pray for answers from her son about what Brin had labeled "the other mystery." She'd been too busy all day to dwell on Stuart and Brin's mother and picnics in the empty inn and a time capsule. Now she couldn't think of anything else.

⚜

Janice stared at the smiling moon face on the window as she listened to Stuart talk about a movie he'd just seen and tried to formulate a way to transition from sci-fi flicks to long-lost love.

"Uncle Stu," Larry interrupted in a conspiratorial whisper. "I did that thing you told me to do."

Stuart held up his hand for a high five. "That's my man. Got it all set?"

"Yep. Can't wait."

The two shared a laugh, and Janice cleared her throat. "What are you two up to?"

"Nothing." The fact that they said it at exactly the same time with exactly the same inflection told her it was anything but nothing.

Stuart deflected her question by giving her the perfect opening for other questions.

"What's new at the inn?" he asked.

"Not much." *Other than hundreds of dollars stolen and then returned and your daughter showing up...* Six more days and she would tell him everything. And ask all the questions flooding her brain.

She told him, in a privacy-respecting way, about their current guests. "The Love Is conference made me think about the one you were involved with back in high school. What was that called?"

"I don't know. Jesus Rally or something, I think."

"Do you still stay in contact with anyone you met there?"

"Ma, that was two decades ago."

"I know, but with social media..."

Stuart ruffled his hair, a gesture of frustration he'd been doing since kindergarten. "When would I have time for that?"

Dead end. She looked around, trying again to find a logical segue. So many couples, staring dreamily across pizzas and garlic bread. Wasn't Valentine's Day enough of a reason to meddle just a tiny bit in her son's love life? "Were you dating anyone back then?"

She studied his face. Stuart had never been a great fibber. There. That tiny tic below his right eye. Dead giveaway. But to what? He hadn't said a word yet.

"Oh, at least a dozen girls that summer. You know me. Mr. Popularity." He laughed, stole a piece of pizza from Larry, and took his turn being the interrogator. "So, about the banquet. Apparently the thirteenth chapter of First Corinthians is the go-to text for Valentine themes. Any problem if I use the same theme as that conference?"

"No problem at all." She opened her mouth to say he should come by for breakfast and meet some of their guests, but stopped herself just in time. Not with Brin, the spitting image of her mother, there.

"Can we get chocolate chip cookies?" Larry, who'd been almost silent since his pizza arrived, stared from his nana to his uncle with pleading puppy-dog eyes.

Janice laughed. "You've been taking begging lessons from Huck, haven't you?"

"Is it working?"

"Yes, it's working." Janice took ten dollars out of her purse and handed it to him. "Get two two-packs."

Larry waved the bill over his head.

"What do you say, buddy?" Stuart prompted.

"Thank you, Nana." His singsongy voice made them all laugh.

"Speaking of chocolate chip cookies," Stuart said, "I've been doing some research on the physiology of love. Do you know why people, especially women, crave chocolate?"

"Because it's delicious?"

Stuart sprinkled parmesan cheese on his last slice of Providence Meatball Pie. "And because eating chocolate releases neurotransmitters that have positive effects on human emotions. Phenylethylamine, which is sometimes called 'the love drug,' causes alertness, quickens the pulse rate, and makes you happy. Tryptophan, an amino acid found in chocolate, causes the release of serotonin, which is a mood lifter."

"Fascinating."

"There's a ton more. One of the fats found in chocolate is called anandamide. It's named after the Sanskrit word for *bliss*. Anandamide activates a receptor which causes dopamine production. Dopamine causes a feeling of intense well-being. And, of course, eating chocolate releases endorphins into the brain, and endorphins are known to decrease levels of both stress and pain."

Janice grinned. "My brilliant son, the doctor. All this knowledge and you're still not—"

"Ma. Don't."

Larry returned with two packages of chocolate chip cookies. Janice took one, opened it, and took a massive bite, chewing to keep from saying anything more.

How long did it take for the stress-relieving, happy-feeling magic to take effect?

⚬━━━⟡⚬⟡⚬━━━⚬

Janice tapped the water from her toothbrush and stared at herself in the mirror. This wasn't going to be one of those nights when sleep came easy. Was Tess or Janice still awake? This might be a good night for watching *Pride and Prejudice* for the eighty-seventh time with a massive bowl of popcorn.

All she had to do was peek out in the hall to look for light seeping out under one of their doors. Once again, a wave of gratitude swept over her. She could be living the life of a lonely widow, feeling displaced and useless. Instead, she felt like she was back in college, sharing living quarters with her two best friends. Always someone to talk to, laugh with, cry with, or pray with. Forty years ago, when the biggest stressors were term papers, final exams, and boys, none of them could have envisioned a friendship that would weather so much. She walked to her closet for her robe and eased the door open.

Beep! Beep! Beep! A sound loud enough to wake the dead shot from the closet.

Fire? Smoke alarm?

No, she knew that sound.

"Stuart!" With a huff of irritation, she turned on the closet light and located the source. Ripping the wires off the motion sensor alarm her son had made in college to catch his room-mate stealing his Mountain Dew stopped the clamor.

And then she saw the note. *Gotcha, Nana!*

Larry. She sank to the closet floor and began to laugh.

Her phone dinged. Only texts from best friends, immediate family, and current guests got through after ten p.m. Tess: *What was that?*

Just a silly toy alarm Larry set. Sorry. Go back to sleep.

Three seconds later, a text from LuAnn to Janice and Tess: *Did you guys just hear that? Is it a fire alarm? Stay in your rooms until we know.*

Janice sent a quick reply, hoping LuAnn hadn't had time to call 911.

Now far beyond the possibility of sleep, Janice walked out into their common area. Her mother had always made warm milk when she couldn't sleep. Add a little butter and salt and pepper, and it wasn't bad. Worth a try.

The milk in the saucepan was almost heated when she heard a tentative knock at the door to the fourth floor.

She leaned close to the door. "Yes?" she whispered.

"It's Brin. I heard something."

From the floor below? Oh, to have the hearing of a nineteen-year-old. Janice turned off the burner and opened the door.

"I wasn't sure if it was okay to come up here, but I thought you should know. I couldn't sleep, so I was going to go down and get some tea. I walked out of my room, and then I heard this weird beeping noise. Did you hear it? It stopped right away, so I figured it can't be a smoke alarm, right?"

"Right." Janice motioned toward a chair as she explained about the alarm.

Brin laughed. "Larry sounds like my kind of kid."

You may have a lot in common, actually. Like DNA. "Hot chocolate?" They'd rarely ever invited a guest into their private quarters. What would Tess and LuAnn say if they woke up? She couldn't exactly explain that she needed time with Brin to find out if she was her granddaughter.

"Perfect."

"So you were having trouble getting to sleep?" *Something on your conscience?*

"Yeah." Brin pulled a phone out of the pocket of her flannel pajama pants. "I had a friend send me screenshots of my diary from back when I was a kid."

You still are a kid. "Oh?"

"Yeah. My mom's in Europe. Did I say that already? She's on a music tour. So anyway, my friend is dog-sitting at our house, so I asked her to take pictures of some pages in my diary. You have to be pretty good friends to let someone look through all your junior high drama, right? Anyway, a few years ago I wrote down everything my mom said about this place."

"Oh?" Janice mixed cocoa powder and sugar with water and stirred it into the heated milk.

"Listen." Brin bent over her phone. "'It's all so romantic. They would meet in an abandoned hotel down by the river and listen to music for hours and dance and have picnics on the floor. And explore. That's the very best part. There were secret passageways and tunnels and—'"

"Wait. St—" Janice stopped herself before blurting her son's name. *Are you telling me Stuart knew about the tunnel before we found it?* How was that possible? Why wouldn't he have said something? She needed to see that picture again. Maybe there was another boy in Marietta who looked just like him whose mother embroidered the Marietta Tigers logo on his shirts. And why was he wearing the shirt anyway? He'd been kind enough to wear it around her once before it mysteriously disappeared, but she knew he'd hated it. "Sorry. Go on."

"They found this old—" Brin grimaced.

"Old what?"

"Stuff. They found some cool old stuff." She tucked her phone back in her pocket. "I tried to find out more before I left, but my mom got this sort of sad look on her face and just said it happened so long ago she couldn't remember. But I know she really could remember."

"What are you hoping to find here, Brin?"

"Oh, just something…tangible, you know? My mom was kind of weird when she was young. She thought that God was in charge of her destiny, and if He wanted them to be together He would make it happen."

Can't argue with that.

Brin shrugged. "I think sometimes you have to make things happen. Anyway, they knew they were too young, and she had to go back to Boston, and so they said they would meet in the same place on a certain date in six years when they were both done with college, but then when she had me she didn't want to burden the guy with a kid because he was going to be a doctor, and so she didn't come. It's like that movie where the woman gets hit by a car because she's looking up at the Empire State Building."

"*An Affair to Remember.*" Lawrence had teased her for being a sobbing mess every time it came on TV. Teased, but watched it with her.

Did Stuart show? Had her poor heartsick boy wandered around in this empty old building waiting for his true love?

He'd been moody the whole summer after college. She'd worried over him, but Lawrence assured her it was only stress. After all, he was about to enter medical school. Janice blinked back tears. "And you don't know his name?"

"No. Well, I know a nickname." Brin giggled. "Neo. From *The Matrix*."

It fit. Stuart wasn't a blue pill kind of guy. Always thinking outside the box, always taking things apart and wanting to reassemble them in a different way. It was part of what made him so good as a doctor and a coroner. "But she must have found out where he is now, with the internet."

"I know. I asked her that. She said she couldn't rewrite the past."

"Sad."

"Right? It's especially sad because of this part." Brin ruffled her bangs with a sigh and started reading from her phone again. "'He promised that when they met again he would get down on one knee and propose to her with a ruby—'"

Squeak. Squeak.

"What is that?" Brin whispered. "It came from below us." She jumped up and strode to the door, pressing her ear against it. "The elevator?"

"I don't think so. The elevator's at the other end of the hall, and it's all metal. This sounds more like... creaking wood."

Janice put her ear to the door. The sound was repetitive, like someone sawing wood with a wooden handsaw. "It reminds me of an old teeter totter I used to play on."

The noise stopped. Soft footfalls followed. And then silence.

July 19, 1863

Ira's chin lolled on his chest as they neared the gangplank. Prudence nudged him. "Wake up!" she whispered through clenched jaws. They couldn't support his weight. "Almost there."

Thunder rolled from the north. Ira stirred, and a bit of strength returned to his legs.

"Headin' home, son?" An officer passed them halfway down the angled boards.

Tabitha managed a slight nod while still holding Ira's arm over her shoulder. "Taking him home to nurse him back to health."

"Good. Good. We'll have need of him when he's strong again, unless this cursed war be done by then. Godspeed."

A raindrop splattered on the dirt-and-blood-caked wood at their feet, leaving a splotch of mud. Fear clenched Prudence's gut. "We have to hide him before the rain. If it washes any dirt off..."

"Those trees." Tabitha motioned with her free arm. "We'll hide there while thee gets the—"

"Tabitha!" a bedraggled-looking woman called as she shuffled toward them. "Who is that?"

Seconds passed, and Prudence was about to jump in with an answer when Tabitha said, "One of my father's hired hands."

"Poor boy. We're heading home in Susannah's wagon. We have her brother and a friend of his. I don't know if either of them will make it, but Susannah is sure their chances are better if we take them home. There's room for this boy. Hurry."

"I—"

"There's a boat coming for him!" Prudence spoke a little too loudly and quickly. "But thy kindness is appreciated."

The woman nodded and moved on.

"If anyone asks, stick with the story of the hired hand." Lifting her skirt, which hung limp without a petticoat, Prudence ran along the bank to the place where she'd tied the small boat. She reached it just as the rain began in earnest.

But she was not alone. A man in a ragged uniform, his arm in a sling, stumbled toward the boat and grabbed the rope that tethered it.

"That's mine!" Prudence yelled over the rising wind.

"Not anymore, it ain't." The man laughed and aimed a pistol at her head.

She let out a helpless scream and pointed behind him. "Is that a snake?"

"What—" The man swung to look behind him, and Prudence used that moment to bend to the side and wrap her hand around a heavy fallen branch.

"Unhand my boat, mister." She swung the branch with all her might, striking his knee and causing him to fall to the ground. She kicked the gun away and snatched the rope out of his hand. She brandished the branch again, this time above her head, and the man staggered to his feet, cursing, and loped away.

And Prudence sank to the ground.

CHAPTER EIGHT

S orry I'm late. I found the woman in the plaid coat!" LuAnn
was almost panting as she closed the back door to the
kitchen just after seven a.m. "I was...walking...by the park,
over by the gazebo...and there she was. Red hair, plaid coat,
three little kids." She pulled off her navy hoodie and dropped
it on a chair. "They got out of a car and went into a house on
Front Street."

Janice stopped slicing banana bread. "Which house? Did
you get the address?"

LuAnn shook her head. "There's an attorney's office sign
out front."

Winnie looked up from arranging strips of bacon on a
cookie sheet. "Nobody I know has attorney appointments
before seven in the mornin'."

"I know. Weird." LuAnn picked up her sweatshirt and
pulled out her phone. "I got a picture of the sign and the house.
I wish I'd thought quickly enough to get a picture of the
woman."

Tess, who'd been unloading the dishwasher, turned to
face LuAnn. "Did you get a license plate number or anything?"

"No. By the time I thought of it, the woman who dropped her off drove away."

"What kind of car?" Janice almost laughed. They'd all become attuned to so many details that had never seemed important to them before buying the inn.

"A nice one. Dark red. A *very* nice one." LuAnn's eyes suddenly brightened. "A Porsche."

Tess shrugged. "Guess we know what we're doing after breakfast."

"Guess so," LuAnn agreed. "I'm off to shower."

Janice held out a hand to stop Tess from pulling a juice glass from the top rack of the dishwasher. "Leave those." She opened the drawer where they kept storage bags and aluminum foil.

"Why?" Tess looked at her like she'd lost it.

Janice pulled two green food prep gloves out of a box and put them on. Pointing to the glasses, she said, "Our prints can't be on these."

Tess's eyes lit up. "You're right—I forgot about that. I wrote down the instructions—I'll get them for you later."

"You're serious." LuAnn halted, one hand on the door.

"I am. We have a perfectly clear partial fingerprint on the heart box." Janice took two glasses from Tess and set them on a tray, then reached for two more. "Whoever is pouring juice has to do it without picking up the glasses. Then leave them on the table and I'll clear." She opened another drawer and pulled out a Pyrex measuring cup. "By then I will be ready to dust."

"Good morning, ladies!" Bart Sandman walked across the showroom floor, grinning at them, left hand extended. The right cuff of his dress shirt was tucked in his pocket. Bart had lost his hand in an IED explosion in Afghanistan. "Is the inn finally successful enough that you're here to actually look at a car?"

Tess shook her head, sending her auburn waves dancing. "I'm sorry, Bart. That day may come, but for now we're here looking for answers."

"Don't tell me, someone left another skeleton at the inn and used a Porsche as a getaway car."

Janice glanced at LuAnn. The man's guess could be more right than wrong. She managed a laugh. "We're looking for the owner of a new red Porsche. She left something at the inn." Not a lie. Not at all.

"Do you know what model? How new?"

LuAnn's mouth twisted to one side. "It looked brand-new. Shiny wheels, like it hadn't been out on the roads much. Not a trace of salt or sand." She glanced at Tess and Janice. "With the ice and snow we had last week, our cars sure don't look like that. It was sporty looking, but not tiny. Three kids fit in back."

Bart rubbed his chin. "Five-seater. Red. That kind of narrows it down." He handed LuAnn a catalog, and she leafed through it.

"There. Pretty sure this is it." She pointed to a Panamera Sport Turismo. "Sporty, but kind of square and SUVish in back."

"Well, that narrows it down more. Anything else?"

"The driver was a woman. At least I'm pretty sure. All I could really see was a black scarf. It covered her head and shoulders, and she was turned away from me. The passenger was a woman in her thirties. Red hair."

"And three children?"

"Yes."

Bart nodded and motioned for them to follow him to a corner desk. Bending over a computer, he typed. "Mm-hmm. Yep. I think I know. Ethically, of course, I shouldn't tell you."

Janice smiled. Bart had given them information in the past. He wasn't a man to be constrained by ethics. Unless, of course, he could benefit from them. "How 'bout we make a little trade?" She hadn't intended to sound like a mob boss in a 1940s movie, but since it came out that way, why not go with it? "You spill, we get Winnie ta make a gallon o' peanut soup just fer you. And we'll sweeten da deal with a dozen pecan rolls. Whatcha say, Bart?"

"I say you ladies crack me up, and it's a deal." He swiveled his monitor so they could see the screen.

Janice took a step back as they blurted the name in unison. "Maybelline?"

❦

Janice yawned. She sat at a table at Jeremiah's Coffee House, sipping on a salted caramel latte as she waited to meet Paige Murphey, her pastor's wife, for their weekly coffee. She massaged her right temple. Her brain hurt from trying to process everything that had happened in the past twenty-four hours. Maybelline. Brin. The strange sound. Wood on wood. Rhythmic. What could it be? This morning, she'd been waiting for LuAnn to return before telling her and Tess about the sound. In the excitement that followed, she'd forgotten.

The other thing she hadn't done was dust the glasses for fingerprints. She'd discovered it took way longer to get a spoonful of candle soot than Tess had claimed. But she'd carefully set all eight glasses on a tray, covered them with a dishcloth, and stashed them in the pantry.

She took another deep breath and closed her eyes, trying to focus on Paige and the baby that would be born in a matter of weeks. Joyful thoughts. What had started as mentoring—the old pastor's wife advising the new one—had turned into a mutual friendship. Janice had to admit that she needed this time as much as Paige might.

"Hi!" Paige swayed toward her, looking beautiful—blooming, as Lawrence would have said.

Janice jumped up and hugged her, a bit awkwardly since Paige was several inches taller, and her pregnancy made it hard for Janice to get her arms around the mom-to-be. They both laughed. "Sit. Put your feet up. My treat today. What can I get you?"

"Promise you won't tell Ben or my OB?"

"Promise. What happens at Jeremiah's stays at Jeremiah's."

Paige's nose crinkled as she grinned. "God put you in my life for so many reasons, Janice. One of them being to get me a double hazelnut macchiato with extra whip."

"My pleasure." Janice strode to the counter and got in line behind two women she knew from church. She greeted Carla and Darinda and asked the obligatory questions about grand-children.

"So…you're meeting with Paige." Though she'd made a statement, question marks danced in Carla's eyes.

"Yes." Nothing else needed.

"I bet it's nice keeping up on all the latest prayer requests, isn't it?" Darinda's smile missed patronizing by maybe a milli-meter. "Keeping your finger in the pot, so to speak." Nope, there went the millimeter.

Grrr. That did not deserve a comment. She wanted to turn and leave, but she wouldn't go back to the table without a mac-chiato in her hand.

"We heard you're having trouble at the inn again," Darinda said.

Again? She made it sound like trouble was a constant thing. Janice had to bite on this one. "No trouble. What did you hear?"

"Cheryl Collins, who cleans over at Putnam Chocolates, told Shelly Williams, who told my daughter, that someone's been stealing from your patrons. And"—Carla bent low and whispered in Janice's ear—"we know who's doing it."

"You do?"

"Yes. There's a young man staying at your inn who has a record." Carla appeared ready to lick her lips over this juicy morsel.

"A record? For what?" Janice wasn't going to let her get away with vague accusations. "Who are you talking about?"

"Well, you can't expect us to know everything. Shelly's husband works for the city, and he knows a lot of police officers, and he told Shelly he couldn't tell her the man's name, but he said you should watch out."

Janice restrained a sigh. "So you don't know anything more than that? Sounds like a lot of hearsay, something none of us want to be repeating."

Darinda huffed. "Shouldn't be hard to figure out. How many young men who could have police records are staying at your inn?"

Janice forced her gaze not to waver from Darinda's face as she calmly said, "Can't think of one person who could possibly fit that description."

It was true. She couldn't think of one. She could think of three.

⚜

Paige took the macchiato with gratitude in her eyes. "Did those ladies try to pester you into telling them what we talk about?"

"Oh, no." Janice made no attempt to hide the sarcasm. "They just wanted to make sure I knew the latest prayer requests."

They shared the kind of laugh only two women who'd filled the same role could share. Paige pressed her hands to the sides of her belly. "How did you do this for all those years? The snide remarks, the stares, the"—she forked the air with two fingers—"'advice,' the looks of patient condescension when, heaven forbid, I suggest something outrageous like letting the teens lead a worship service."

Janice nodded. "Not only was I in your shoes thirty years ago, I also became one of those old biddies who didn't like change. For a time, at least."

"You are not an old biddy! I understand being resistant to trying new things. You just needed a little time to adjust. Some of these people planted their feet on one side of the line forty years ago, and they've grown roots. Nothing's going to get them to move."

"Then you simply mow around them, my dear." Janice held up her latte, and Paige tapped it with her mug.

"What would I do without you, Mama Janice?"

Janice blinked back sudden tears. She'd thought her days of counseling had ended when Lawrence died. "I need you too, Daughter Paige." She winked. "You keep me young and let me vent, and we always seem to bring each other back to the right place."

"Praise God for that." Paige took a sip from her mug and sighed again. "What's new with your kids?"

"Stace is fine. Larry's adorable."

"And Stuart is not so fine?"

"Stuart is single. I'm getting desperate."

"But he's not?"

Janice ran a fingertip around her lime-green mug. "Not that he lets me see. It's like he's got this fantasy of this perfect woman. I worry that he'll miss the one who's right for him because he's waiting for someone who doesn't exist." She made it all sound hypothetical, though in her gut she was pretty sure that was exactly what her son was doing—waiting for someone who was as perfect as his faded memories of a girl he'd met twenty years ago.

"Maybe she is out there."

Janice laughed. "Whoever she is, I've been praying for her for thirty-six years." An involuntary inhale startled Janice. Whom had she been praying for? Was it possible she'd been praying for Brin's mother all along?

Janice shook her head and changed the subject. "How's Ben doing?"

"He's taking on way too much." Paige rolled her shoulders. "I'm worried about him. I suppose I'm being selfish, but I want my husband around after the baby's born."

"Not selfish at all. That baby needs to bond with his daddy." A twinge of old angst pinched behind Janice's sternum. She and Lawrence had dealt with the same thing when Stacy and Stuart were about six and eight and Lawrence was rarely home. Thankfully, Lawrence had listened. "One of your roles as his helpmate is to help him see that. What do you think he can cut out of his schedule?"

"Oh..." It came out on a groan. "It's all good stuff, and he's so good at doing the good stuff." Paige sat up and kneaded her lower back with both hands. "He just took on something I guess Lawrence did on a regular basis."

"What's that?"

"He's been leaving the house super early a couple of mornings a week and going over to Harmar to talk to a bunch of fishermen. It's a good thing, right? But didn't it scare you? I've seen some of those men. They're...earthy. Not that that means anything about their character, of course. But it could. We ran into a couple of them at Walmart, and Ben was joking around with them like they were old buddies. I don't know, maybe it's just overactive pregnancy hormones, but it worries me."

"Was one of them named Axel?"

"Yes. What a character, huh? Ben told me a little about his story. You probably know all about him because of his sordid"—Paige closed her eyes and took a long, controlled breath—"connection with the inn."

"No. I don't. I— Paige?" Janice reached out and grabbed the sloshing macchiato as Paige's face pinched in pain. "You okay?"

"I don't...know. I've been having contractions all morning, but they've been so mild. But now..." Eyes wide, she took a long, slow breath. "I think...I'm...in labor."

⚜

Janice turned onto Butler Street. "Candle blow." She'd taken Lamaze classes before Stuart was born and then again as a coach when Stacy was pregnant with Larry. It was all coming back to her. "Let me know when it ends."

The contraction lasted until she put her blinker on for Second Street. Sixty seconds, she'd guess. This one was six minutes from the last one. They weren't regular. "How strong are they?"

"Not terrible." Paige massaged her belly. "Ben's going to meet us there?" It was the third time she'd asked.

"He'll be there when we get there."

"It's too early." Paige gripped the door handle. "I'm scared."

"Larry was born a month early. He spent two days in the NICU for observation, but he was fine. Didn't even need oxygen." She patted Paige's hand, pressed in a fist, on her swollen belly. "Let's pray."

As Janice prayed, Paige's fist relaxed. Janice turned the car into the Emergency Room entrance. Paige had called her obstetrician's office, and they'd told her to go in and get checked.

Ben was waiting in the parking lot, looking as terrified as Paige. As he embraced his wife, Janice touched his arm and attempted the same reassurance she'd offered Paige. "There's a lot they can do to stop labor if they need to. And four weeks really isn't all that early. Paige said at her last visit they figured the baby was five pounds so . . . " She gave up when she realized her words were falling on deaf ears. With a protective arm around his wife, Ben ushered her toward the ER entrance.

Janice stood in the parking lot. Alone. Feeling suddenly unneeded. Again. The strangest things triggered grief and the sense that she'd lost her identity when she lost Lawrence.

She watched Ben open the door, his hand low and reassuring on Paige's back.

Little things. That's what she missed. Like a hand on her back. Like someone to open the car door or leave a note on the mirror or say "I love you" before they switched off the lights at night.

Putting her hand on the car door handle, she closed her eyes. *Lord, forgive me. It does no one any good for me to dwell on the past. I'm feeling a little empty right now. Sometimes I wonder what my life is—*

"Janice?"

She opened her eyes to see the Sams walking toward her from the direction of the ER door. Sam had his arm around Sammy. Both faces looked ashen. Janice rushed toward them. "What happened?"

"Just a little arrythmia." Sammy smiled. "I got a little dizzy. I'm fine now. They adjusted my meds and told me to take it easy for the rest of the day." She smiled up at her husband. "It happens. I usually just wait it out, but—"

"But I'm not taking any chances on losing her." Sam squeezed her and lifted a trembling hand to her face. "Gotta take care of my bride." Sam, tall and broad-shouldered and incredibly fit for a man in his seventies, seemed to age before her eyes as concern for his wife overwhelmed him.

"Where's your car?" Janice turned away from them, under the guise of looking for their vehicle, to hide the sudden flash of tears. "I'll drive you back to the inn."

"That would be wonderful." Sammy patted Janice's arm. "I'm not so sure I want Sam behind the wheel when he's still shaking like this." She held up her husband's hand to prove her point. "Thank you, Janice. You know, I don't think I've ever met more kind and considerate people than you and Tess and LuAnn. God certainly has His hand on you three."

"Yes. He does." *And thank You for the reminder.*

July 19, 1863

Lightning ripped the inky sky, a gash of white that disappeared as quickly as it materialized. From the forboding clouds above them, rain pelted down on the little craft as it fought wind and current.

"Tabitha!" Prudence yelled over the torrent. "Come up here!" She craned her neck as Tabitha moved, slow and heavy, struggling against her sodden skirts and the swaying boat. As Tabitha, leaning hard on Prudence's shoulder, swung one foot over the seat, Prudence slid to the right and handed over an oar. "Put on thy gloves. We will make better time this way." In truth, she wasn't sure they would. Two exhausted women bobbing like a cork in the angry river would make slow headway, but the effort would keep Tabitha warm.

"I don't have gloves."

Without a word, Prudence slipped hers off and handed them to her friend.

"No. Thee can't—"

"I am a farm wife, remember? These hands are used to work."

And accustomed to the feel of the oars.

How many trips had she made in this skiff? But most often over the years it had been a trip across the Ohio and back and, on both sides of the river, they did what they could to make sure the crossings were not in inclement conditions.

Sometimes it couldn't be helped. She'd dodged chunks of ice and dealt with flood waters, but this was the worst storm in her recollection, and they were traveling upstream. "Lord, we implore Thee for Thy help."

Ira's boot rested against Prudence's, and she felt the vibration of his shivering.

Just when she wondered if she could manage one more stroke, and as Tabitha's shoulders began to shake in a sob, she saw the lights of the Riverfront House, welcoming them to a place of safety.

They rowed toward the bank, toward an outcropping of rock and bushes. She'd tied the skiff to a low branch in that very spot more times than she could count. Just to its left was the entrance to the tunnel that, at least to her knowledge, hadn't been used in months.

Her legs almost gave way when she stepped out into the thigh-deep water. She roused a feverish Ira and, between the two of them, she and Tabitha got him out of the skiff.

"Only a few more feet. We're almost there."

"No!" Ira shook them off as if they were flies. "Let me go. I have to get to General—" With a massive splash, he fell facedown in the water.

CHAPTER NINE

Janice pushed through the swinging door with a tray of steaming soup bowls. Her stomach rumbled. The lunch crowd should thin in an hour, and she'd find time to grab a bowl... or two. She served the grandma with the mischievous little grandson named Johnny, leaving a snickerdoodle at his place with a wink. As she stepped to the next table, the door chime rang, and she looked up, ready to smile a greeting.

Or not.

Axel Barrett shuffled in, followed by his fishing cohorts.

She looked around. She was the only server in the café.

Axel waved at her.

"Welcome to Wayfarers Inn. We have a table by the window." She gestured toward the corner. "Lovely view of the river."

The tallest one—Stick?—laughed. "Like we never get to see it."

"Today's soup choices are Chicken Tortilla and Split Pea. I'll give you a minute to decide. What can I get you to drink?"

"Iced tea all around, Mrs. Eastman." Axel seemed far less movie-pirate-scary here on her own turf.

Janice walked double-time into the kitchen. "Axel and his gang are here." Yes, she was being melodramatic, but everything that was happening lately seemed to call for a bit of melo-drama.

LuAnn froze, mid tortilla chip smash. "What do they want? Did he say anything about you talking to Marie? Do you think he suspects us of suspecting him? Is there going to be trouble?"

Janice knew her silver-haired friend with the Walter Mitty imagination well enough to guess she was picturing a *Bam! Pow! Thwack!* wild west barroom fistfight.

"They're here to eat."

Tess ladled tortilla soup into a bowl LuAnn had just filled with crushed chips. "Why? If they've ever been here for lunch, none of us saw them, right? So they're here for a reason. They have to know we're onto them."

"But we're not." Janice grabbed a chip, but her mouth was too dry to eat it. "All we know is Axel lied about having Franky's tackle. We don't know that he, or any of them, were in the boat the other night. Maybe somebody borrowed his boat without asking."

Winnie chuckled. "That's called stealing in my book. Looks like you've got your work cut out for you." She held out a basket of warm corn muffins to Janice. "People open up to you. And these will help prime the pump."

Reluctantly, Janice took the basket. "What should I say?"

Tess turned away from Big Red. "Ask 'em if they want ta make a deal. They spill the beans about who stole RJ's bag, or you'll spill the peas on them!" She slapped her knee. "Man, I crack me up."

LuAnn guffawed, and Winnie and Tess joined in.

Janice gave an exaggerated eye roll. "You people are no help! I'm walking into the lion's den armed with nothing but corn muffins, and all you can do is laugh?"

Tess grabbed a wooden spoon. "I'm right behind you, sister."

"Me too." LuAnn brandished a paper towel roll. "We got your back."

In spite of herself, Janice smiled. A smile that lasted until six feet from the table in the corner.

Noah, wearing a black jacket with *Love Is* embroidered on the back, backpack slung over one shoulder and a long, narrow bag in the other, walked over to the table and placed a stack of bills in Axel's outstretched hand.

As Janice approached the table, slightly trembling muffin basket in one hand, shaky coffeepot in the other, Noah darted for the front door. Janice caught his eye as he glanced back toward Axel's table before opening the door. When she turned her attention back to the fishermen, Axel's smile was aimed in her direction.

Janice held his gaze. "I see you met one of our guests."

"Nice kid. What a charming place you have here."

"Thank you. Did you have business with Noah?" Where was this weirdly out-of-character boldness coming from?

"Yep. I do a little resale business on the side. Fishing stuff."

Sure you do. And "on the side" of what . . . your breaking and entering business? Her thoughts countered what she'd just told Tess and LuAnn. They had suspicions, but no evidence. Yet.

"You know, it occurred to me after you left that I'd had more than a few conversations with your husband over the years. We had some splendid debates at the Busy Bee on Saturday mornings."

Why had Lawrence never mentioned it? Had she been too preoccupied to listen? "I understand Pastor Ben Murphey has taken over for him."

"Yep. Boy's not quite as good a debater as your husband."

"Was my husband able to persuade you with his message?"

"Persuade?" He grinned. "Well, let's just say that, as my time gets closer, I'm considering it all."

Well, that was more than she'd expected. She poured coffee and took Stick, Bobber, and Raven's orders. Two split pea, one tortilla.

The door chime turned her attention away from Axel as she was about to take his order. She smiled at the familiar camo jacket and felt her shoulders relax. Tory Thornton, Wayfarers Inn's handyman and one of her favorite people in Marietta. Janice had taught with him years ago, and was trying to get used to calling him "Thorn" like everyone else in town. She always felt a little calmer when he was in the building.

Thorn waved at the men at the table. "Hey, Axel. Guys. Come to see what life on the other side of the river's like, huh?"

So Thorn knew Axel. She made a mental note to pick Thorn's brain later.

When the men finished their easy banter—which told her nothing about their relationship—and Thorn walked off to an empty table, she turned to Axel.

Axel folded his large, scarred hands around a black mug. "I imagine you think I deceived you."

"Well, we..."

"You talked to Maria."

"Yes."

"Apparently she left a box of Franky's things in my boat without letting me know."

She nodded, waiting for him to continue.

"The lure you found...I think that had to be one that fell off one of Franky's lines. Could have been months ago. It looked like it had been pretty water-logged. I think you got yourself a Franky original. Quite a find."

"Quite."

"I'd like the tortilla soup, please." Axel unfolded his napkin and set it on his lap.

"Right away."

She brought their soup, refilled their muffin basket once and drinks twice, returned to bus the table when they left...and picked up a tip equal to the cost of their meal.

The last customer walked out the door, and Janice collapsed onto a chair in the kitchen and pulled her phone out of her apron pocket. A text from Ben caused a sigh of relief. *False labor. P resting. Thank you.* He'd added a heart emoji.

Thank You, Lord. Janice gave a weary smile to Tess, who plopped into a chair looking as tired as Janice felt.

"Powwow," was all Tess could say.

"You girls go talk." Winnie waved at them with a dish towel. "I've got this."

"Are you sure?" LuAnn set a tub of dirty dishes next to the sink. "There's still a lot—"

"I'm sure. You all go solve the mystery and figure out who's cookin' in my kitchen for the banquet. I'm this close"—she held up her thumb and forefinger, less than an inch apart—"to canceling my weekend plans so I can stay here and—"

"Oh, no you don't!" Janice stood and headed for the coffee-pot. "We got this." She stuck her tongue out at Winnie, who responded by throwing the dish towel at her.

The Inn Crowd convened in their fourth-floor sitting room. Janice filled them in on her strange encounter with Axel and gang.

"He never gave Noah anything in exchange for the money?" Tess set a bowl of red grapes on the coffee table.

"Not that I saw."

LuAnn slipped her shoes off and stretched out her long legs. "So what's the connection between Noah and Axel?"

Janice positioned a throw pillow behind her back. "Totally unlikely alliance. What was the money for? How could those two have met? No idea."

"I think what you saw today is a red herring." LuAnn popped a grape in her mouth.

"You and your literary devices." Though Tess razzed LuAnn, it was clear she was considering the theory. "So Noah made a show of giving Axel money as a diversion?"

"Yep."

Janice twirled a strand of hair around her finger. "What was his—or their—objective?"

"No clue." Tess stretched her neck from side to side.

LuAnn picked up the ever-present notebook. "We have to record the clue even if we have no clue if it's really a clue."

Tess rolled her eyes. "Let's do a recap of everything we saw and heard today." She pointed at LuAnn. "Did you see anything notable at breakfast?"

"Oh!" LuAnn said. "I almost forgot. I told Cameron I heard him say he stayed with a friend when he first got to town. I said we know almost everyone in Marietta and asked who it was."

"Aaand?" Tess played into LuAnn's hands, leaning forward and resting her elbows on her knees.

"And you aren't going to believe it."

Janice copied Tess's pose, letting LuAnn have her moment of suspense. "Who?"

"Thorn."

Their mouths were still gaping when Janice's phone rang. Stacy. "Hi, sweetie."

"Would you mind watching Larry again for a few hours? I hate to ask, but the sitter filling in for the nanny just called and—"

"No problem. Want me to come get him?"

"No, but thanks. She brought him to the clinic. I've got a short break, so I'll drop him off. I'm sorry I have—"

"No sorries." Being a single mom was tough. "Bring him over. See you in a bit."

Tired though she was, her grandson always managed to give her spirits a lift. And Tess and LuAnn—and Tom and Huck—loved having him around. They were having leftover tortilla soup and corn muffins for supper, perfect for the six-year-old, who had once declared he was only going to eat quesadillas and salsa for breakfast, lunch, and dinner when he grew up.

In less than ten minutes, Larry came bounding in.

"Hi, Nana! Where's Tom and Huck?" Larry flung himself at her, hugging her waist. "Upstairs?"

"Yep. Aunt LuAnn just went upstairs. Tess and I will make popcorn and be up in a few minutes." She was pretty sure he'd stopped listening after the first word.

In the kitchen, Tess plugged in the air popper. Janice got a stick of butter out of the fridge, then went in search of the cheese powder Larry loved. On her way to the pantry, she looked around the kitchen, which still, five months after the inn opened, made her heart go pitter-patter. Ceiling-high white cupboards, white subway tile behind long stretches of counter. She loved the black and white theme, with red accents like the vintage canister set they'd found at a flea market and the old red-handled utensils that hung from rustic metal hooks above the kitchen's focal point, Big Red. The 1954 O'Keefe and Merritt Aristocrat gas stove was a true treasure. She glanced at Tess. "Do you ever wonder if someday you'll wake up back in your rented house and realize this life we're living is just a dream?"

Tess laughed. "We are blessed," she called over the noise of the popper. "Do you ever feel guilty for being so...content?"

Janice waited until the noise stopped before answering, using the time to melt half a stick of butter in the microwave.

"You were listening in on my thoughts again. I never told anyone, but I used to keep a running commentary in the back of my journal about all the things I could do if I wasn't married to Lawrence. Not because I was unhappy, just because I thought maybe I could be prepared. Dumb thought."

Tess poured the butter on the popcorn and salted it. Janice turned off the lights, and they walked to the elevator together.

After starting the elevator, Tess looked at her. No judgment, just interest. "What was on your list?"

"Things Lawrence wasn't interested in. Broadway musicals, a river cruise in Europe, living in a house filled with antiques."

"One out of three isn't bad."

"Not bad at all. And this place is as entertaining as the other two."

Tess nodded. "You know what I'm discovering? I like who I am here. It feels right."

"I'm still working on it." Janice thought of the meltdown she'd almost had in the hospital parking lot. "But that gives me hope. We're 'finding ourselves' in *our* sixties like everybody said we were supposed to do back in *the* sixties."

They got out of the elevator on the fourth floor. Janice peeked into LuAnn's apartment. "Lu? Is Larry with you?"

"No." LuAnn walked out of her sitting room, notebook in hand. "He took Huck. They must be hunting for the slimy tennis ball."

They walked down the hall together. Janice set the cheese powder on the kitchen table and looked around. "Larry?"

The silence that answered sent a chill up her spine.

"Larry?" She strode to her apartment and did a quick search. Tess and LuAnn joined her.

Silence.

She ran to the door to their floor, then down to the landing on the third. Silence. She ran down another flight of stairs. All the guest room doors were closed. No sign of Larry or the dog.

Her searching grew more frantic by the second. Tess and LuAnn joined her on the main floor. Grabbing Janice by the arm, Tess demanded eye contact. "He's in the building, Janice. I see the panic in your eyes, but he's here. He's too scared of the dark to go outside, you know that."

Janice nodded, her gaze drifting to the basement door. "He couldn't... could he?"

"I'll search the basement. And the tunnel. You go upstairs. He's probably under a bed playing a trick on you."

LuAnn put her hand on Janice's other shoulder. "He's hid on us before, and we found him within minutes."

"Very, very long minutes."

"I'll check the kitchen. You go upstairs."

Anxiety knotting her stomach, Janice did what she was told. *Please, God.* They were right, he had to be in the building. Irrational fear had been part of her daily existence most of her life. She'd learned to control much of it, but there were still those times...

Like now, when she stood in her bedroom staring at the little dog, who sat, looking forlorn, in front of the closet door.

The door that hid a trap door that led to a ladder that led to other trap doors all the way to the cold, hard basement floor. Trap doors that should be locked from the underside. She stared down the shaft at a glimmer of light that shouldn't be there.

O Lord, hold on to my boy.

CHAPTER TEN

Janice gripped the closet frame and fought a wave of dizziness as she looked down the ladder shaft. "Larry?" Her voice echoed back at her. "Honey, are you down there? Answer Nana."

Silence. Then a soft whimper. "N-Nana. I'm scared."

Pent-up breath rushed out of her. Tears stung her eyes. The voice hadn't come from the bottom. It sounded like he was only two floors down.

"Hold on, baby. Nana's coming." Taking the deepest breath she could manage, she bent to her knees.

She'd watched LuAnn do this with ease. And grace. What did she do first?

She turned on all fours and lowered one foot over the edge.

"I see your leg, Nana."

"See? I'm almost there. Just keep looking up at me." *Don't look down.* That's what you're supposed to say to people who are afraid of heights, right? *Don't look down. Don't look down.* She grasped the wood frame with sweaty hands, and as her left foot found the third rung, her right hand moved to the first. "'I lift up my eyes to the mountains,'" she whispered. "'Where does my help come from? My help comes from the LORD, the Maker of heaven and earth. He will not let your foot slip—'"

"Don't step on my heart, Nana!"

She froze, her own heart on the verge of stopping. "What?"

"My heart! It's right by your foot!"

Another pulse skip. Was he hurt? The boy knew the names of body parts, but... "Your *heart?*"

"My candy heart. It's by your foot."

"Oh, Larry, I'll buy you a million candy hearts after we get out of here." And how, exactly, were they going to accomplish getting out? Why hadn't she made a plan before jumping in like Wonder Woman? Could she crawl over him? Would her presence give him the courage to step down to the next closet where they could exit? "Can you put your hands real close together and your feet—"

"Janice? Larry?" LuAnn's shouts from below landed on her ears like an angel chorus.

"Can you see him, Lu? I can't tell how far down he is." Janice kept her eyes fixed straight ahead.

"I've got him." The ladder trembled as LuAnn climbed. "You can't fall now, sweetie. Just step down. Three big steps and you'll be safe in Lily and Lace."

"That's a girl room."

LuAnn's laugh echoed up the shaft. "Yes, it is. There. Now run up to Nana's room. And nowhere else, got it?"

"Got it."

"So, Nana." LuAnn's voice ricocheted off the walls. "Are you okay climbing back up, or should I come up there?"

"I'm good." Surprisingly, she was. The last time Larry had disappeared, searching for him had nearly been the death of her. Baby step by baby step, she was conquering her fears.

"I'm here, Nana." Larry's voice came from above her. "You can do it. You're really brave. Uncle Stu said you're wimpy, but I think you're really brave."

He said *what?* Any trace of anxiety disappeared. She climbed to the top, and with Larry tugging on her arm, hoisted herself onto the closet floor.

An audience of three cheered. Sitting back on her heels, she gave a weak smile. "What were you doing in there, buddy?"

"Huck was chewing on the opener thing, so I pulled on it, and the ladder was there, and I wanted to know where it went to, so I climbed down. I never get scared on our play set or on the high slide at school. But this one goes straight down like a wall, and then I climbed through a box thing, and then I saw the candy heart, and when I reached for it the ladder wiggled, and all a sudden I got scared, and then I heard you."

"Candy heart?" Tess leaned against the closet door. "Where was the heart?"

"On the ladder."

"Just sitting on one of the rungs—the things you step on?"

"Yep."

"Hmm." Tess looked at Janice, then back at Larry. "Did you see any words on the heart?"

"Yep. Just one. It didn't mean anything though. It just said 'I'm.'"

LuAnn mussed his hair. "Larry Boy, you might just be our next honorary Wayfarers Inn sleuth." She stood, brushing the knees of her pants. "And now, I'm going to make sure every trap door is locked."

<hr />

"I have an idea." Janice rested her elbow on the arm of a wing-backed chair in the reception area. Her spoon drew stripes in a mound of Whit's chocolate-covered strawberry custard. Strawberry custard with fresh strawberries and dark chocolate flakes—the perfect antidote for the overload of adrenaline caused by a sometimes fearless six-year-old. Stuart was right about chocolate. "Let's do a family-style breakfast in the morning at seven and sit with our guests before the café opens."

Tess pulled her spoon slowly from her mouth, lingering over her last bite. "I like it. We can get up extra early and get things ready before we eat so Winnie isn't overworked."

"That'll give us time to really talk to each person." LuAnn turned a page in her notebook. "We should have questions, conversations starters. What do you do for a living, how did you get involved with Love Is, where do you live, why did you need eight hundred dollars…"

Tess and Janice laughed. They'd decided to wait downstairs for the Love Is people to return. Janice had started a fire, and while they waited and indulged, they updated the Clues and Suspects list.

Tess ran the bottom of her spoon over her custard, making it level with the top of her bowl. "What do we have so far?"

LuAnn, the disciplined one who'd taken only a small scoop of custard, tapped her silver pen on their Suspects page. "The redhead in the plaid coat. Cameron, because he's left-handed. Natalie, because who believes she spent two hours at Walmart? And Noah, because of the money he gave Axel. And then there's Axel and his buddies because fishing stuff that might have been his fell out of the boat, and he took money from Noah, and we all have the gut feeling he's hiding something. Anyone else?"

Janice ran her tongue across her teeth, dislodging a strawberry seed as she thought about the question. "Isn't it possible we're looking at more than one thing going on here? What if the person who left the box of chocolates is not the person who stole RJ's bag?"

Tess nodded. "Or what if the person who left the chocolates told someone she was going to do it, and that person used the opportunity to steal the bag?"

Janice got up and added another log to the fire, sending sparks skittering up the chimney. "What if Franny had the candy delivered but then got a flat tire, and the heart box has nothing to do with the theft?"

"Seems odd..." Tess stared into the fire. "Two separate people using candy to leave messages? And what kind of thief leaves an 'I'm sorry' message in candy hearts? If that's what it was supposed to say. We're just guessing at that. Was 'sorry' meant to be part of the message and 'I'm' the other half? And did it get kicked under the closet door, or did someone drop it while they were scurrying up...or down? And why would somebody steal eight hundred dollars and turn around and give it back a couple of days later?"

Janice stirred her custard, watching strawberry chunks swirl around bits of dark chocolate. "We have to find out where RJ got his bag."

"You want one just like it?" LuAnn teased. "Schafer Leather Store is only two blocks—"

"I want to know how old it is and where he got it. I think we've been focused on the wrong thing all along. It was never about the money. It was about the leather bag."

LuAnn's lips parted. "So you think—"

The sound of the front door opening caused them all to turn. Noah came in first, alone. Ignoring them, he made a beeline for the stairs. "Good night to you too," LuAnn muttered.

Natalie walked in next. It was the first time Janice had seen her looking slightly disheveled. Mascara smudges left shadows under her eyes and the blush on one cheek was rubbed off. Janice stood. "Would you like a cup of tea or hot chocolate, Natalie?"

Wrapping her arms across her waist, Natalie looked from Janice to the fire and back again. "Tea...would be nice."

"Come sit down." Janice motioned to the place she'd just vacated. "Chamomile, mint, or apple cinnamon?"

"Mint, please."

As Janice walked toward the café, Tess and LuAnn jumped in with questions about the weather and the conference. When she returned and set a mug of mint tea in front of Natalie, they were talking about a session RJ had taught on sacrificial love.

"I told RJ when I started with Love Is that I was new at this, but I wanted to learn. I just wasn't quite prepared for how it would hit me." Natalie took a tissue from the box on the coffee table. "He talked about the Good Samaritan and laying down our lives for our friends. I would do that for family or close friends, but I don't know about a stranger. I would stand in front of a truck or take a bullet for my sister or my mom or grandparents..." Her shoulders shook, and she reached for another tissue. "I'm sorry. I'm not usually this emotional."

"No apology necessary." Janice settled on the love seat. "It sounds like you were right where you needed to be tonight."

Natalie nodded and blew her nose. "What if..." She squeezed the tissues in a tight fist. "What if loving one person means you have to—"

RJ, Franny, and Cameron came in, whispering and laughing quietly. RJ strode over to the circle of chairs by the fireplace. "Ladies, thank you for your prayers. What an incredible night. We had people show up who hadn't even registered. Franny shared her testimony and had everyone in tears."

Tess pressed her hands together and looked at Franny. "We'd love to hear your story."

Franny gave a tremulous smile and slipped out of her coat. "I don't want to keep you up, so I'll try to give you the condensed version."

Natalie stood. "I'm going to head to bed."

Janice got up and walked her to the stairs. "You didn't get to finish what you were saying."

Natalie shrugged. "It's okay. Maybe another time." She looked up at the ceiling. "I just...have so much to learn about...doing things right."

"We all do." Janice put her hand on Natalie's shoulder. "It's a journey. Don't be hard on yourself for not getting it all right away. I'm in my sixties, and God is teaching me new lessons every day. And I still make huge mistakes."

"Thanks." With a soft smile, Natalie said good night and walked up the stairs.

Janice went back to her place on the love seat and listened to Franny.

"...in college and this guy came to talk to our group. He talked about growing up on the street and getting into a gang, and then God saved him, and his life did a complete one-eighty. It hit me that I had no story, no dramatic testimony. So I asked God to give me a story."

Franny twisted the ring on her right hand. LuAnn reached over and rested her hand on Franny's arm. "I'm guessing He did."

Tears glistened in Franny's eyes. "I was back home, two days before Christmas, and my mom and I were shopping. I was driving. The roads were a little slick, so I was taking it slow. But then my mom got a phone call from my brother. He'd just called 911 because my dad was having chest pain and couldn't breathe. He'd overheard the EMTs saying they didn't think he'd make it to the hospital. So I turned around and...there was ice at an intersection and a pickup slid right through. I tried to stop, but I was going too fast and...we hit the side of the truck head on."

Janice, aching for Franny while reliving the moments after the call about Lawrence's accident, reached for a tissue for herself.

"My mom died instantly. My pelvis was fractured, and I had a concussion..." Franny blew her nose. "They let me see my dad in the ER. I got to hold his hand for about ten seconds before he died."

"Oh, sweetie," Janice whispered.

Brin came in, looking as bedraggled as Natalie had. Janice extended a hand, beckoning her to join them, but Brin simply shook her head and walked upstairs.

"I couldn't live with the pain, not the physical pain or the guilt or the grief." Franny looked at Janice, then the other two and gave a wobbly smile. "I spent my inheritance, the money my parents had spent a lifetime working hard for, on drugs." She swept both hands across her eyes. "I lost everything." She stopped, took a few slow breaths, and folded her hands. "Three years ago, I was living in my car."

Tess put her hand on Franny's shoulder. Janice touched her arm.

"I got arrested for stealing and forced into rehab. I learned to make jewelry in rehab. And that's where I met Jesus again." She looked down, a shy smile tugging at her lips. "And RJ."

CHAPTER ELEVEN

One of those nights again. Janice woke and stared at the red numbers projected on her ceiling. 2:54. They'd all been too exhausted to process Franny's story together, but she wondered if Tess and LuAnn were also staring into the darkness. They should have taken the time to talk. This was huge. Though Franny's story wrenched their hearts and showed them once again God's power to transform a life and not waste mistakes, they needed to face the facts. They had two recovering addicts under their roof. And, if Darinda and Carla could be trusted, a man with a criminal record.

She tried counting blessings, and sheep backward from a thousand, but sleep still eluded her like a puppy being chased by a six-year-old boy. Time to get out of bed and do something constructive.

Her bathrobe, with its wide, baggy sleeves, wouldn't do. She changed into yoga pants—the ones she never used for yoga—and a Cincinnati Reds sweatshirt and padded downstairs.

When they'd first moved in, she'd been afraid to go down to the main floor alone at night. The building was so big and made so many unfamiliar sounds. Pipes rattling, the refrigerator humming, the new AC unit kicking in. Now, though it still felt a little too eerie to hang around too long, and she still didn't love going to the basement laundry room by herself, she wasn't afraid to go down to the kitchen and get something out of the pantry. Like a tray of glasses. And candles and a box of baking soda.

One lingering fear stood in her way. Mice. Months ago, they'd found "evidence" in the pantry, and Janice had run out and purchased every mousetrap known to woman. She'd expected more little visitors with the onset of cold weather, but apparently word had gotten out in mouse world that the Wayfarers Inn pantry was not a safe place. They hadn't seen any droppings or chewed corners on cereal boxes since August. She turned on the pantry light, braced her shoulders, and stood on tiptoes as she opened the door. Nothing. Not a squeak or a scamper.

With everything she needed stacked on the tray, she turned off the pantry light and gave the door a firm tug until she heard it latch. If only she could do the same with unwanted thoughts.

The glasses *tinked* against each other as she walked up the stairs. The elevator made too much noise, and she didn't want to startle Tess or LuAnn if they were, indeed, staring at the ceiling.

Upstairs, she turned on the light over the stove and assembled everything on the counter. She glanced up at the smoke detector and hoped her mad scientist project wouldn't set it off. No more squawks in the middle of the night.

She lit a candle and held it to the bottom of the Pyrex measuring cup until a layer of black residue covered the bottom.

With a small metal spatula, she scraped the soot into a small bowl. Blacken. Scrape. Repeat.

Squeak. Squeak.

The same noise she and Brin had heard. This time it reminded her of Stuart, standing in his crib as a toddler, twisting the wooden spindles on his crib until they squeaked. Where was it coming from? She blew out the candle and looked down the hallway. Maybe LuAnn had taken Huck outside.

LuAnn's door was closed. So was Tess's.

Squeak. Squeak. The sound seemed farther away now.

On tiptoes, she snuck back to the hallway and to the stairwell door. The latch clicked as she opened it.

The sound stopped. Soft footsteps followed. She listened, waiting for a guest room door to open, but heard nothing. Should she wake Tess and LuAnn?

"If you're worried about anything, call me. Doesn't matter what time of day or night." Tory Thornton's words when they'd hired him to be their handyman. She went into her room and got her phone but stopped with her finger poised over Thorn's name. This was silly. She wasn't going to wake him for what could end up being just her imagination. Guests had a right to walk downstairs. Maybe someone was hoping to find coffee or a snack.

That didn't explain the noise. Brin had heard it the first time. It wasn't all in her head. She tapped her phone.

"Thornton here." His voice sounded wide awake. Must be his military training allowing him to be instantly alert.

"This is Janice at the inn. I'm so sorry to wake you. It's probably nothing, maybe just one of our guests wandering around, but I heard this weird squeaking noise, and—"

"Where are you?" There was no trace of Thorn's usual easygoing demeanor. He was all business.

"Up on the fourth floor."

"Stay there. Keep your door locked. I'll be there in five and call you after I'm sure it's clear."

And he was. Pressing close to the single window in their kitchenette, she saw the lights of his Jeep arch over the trees as he drove up next to the building. She watched the time on her phone as she waited. Eleven minutes passed. She jumped when her phone buzzed.

"There's no one down here," he said. "I searched the basement. The tunnel's locked, and so is the loading dock. How about you come down and tell me more about what you heard?"

"S-sure." She stopped on the third-floor landing, scanning each door in the red glow of the Exit sign. Nothing out of order. She took two steps and felt something under her bare foot. Sand? She looked down.

Sawdust. She turned on her phone flashlight and looked around. No sign of where it had come from. Had someone tracked it in? She scooped the tiny shreds into the palm of her hand and went down to show Thorn.

"Sawdust all right," he said. "Show me where you found it."

She led him to the spot. He found several more crumbs in the second-floor hallway. Thorn left her standing there and checked the other floors. When he returned, he shook his head and motioned for her to follow him down to the kitchen. "Now, tell me what you heard."

⚜

At 6:55 the next morning, the Inn Crowd stood in a line at the base of the stairs.

Tess, in the middle, nudged Janice and LuAnn. "We look like cruise ship greeters."

Janice hummed the opening measure of the *Love Boat* theme song as Natalie descended the stairs. Natalie smiled back. Perfect hair. Perfect makeup. No sign of the dark circles Janice had tried to cover on her own eyes this morning. Natalie appeared to have had a restful night. *Next.*

The Sams were next, although they came off the elevator, hand-in-hand. "What's this we hear?" Sammy asked, waving one of the breakfast invitations LuAnn had printed up and slid under each door. "Breakfast with our hosts?"

LuAnn nodded. "We're going to join you this morning."

"It's kind of selfish, actually." Janice stifled a yawn. "It gives us a chance to sit down with our guests and get to know them."

Sam tipped an imaginary hat. "We are honored."

Janice studied each person as they walked down the stairs, mentally giving each one a rating on a scale of one to ten, ten being bright-eyed and bushy-tailed, one being, as her mother would have said, plumb tuckered out. Cameron—6. Noah—8. RJ—10. Brin—10.

And Franny—2.

The spread laid out on the harvest table was worthy of one of those home and garden magazines. A red-and-white gingham cloth covered the table. White plates, except for the three red ones, red linen napkins, Kerr canning jars for glasses.

"Leave the red plates for us!" Tess called over the chatter. "They are strategically placed so we can mingle."

"Perfect," Tess whispered as Winnie set two platters towering with golden biscuits on the table and LuAnn filled glasses with fresh-squeezed orange juice. Scrambled eggs, country fried potatoes, bacon, a massive fruit bowl, biscuits and gravy, and heavy white cups filled with hot coffee completed the culinary masterpiece.

Tess, LuAnn, and Janice took their places, prepared to interrogate—in a cheery-Miss Marple kind of way—their possible suspects.

"So you know Tory Thornton." Janice, sitting between Cameron and Natalie, began with her focus on their resident psychologist.

"Yep. Small world, huh? We met at the—oh, I guess you'll have to ask him about that. Anyway, I was just drawn to the guy. We touch base once in a while, but it was good to spend some face-to-face time with him."

"He's a good man." But why the secrecy? Where had they met? "I used to teach with him."

"Did you know him when his wife and daughter died?" Cameron turned toward her, giving her his full attention.

Empathy softened his voice. She could see why he made a good psychologist.

"Yes. It was so sad. He was completely broken." The man who had come to her rescue last night was a changed man from the Thorn who'd quit teaching and, she later found out, become practically a hermit for the next eight years.

"He speaks highly of you three women. You literally saved his life by hiring him."

"He's been such a help to us." Just as she was trying to decide how to redirect the conversation, Cameron reached for the salt, which caused his sleeve to slide up over his wrist. A wide Band-Aid replaced the white gauze bandage she'd seen when he first arrived. "What did you do to your arm?"

Cameron tugged his sleeve. "Nothing serious. I was helping a friend the other day and scraped it."

Very vague.

He swiveled back and picked up his fork. "Guess we shouldn't be letting this incredible food get cold."

Catching the hint that her time of questioning Cameron was over, she turned to Natalie. "How's the food?"

Natalie pointed at the biscuits with an eggshell pink nail. "These are heavenly."

Janice nodded. "We've often told Winnie we're sure her biscuits will be on the eternal banquet table in heaven."

Natalie smiled. Her look was more understated today—crisp white blouse, navy skirt, and blazer. She tucked a stray strand of hair up into the bun on the back of her head. Not a messy bun, this one looked like a perfectly symmetrical doughnut.

"Other than making hotel reservations, what's your role with the conference?"

"I handled the conference registrations, and I'm in charge of the check-in table and the information booth."

"I gathered you hadn't actually met RJ until this week. How did you two get connected?"

"Through a mutual friend." Natalie ran her finger along the side of a butter crock filled with conversation hearts. "Were any of the antiques here when you bought the building?"

"We've found a few small things, and some of the furnishings were given to us."

"My—I heard you found an old journal." Natalie took a sip of coffee.

"Yes. It was written by a woman who worked here back in the 1850s."

"That must be fascinating," Natalie said. "I never cared much about history until the last few years. My grandma is really into it. What did the woman do here? Was she a maid?"

Janice jabbed her fork into a piece of pineapple. How had her attempt to learn more about Natalie gotten turned around so she was the one answering questions? "Yes. Life for women was very different back then. We have it comparatively easy today. Where do you live, Natalie?" Awkward transition. "And what do you do for a living?" Was that even a socially acceptable question these days?

"I just moved to Columbus. I worked in DC for about ten years, for the same company. The pace is just too fast for me there." Natalie took a forkful of potatoes. "Why do we make busyness such a virtue?"

"Excellent question. We all need to slow down. What did you do in DC?"

"I worked for several companies." Natalie dabbed her mouth with her napkin. "I usually just have fruit and yogurt for breakfast and then a five-mile run. If I ate like this every day..." Natalie's phone vibrated. She turned it over, and Janice read the single word on the screen. *Gramps.*

"Sorry." Her face a mask of worry—or fear—Natalie set her napkin on the table and stood. "I need to take this call." She got up and almost sprinted toward the stairs.

July 21, 1863

"Where am I?" Delirious with fever, either brought on by infection in his head wound or pneumonia from the water he'd inhaled before they'd hauled him out of the river, Ira thrashed on a pallet of quilts on the floor of the hidden room.

They had survived two nights and two days without detection. Tabitha had gone home but would be back again at nightfall with food and water.

Huddled in a heavy quilt to ward off the chill from the hard-packed dirt floor and the stone walls surrounding her, Prudence prayed and slept in fitful spurts. Her prayers would meld into her dreams and her dreams blend into prayers.

"Where am I? Let me go. I must go. Jennie. The baby."

They were the first lucid words Ira had uttered since they'd brought him here.

"Thee is safe. At an inn." Prudence turned up the wick on the lamp and crawled over to him.

"Ohio? Virginia? Where am I?"

What would it hurt to tell him? "Marietta, Ohio."

"What is the date?"

"The twenty-first of July."

Ira blinked, tried to raise his head, but sank back on his pillow. "Who...are you?"

She'd dreaded this moment. How should she answer? "I am...Euphemia Collins."

His eyes shot open as if he'd been struck. "Effie? Little Effie? You're alive," he whispered. "I'd hoped, but..." A sad smile curved his lips. "I'm so sorry I hurt you. That day...I became...my father. I could not stand that. I left, and did not return."

She knew she should rejoice. He had not become his father after all. But the deep-seated bitterness she had tried to release to God had still left a remnant. "But thee still fights for the cause."

"For the cause of freedom."

"Freedom to be a separate slave-holding nation. That is not true free—"

"No! Effie..." He squeezed his eyes shut.

She waited, thoughts in turmoil as he appeared to have fallen back asleep.

"I came...north...West Point. I worked for Mr. Pinkerton. When the war began I enlisted...in the Union."

It was Prudence's turn for a look of shock. "But thy uniform..."

Ira nodded in a way that seemed painful. He patted his chest. "My...satchel."

"It is beside thee."

He reached out and clutched the strap. "Help me...sit up."

She bunched her quilt behind him and propped him against it.

He stared at her, now eye to eye. "Effie."

"My name is Prudence now. Prudence Willard."

A strange, slow smile lifted the corners of his mouth. "You are the Eagle."

"Pardon?" Was he delirious again?

"The boat, this room, Marietta... I have heard the stories of the Melungeon woman who brought many to freedom. They call you the Eagle." His eyes closed again. "'As an eagle stirreth up her nest, fluttereth over her young, spreadeth abroad her wings, taketh them, beareth them on her wings.'"

"That verse is about the Lord." Her voice grew hoarse, her throat tight.

"And you. You protected, bore them to safety. The eagle feather... means safety."

Tears stung her eyes as Ira drifted back to sleep. An hour passed before he spoke again.

"I need your help, Effie."

"In what?"

Ira looked down at his satchel. "I have been gathering... information." He searched her face. "I have a message that must get to Major General James McPherson. There is a plot... to kill... the president." He gripped her hand. "You must stop it, Effie."

CHAPTER TWELVE

They were clearing tables after the breakfast crowd when Thorn walked in. Janice greeted him. "Hope you were able to get to sleep when you got home."

"Slept pretty good," he said, though his eyes looked weary. "Everything okay here?"

"Yes. No more things—or people—that go bump in the night." She motioned toward the kitchen. "I haven't had a chance to tell Tess and LuAnn. Do you have time to join us for a powwow?"

"Sure." Thorn unzipped his camouflage jacket. "If there's a cinnamon roll and some good strong coffee involved."

"Deal." She walked ahead of him to the kitchen where she asked Tess, LuAnn, and Winnie to sit at the table. Janice told them about the noise and the sawdust.

"That's just a bit too scary for my likin'." Winnie rested her elbows on the table and pressed folded hands to her lips. "Don't you ladies think it's 'bout time to get Chief Mayfield in on all this?"

"All what?" Thorn looked from Winnie to Janice.

"Oh, there I go." Winnie closed her eyes and shook her head. "Lettin' my mouth run ahead of my brain."

"It's okay." Tess patted Winnie's arm. "I think we should bring Thorn in on this."

The women took turns telling him about the missing leather bag and all that had taken place in the past five days.

When they finished, he sat back, folded his arms, and tapped one finger against his mouth. "Hmmm."

Janet interrupted his thinking. "How well do you know Axel Barrett?"

"I've known him for a few years," Thorn answered. "I'm not sure anyone can know Axel *well*. He's made more than a few bad decisions, but I hear he's trying to turn his life around. I think your husband played a part in that."

"I've heard that."

"So what do you think of my buddy Cameron?" he asked.

"Seems like a nice guy," Tess said. "He said he stayed at your house the other night."

"Yep. Got here later than he'd planned. He stopped to help somebody, so he was soaked and pretty beat when he got here, but we still had a good visit."

Janice could almost hear the wheels turning in LuAnn's head as she mentally recorded the conversation. The details were raising Cameron toward the top of their suspects list. "How did you two meet?"

Thorn's laugh rumbled. "He didn't tell you, did he? Always a rules guy. We met at the VA hospital over in Cincy. He was doing an internship. I was...well, getting my head checked out."

Thorn suffered from PTSD. He'd been open about his struggles when they hired him. "I bet Cameron is good at what he does," Janice said.

"He is. Solid guy. I think you can take him off your suspects list, ladies."

"What? We..." LuAnn stuttered.

Again, the warm, rich laugh. "I can always tell when you girls are putting on your Sherlock hats."

"You can?" Tess squeaked.

"Yep. You start firing questions like a paintball scattergun."

Janice dropped her dish towel and headed for the pantry door. "I have an idea." Not knowing exactly what she was looking for, she rummaged in the pantry until she found the perfect thing.

Tess tipped her head to one side. "Your idea is oatmeal?"

"Have you no imagination?" Janice held the cardboard canister up for all to see. "This is a suggestion box. I'll cut the top off and pretty it up and put a slit in the cover and put some note cards next to it, and we'll announce to all of our guests that they can put suggestions in it."

"I'm not so sure I like that idea." Winnie wrung out a dishcloth and began wiping off the table. "Not sure I want everybody criticizin' my food."

"Nobody's going to criticize your cooking." Janice shook her head. "It's the rest of us who have to worry. What if they don't like what we put in the goody baskets in their rooms or the way we fold towels?"

"I think we're all woman enough to handle some constructive criticism," LuAnn said.

Janice opened a drawer and pulled out a pair of scissors. "And we'll tell them to give lots of details and sign their names."

Tess scrunched her mouth to one side. "There's more to this, isn't there?"

"Well, there might be. I've looked at all the signatures on the charge slips and none of them look like the handwriting on the sticky note that was on the box of chocolates. But a signature isn't a good sample of anyone's handwriting."

"Ah!" Tess's eyes brightened. "Brilliant."

LuAnn opened a drawer and pulled out an unopened pack of index cards. "What's the Christian version of killing two birds with one stone?"

Winnie threw the dishcloth at the sink. "Killing one giant with one stone and a whole lotta faith."

***

Janice sequestered herself in the tiny office under the stairs. She had so much to do. So why was she sitting here like a kindergarten teacher, surrounded by scissors, tape, and construction paper, instead of doing what she was supposed to do? She set the finished suggestion box aside.

Panic clawed at her insides as she stared at the square marked BANQUET on the wall calendar. Four days. She'd ordered the food, and Tess and LuAnn had assured her the three of them and Brad could handle the cooking and serving. She wanted desperately to believe them, but they'd never done anything on this scale before. She knew several women who were skilled in the kitchen and who might jump at the chance to earn a bit of spending money, but this wasn't a funeral lunch with ham sandwiches and potato salad in the church basement. Why had she planned such a fancy menu?

And there was a selfish element at play too. Stacy had taken her shopping for a dress weeks ago. Dark blue, covered in tiny blue sparkles that glinted silver when she moved. She loved the swishy skirt and the sheer scarf that went with it. She'd seen it as a statement. A turning point. It was the first dressy outfit she'd bought since Lawrence died. She had appointments all set for her hair and nails.

She'd have to cancel her Saturday primping. Too much to do.

But first, she'd try one last caterer listing. She was just tapping in the number for Country Catering when her phone buzzed, signaling an incoming call. Maybelline.

"Hello?"

"Janice. I had hoped, after our talk, that you'd let me in on what's going on over there. Everyone's talking about the mystery afoot at Wayfarers Inn."

Janice squeezed her eyes shut. Once Maybelline found out about the theft, everyone in Ohio and West Virginia, and probably a few in Pennsylvania, had probably heard about it by nightfall. "Mystery? You know, there is one, now that you mention it. LuAnn saw you in a brand-new Porsche the other day. Was that your car?"

"Why would I be driving a car that wasn't mine?" Maybelline sputtered. "Of course it's mine."

"So you sold the little brown car and got something snazzy, huh?"

Maybelline had been driving the same car, a rattly little nondescript sedan, for at least twenty years. As far as Janice knew, her job as curator of the Marietta Underground Railroad Museum was purely voluntary. It was truly none of her business, but it all seemed strange.

"Well, a girl's gotta splurge once in a while."

A manicure and pedicure would be a splurge. But a $95,000 car? "LuAnn said you were dropping off a young woman and her kids. She thought the woman looked familiar but couldn't think of her name."

She waited... through three breaths. Maybelline's, not hers. Was she okay? Her breathing sounded tight, difficult.

"Maybelline? Are you all right?"

"Of course I'm all right." The terse words were shadowed by what Janice could only interpret as anxiety. "I was just giving the young woman a ride. She...lives near me. Now, back to your mystery. Have you found the satchel yet?"

How could she get out of a yes or no answer? "You mentioned a legend. What do you know about the bag?"

"Just that it could be a hundred and fifty years old and contains something extremely valuable."

What? Janice leaned against the back of the swivel chair, faking a calm posture and hoping it was reflected in her voice. "We're not missing anything like that."

"Well, maybe you're not missing it, but someone's looking for it. If you'd like help, I'd be happy—"

A tap at the office door gave Janice a reason to politely decline whatever Maybelline was about to offer. But Maybelline's last words left her with nothing but questions. *Please find it before anyone else does, Janice.*

———

"A hundred and fifty years old?" Tess's eyes narrowed. "Did you get a look at RJ's bag? It's not possible he would be carrying around something that old, is it?"

Brad Grimes had joined them for supper on the fourth floor. With four pairs of hands working together, they had a spread of taco fixings arranged on the kitchen table in no time.

Janice shook her head, but the gesture lacked conviction. "I'm sure it was one of those bags made to look old. Shabby chic or whatever they call it these days. It reminded me of one of Stacy's favorite purses. And when did it become cool for guys to carry bags that look like purses anyway?"

"Murses. That's what Jeffrey called them." Tess passed the salsa to LuAnn.

Brad cleared his throat. "It's a man bag, ladies. Back to your mystery. Janice, repeat what Maybelline said about your plaid coat suspect."

Janice slathered sour cream on a tortilla and reached for the meat. "All she said was the woman lives near her, and she was giving her a ride, but she was clearly evasive about it."

LuAnn wiped her hands on a napkin and flipped a page in the ever-present notebook. "Let's go back to our first clue and make sure we've got everything down." For a "different perspective," she started at the bottom of the list, stopping after each one to add new information. "Fishing lure. That one sure opened a can of worms." She winked and grinned. Brad laughed and gave her a high five.

"Good one, Lu." Janice rolled her eyes. "We know Franky made the lure, but that's about it. What about the *WW*? Was it Axel's boat? Was there really a new guy with white curly hair and a peg leg?"

Brad laughed. "I sincerely doubt it. They were having fun at our expense."

Janice told Brad about Axel coming into the café and his interaction with Noah.

"Is Noah from around here?"

All eyes turned to Janice.

"So maybe I did a little research on him. Noah Nichols is not on Facebook or Instagram, but he does have a LinkedIn profile. He's from Cleveland, and he does just what he says he does. I suppose you'd call him a freelancer—he hires out to run sound and light equipment. We need to ask RJ how well he knows him."

LuAnn made a note. "I'm going to put a star by all of our to-dos, and we can divide them up. On to the sticky note. Did you finish the suggestion box, Janice?"

"It's done, but I didn't put it out. I thought we could mention it at breakfast tomorrow. If I just leave it on the front desk, we might have café customers adding their ideas. Right now it needs to be just for our guests."

"Good point." LuAnn read a few more clues. "Anything else?"

"Can't think of anything." Janice shoved aside the tiny voice that told her she should tell them about the picture of Stuart. *Talk about a can of worms*…As soon as the banquet was behind them, she'd have time to sort it all out. She had to get more details from Brin and come to terms with it all herself before she could share it with her friends. Right?

CHAPTER THIRTEEN

"N o one will notice we've simplified it a little," LuAnn said. The Inn Crowd sat at a table in the café, working out banquet details while they waited for their guests to return. LuAnn drew a neat straight pencil line through "cherry-thyme pan sauce" on the list. "Winnie can bake the squash rolls tomorrow, and we'll stick them in the freezer. All we'll have to do is put them in the oven for a few minutes right before we serve on Sunday."

Janice sighed. "The parmesan-garlic potatoes are easy. I guess we could eighty-six the crisp fried kale and just add some parsley to the carrots. But we're not skipping the maple-glaze-and-sugared walnuts. We can make the bread pudding and caramel sauce ahead of time and just warm it up." She took the pencil from LuAnn and crossed out *kale*. "I guess it's still doable. I just pictured all of us dressing up and being served for a change." She pointed to LuAnn. "*You* are not serving. You are sitting with your *date*." In music, her treatment of the last word would be known as a dynamic accent. And it received the expected glare in return.

As LuAnn opened her mouth to give some version of "It's not a date," the front door opened and the Sams walked in, huddled together under a massive black umbrella and lugging three large paper bags with string handles. Janice jumped up to help them. She took the umbrella and folded it. "Did you have a fun evening?"

"The best." Sammy giggled as she brushed a salt-and-pepper curl away from her forehead. Her eyes absolutely sparkled when she looked at Sam. "We were at the Brickhouse Cardio Club."

"In Parkersburg?" Though Sam clearly had some kind of fitness routine, Sammy was a bit more...rounded, and there was something fragile about her. Janice couldn't quite picture her in workout clothes at a gym. A slow spin class maybe? "Working out?"

Sam laughed. "Ballroom dancing. We used to go, years ago, the four of us. It was time for a refresher course."

"You two are an inspiration." She knew other couples who'd been tight foursomes and then ended up as a twosome with different partners. When Darinda had once not so politely asked if she thought she'd ever date again, she'd said no. In truth, the thought that had crossed her mind then was that it would have to be someone she'd known for a long time. No surprises, not at this age. She cast the envy aside with a smile. "Looks like you did some shopping too."

"Yes." Sammy set her bag down and slid out of her damp coat, with Sam's help. "Before dinner we stopped at the Antique and Salvage Mall."

On closer look, Janice could see the bags looked slightly crumpled, and each from a different store. Macy's, Boston Store, and a logo she didn't recognize. "Did you meet Harry?"

"What a character." Sam reached into one of the bags and pulled out something wrapped in newspaper. "And we met the woman who runs the Underground Railroad Museum. We're checking that place out tomorrow."

"Funny little lady. I've never seen hair that shade of red before." Sammy took the paper-wrapped bundle from Sam and began unwrapping it. "When she found out we were staying here, she started telling Harry about a legend of an old satchel that went missing back in the Civil War. But you know all about that."

"Actually, we've never heard the details." Maybe she should have stayed on the phone a bit longer with Maybelline.

"The legend says there's something extremely valuable in an old leather satchel hidden here in the inn. She implied you three must have found it when you were doing renovations." Sam stared at Janice as if he was about to recite her Miranda rights. "Is it true?"

Just as Janice was starting to feel like a bug under a microscope, Sam laughed. "The woman is quite the storyteller."

LuAnn gave a weak version of Sam's laugh. "Maybelline and her stories. You'll really enjoy the museum. There are so many legends surrounding the town's involvement with the Underground Railroad. A lot of true stories but some that can't be corroborated. Have you heard of William Still? He helped free almost as many slaves as Harriet Tubman. His great-great-great-granddaughter lives in town. And you've probably heard about the quilt that went missing here a few months back. People used to think railroad conductors used symbols on quilts to create maps telling runaway slaves where to go, but in reality—"

Sam held up his hand. "Miss Sherrill, are you trying to change the subject?"

Tess pointed at the tiny cream pitcher Sammy had unwrapped, clearly trying to distract Sam from focusing on LuAnn's attempt at distraction. "That's so cute."

"Isn't it? Harry said it dates back to the Civil War, which brings us back to the missing satchel. In case you're not, you should be aware that Maybelline Rector said you don't have the right to hide something of historical value to the entire community and she's going to the town board and the historical society to insist they make you produce the evidence."

Janice took a half step back. "Actually, *if* we had found something like that, it would belong to the inn."

Sam's eyes twinkled. "I know that, and you know that, and the law knows that, but I have a feeling that woman could create quite a ruckus."

Janice sighed. She had *exactly* the same feeling.

***

"Why hasn't anyone mentioned this legend before?" LuAnn ran her fingers through her hair. "Maybelline's not the quiet type. And it can't really be a legend if nobody talks about it ever, can it?"

Janice added another sugar packet to her decaf. "Two satchels are missing? How bizarre is that? There's no chance RJ's satchel is the one from the legend, is there?"

"No." Tess waved the question away. "He's never been here. How could he—"

"What if he knew where it was and came in sometime, maybe wearing a disguise." LuAnn looked at the front door and then the basement stairway. "Maybe it was a long time ago, before we put a lock on the tunnel. He stole the bag, but it didn't contain what he thought would be in it, so now he's returned to find the valuable thing. He's the one you heard making the weird squeaking noise in the middle of the night."

Tess stared at LuAnn like she'd lost her last marble. "And then he left the box of chocolates by the door before he came in. With a note he wrote to himself telling himself to meet himself at Austyn's."

LuAnn smacked her lips. "Maybe his name isn't really Johnny. Maybe the candy was meant for someone else."

"Ah! You guys!" Janice sank both hands in her curls and pulled. "We could make ourselves crazy like this."

"Been there, done that." LuAnn laughed. "What else is new?" She stood and stretched. "Okay, watch this." She closed the notebook and held it by one corner, letting it swing back and forth. "I am putting the notebook to bed." With that, she turned and walked into the kitchen.

"And I am putting myself to bed." Tess yawned and slowly got to her feet. "We don't need to wait up for our peeps, do we? I, for one, am too tired to do any more interrogating."

"Sleep well. I think you're right. I could use a longer night's sleep than the last couple of nights." Janice watched Tess shuffling toward the stairs. Five more days and she'd be able to sleep like a baby. She needed to think of a way to celebrate the coming of Monday, a way to revel in the banquet aftermath...and keep her mind off the deposition. Maybe she'd stay in bed all morning with a good book. She closed her eyes, savoring the thought. A bubble bath and comfy clothes and—

The door chime shattered her evening daydream.

Once again, Noah was the first one back. Knowing he probably wouldn't respond, Janice looked up and smiled, but didn't call out to him. To her surprise, he walked toward her. And stood there, looking at the floor.

"Want to sit down for a minute?" Janice felt as though she needed to speak to him the way one would talk to a skittish horse.

Noah nodded, hesitated, then sat on the love seat.

"You must be so tired." She bent forward, showing by her body language she was ready to listen. Then again, maybe that was too intimidating. She sat back. And waited.

Noah rubbed his thumb over a tattoo on his arm. A semi-colon. She'd seen them before and knew what it stood for—your story isn't over yet. It was meant as a symbol of hope and encouragement for those struggling with depression or thoughts of self-harm. Had he gotten it as a reminder for himself, or in memory of someone he'd lost? He glanced up, making eye contact for a brief moment. "Uh...Natalie said maybe I should talk to you. She said you're easy to talk to."

Janice simply waited.

"My dad...left my mom and me when I was nine. He was supposed to pay child support, but he never did, and he never wanted anything to do with me. Now he wants to meet with me. He says he's sorry and he wants to get to know me." He swiped a hand across his eyes. "This morning, Cam talked about loving people even when they don't deserve it, but I...can't."

Janice looked up to see LuAnn settle into a chair in the café and bow her head. *Thank you, my friend.* "Noah, sometimes loving people who haven't done anything to make us want to love them feels impossible. You've heard people say 'Fake it till you make it,' haven't you?"

"Yeah."

"Well, I heard a very wise pastor give a different twist on that. He said, 'Fake it till *He* makes it.' What he meant was, do the right thing, act the way you know you should act, all the while trusting that God will supply the feelings that match your actions."

"Huh." Noah twisted a button on the sleeve of his jacket. "Okay." He stood up. Still looking down, he said, "I don't know if I can, but..." He glanced at her, so briefly Janice would have missed it if she'd blinked. "Thanks."

Noah was halfway up the first flight of stairs when Brin came in. She took her mittens off and clutched them in both hands. "Can I talk to you?"

"Sure."

The clock chimed once for nine thirty as Janice motioned for Brin to sit down. LuAnn got up and, pointing to herself, made a gesture that asked, "Do you need me to stay?" Janice shook her head and stifled a yawn. She'd wanted God to give her opportunities to minister again, but she wasn't at all sure she was ready to put up a shingle for Revolving Door Counseling Service. "What's up?"

"I just got these texts. I don't recognize the number. Here." She held out her phone.

Janice gasped as she read the message.

Find the time capsule by midnight Friday and wait for instructions.

The next one was even more chilling.

Ask your mother where it is. Or I will get the information from her myself.

Brin's shoulders rose and fell rapidly. She appeared on the verge of a panic attack.

"Breathe." Janice put a gentle but firm hand on Brin's shoulder and ushered her to the love seat. "First of all, tell me what this time capsule is. What does it look like? Did your mother tell you?"

Brin sniffed, and Janice handed her a tissue. "She said it was an old leather bag they found."

Janice would've bet the inn that's what she was going to say.

"We're going to find it." She could say it with complete confidence, because, no matter what it did to Stuart's peace of mind and concentration, she would talk to him and tell him everything before Friday night. If they didn't find the time capsule on their own.

"I d-didn't tell you everything." Brin's bottom lip quivered.

"Okay." Janice willed her pulse to even out. Whatever Brin was about to say, it probably concerned Stuart. "What didn't you tell me?"

"The time capsule. It had letters and drawings from the Civil War in it."

Janice pressed her hand against her chest. The legend was true. No wonder Maybelline was eager to find the bag. And Stuart had found it twenty years ago? "What did they do with it?"

"They made a time capsule and hid the leather bag in it...or the bag was the time capsule. I'm not sure. Anyway, they each wrote letters and put them in the time capsule and put in other things that were special to them, and then they hid it. They were going to open it together when they met in six years."

"Where did they hide it?" A torrent of other questions flooded Janice's mind, but she forced herself to start with one.

"I asked my mom about it before I came here. I pretended to be just casually looking through my old diary, you know? She said it was under the stairs. That's all. I told this...friend about it, and she said I shouldn't tell anyone else. She said I should find it myself and keep it a secret."

Brin stopped for a breath, and Janice felt she'd lost hers. The time for secrecy was gone. Maybe it was time to call Chief Mayfield. And Stuart. But not tonight.

"I think...we have to tell Tess and LuAnn."

"Okay. Now?"

Janice gave a slow nod. "Yes." Even if Tess was already sound asleep. This couldn't wait any longer.

Brin got up and strode toward the stairs. Janice stopped her. "Could we...still keep the part about your mom's relationship with the boy...and the picture...to ourselves? Maybe just say your mom was here with a friend."

"Why?"

"I just think...it would complicate things. They might know the boy."

"But wouldn't that help? If we could find him, he could tell us right where they hid it."

"We will look for him, but let's just keep that part to ourselves for now."

Brin squinted through her glasses. "You know who he is, don't you? I know he's probably married with a bunch of kids. I'm not trying to fix him up with my mom or anything. I just want to find the time capsule for her."

"Let's just give it a couple of days."

"Why? What...is he in prison? Is he sick? Does he have a terminal disease? Is he famous? Like a politician? Is he running for office and you don't want to mess up his reputation by people knowing he broke into an abandoned building with his girlfriend when he was sixteen? Why are you protecting him?"

"He's a highly respected man in town, and I just think we should approach this...carefully."

"Fine." With a shrug, Brin turned toward the stairs. "I don't get it, but okay." She stopped and turned. "For now."

LuAnn brought mugs of hot chocolate to the coffee table in their fourth-floor sitting room. Brin took out her phone and showed LuAnn and Tess the texts, then launched into what seemed to be a more embellished version of the story of her mom and "a friend" finding a leather bag in the inn.

"You're sure it was this building?" Tess was still squinting in the lamplight. She had been asleep. "There are a lot of old buildings in this town."

"I'm sure. My mom showed it to me on Google Earth, and then one time I looked up the address again, and I found a newspaper article about you guys buying it and fixing it up, and I've been wanting to come here, but my mom didn't want to. I check all the local news for Marietta, and when I saw the thing about the Love Is conference I knew it was a sign that I was supposed to go. My mom had a tour planned in Europe, so she didn't even have to know I was coming."

LuAnn puffed her cheeks out with an exhale. "Who did you tell about the leather bag?"

"My best friend back home. And the Love Is people. I emailed to find out if I could still come to the conference if I'm not a Christian and, because I talk way too much, I told them about the time capsule..." Brin's lips drew back, showing clenched teeth. "Then this girl who was also going to the conference somehow found out I was going and friended me on Facebook and messaged me and said we should meet up when we got here and...I kind of told her everything too."

Janice winced and saw a similar reaction from Tess and LuAnn. "Who told you not to tell anyone else about it?"

"That girl. She asked all sorts of questions about me and my life and my family, and before I knew it I was telling her all about my mom and the boy and what they found. I told her I'm going to be taking photography classes, and I want to make movies someday, and she said this would make the best movie, and I shouldn't tell anyone because someone might steal my idea."

Janice slid forward on the love seat. "Have you met up with her yet?"

"No. Right before the conference started, she sent me a message saying she got the flu and she couldn't come."

"What's her name? If you were messaging on Facebook we can look at her profile."

Brin tapped her phone and handed it to LuAnn.

"Nan. That's it? She only goes by her first name? Do you know her last name?"

"No. And there isn't even a picture of her."

LuAnn *tsk*ed. "She opened her Facebook page on January 3 of this year."

Brin closed her eyes. "I guess I got played, huh?"

July 21, 1863

Ira snored so loudly Prudence feared they would hear him on the first floor. But his deep sleep was what she had prayed for. Moving like a slinking cat, she inched around his pallet and lowered to her knees at his left side, setting the lamp on her right, turned as dim as she could make it and still be able to read. Her hands trembled as she eased a strap through a loop on the front of his satchel. She lifted the flap and slid her hand in and pulled out a book. No, not a book. A sheaf of ragged-edged pages pressed between two thick pieces of leather and tied with a rawhide thong. She untied the cord and lifted the top covering.

Pictures. The page was covered in drawings, small vignettes of battle. Her stomach lurched. It shouldn't have shocked her considering the wounds she'd dressed in the past week, but the graphic depictions made her press her hand to her mouth.

Page after page of charcoal drawings. And maps. She recognized the curve of the Ohio River where it met the Muskingum. Symbols—squares, triangles, and letters, dotted the map. Marking battles? Battles that had occurred, or battles planned?

Ira groaned, and she stuffed the papers back in his satchel.

Who was Ira Fitzhugh? A spy for the Union? Or a traitor to the republic? How did she know she could trust him? Was he telling the truth? Could she, *should* she do what he asked of her?

Lord, stop me if this is not Thy will.

Chapter Fourteen

The next morning, once again, Tess and Janice hovered near the bottom of the stairs, ready to greet their guests. And observe. Winnie had made a simple breakfast for their second attempt at finding out information from the Love Is crowd. Ham and Swiss quiche and "berries in a cloud." Janice couldn't be sure, but she thought Noah smiled at her for a split second before heading to a table against the wall.

To Janice's surprise, Brin was the next person to come down to breakfast. "You're up early."

"Yeah. I didn't sleep all that great."

"Not surprising," Tess said. "Don't worry, we'll get to the bottom of this."

Brin nodded. "It wasn't just all bad stuff keeping me awake."

"Oh?" Janice and Tess said together.

"I've been thinking about what I want to do next. I took this semester off to figure out what I really want to do with my life and..." She swept her arm out. "Right now, this is it."

Tess stared blankly. "This... what?"

"I want to work at a B&B."

Janice stopped her lips from spreading in a grimace. She couldn't exactly tell Brin they couldn't hire her because she was on their Suspects list. "Well, that..."

"Sure!" Tess blurted. After eye contact with Janice she added, "You'll have to fill out an application, of course, and we'll do a background check."

"Great. No prob. I haven't been arrested for anything. Not recently, anyway." Brin laughed. "I'm a hard worker. I can start today. They just have boxed lunches at the conference, and I'd way rather be here anyway."

"Okay, well..." Tess gave Janice an apologetic look. "Meet me at the front desk, and I'll give you an application.

Brin bounded off, curls bouncing, and Janice glared at Tess. "What were you thinking?"

"Sorry. I know we should have talked about it first. But we do need the help, even if we just have her bus tables. And, there is that old saying...something about keeping your friends close and suspects closer."

Janice couldn't help but laugh. "Okay, but if this turns out bad—"

"It's on my head, I know." Tess wrinkled her nose and gave a quick shrug, then met Brin at the front desk.

At five minutes after seven, Natalie floated onto the scene, wearing a black midi dress with a slit on the side that ended at a modest spot just above her knee. A black and red scarf was artfully knotted at the side of her neck. As she padded silently down the steps in ballet flats, she reminded Janice of a character in one of Stuart's favorite superhero movies. Catwoman or Batgirl—someone who could sneak up on you without your knowledge. Janice greeted her. "Good morning. Hope you slept well."

"Definitely. Everything about this place is comfy." Natalie's red lips shimmered as she smiled. "I can't thank you enough for making us feel so welcome."

"Our pleasure. I'm sorry we didn't get to talk longer yesterday. Was everything all right?" Janice didn't mention that she'd read the name on Natalie's cell phone. "You seemed concerned."

"Just a work thing." Natalie straightened her scarf.

"You mentioned working in DC, but you left me curious what line of work you were in." *Did you mean DC comics and not Washington DC?*

"I worked for Capitol City Tactical. I taught Urban Escape and Evasion classes."

Innnnteresting. Janice kept her face muscles relaxed as she asked Natalie for more information.

"Imagine if we had an EMP, an electromagnetic pulse that wiped out all electronics, including vehicles. What would happen to our society?"

Natalie couldn't know she was talking to someone who had suffered, in her younger days, with doomsday phobia. Janice slowed her breathing. "I imagine we'd have total chaos. Anarchy."

"Exactly. The classes teach things like how to acquire supplies and maintain order."

"Fascinating. How did you get into that line of work?"

Natalie shrugged, a gesture she made with elegance. "I was in the navy, four years active duty, and when I got out I couldn't picture myself behind a desk. I'm kind of an adrenaline junky, so I looked around for jobs that hire ex-military. It's a perfect fit."

"Who are your clients?" Janice thought of Thorn saying they shot questions like a paintball scattergun when they were in sleuth mode.

"We get a lot of survivalists. And a surprising number of gamers. We aren't all couch potatoes, you know."

"So you're a—"

Natalie rested her hand on Janice's arm. "I don't want to keep you from your other guests, and I'd better eat before we have to leave." Natalie nodded at Tess, who was coming toward her with a long-stemmed glass filled with berries and whipped cream. "Nice chatting with you."

Too many questions, Janice. No one wanted to feel like they were being cross-examined.

Several minutes passed before Franny, wearing a long black sweater and bright yellow tunic over black leggings, joined them. Janice admired her jewelry—a necklace with matching earrings made of flat, black beads with hand-painted yellow daisies. A silver, petal-shaped charm on the necklace said "Joy." She wore a large daisy pin on her sweater.

"More from your line?" Janice asked.

"Yes. I'm working on a whole Joy collection." Franny pulled a business card out of a pocket behind her Love Is name tag. "I'm doing some online things to raise money so I can hire a professional photographer and upgrade my catalog."

"Sounds like you're a very goal-oriented person." Janice tried not to let her thoughts stray to other ways Franny might be trying to raise funds.

"Gotta be." Franny winked. "Jewelry is a cutthroat business." She laughed and headed for the table where Noah sat alone.

Cameron came bounding down the stairs. "Good morning, all," he called out.

"Good morning," Janice said. "Have a seat, and we will serve you. Black coffee?"

Cameron gave a firm nod. "The only way a good cup of java should be enjoyed."

"I heard good things about your talk on unconditional love."

"Oh? That's a tough one." He rubbed the stubble on his chin. Hunger must have won out over shaving this morning. "I get more pushback from that session than any."

"Understandable. We live in a culture that tells us to distance ourselves from people who make us uncomfortable."

"Exactly." His momentarily serious countenance morphed into a grin. "But we keep on keepin' on with the message." His phone rang, and he pulled it out of his pocket, nodded to Janice, and walked off.

She couldn't help but like him, but as she watched Cameron head to a table in the far corner of the café—as far away from the others as he could get and still be in the same room—and angle toward the wall as he talked on the phone, questions overshadowed the draw of Cameron's charisma.

She was about to saunter over to Cameron's table with a pot of coffee—intent on filling his cup and her curiosity—when RJ came down the stairs. LuAnn, a tray of quiches in her hands, whispered to Janice. "Looks like he slept well."

Give the man a ten.

"We should try to corner him and ask where he got his bag." LuAnn smiled up at RJ as she talked in a hushed tone, barely moving her lips.

RJ grinned as he hopped off the bottom step. "It's a beautiful day in the neighborhood."

Janice glanced toward the front windows, at the dark, low clouds that shrouded the river, then back at RJ.

"Ah, what's a little rain?" He smiled a dashing smile.

Janice couldn't help but return the smile. "RJ, can we talk to you for a minute? In the library?"

"Sure...?" RJ looked confused... or worried.

"Thanks. I'll get Tess and LuAnn and meet you there. It won't take long. We just want to ask you something."

When they'd all gathered, Tess said, "We just wanted some details about your leather bag."

"That old thing?" RJ now looked perturbed as well as confused. "I really don't care if I ever get it back. I have the money. That's all that matters."

The three women exchanged looks. They'd decided not to tell him about the legend. Not yet, anyway.

Tess cleared her throat. "Have you thought of the possibility that someone wanted the bag and not the money?"

RJ stared at Tess and gave a sputtering, incredulous laugh. "Nobody wants that old thing."

"Where did you get it?" LuAnn asked.

"It used to be my uncle's. He was going to throw it out a few years ago, and I asked if I could have it. I was in college and used it as my book bag."

Janice studied him. His answers seemed genuine. "Do you know where he got it?"

"No idea. What's the big deal? I've seen people with bags like that. What do you know that I don't?"

LuAnn glanced at Janice as if wondering if they should tell him everything. "We're just trying to figure out what happened. Why would someone take your bag in the first place, and then why return only the money?"

"Maybe they lost the bag. Or spilled coffee on it. Could be lots of reasons." He ran his hand through his hair. "Of course I'm curious about who took it. My theory is that someone was just pulling a practical joke, but when they found out how much money was in it, they knew it wouldn't be funny, so they returned it."

Creases formed on Tess's forehead. "We...found something, another conversation heart. Outside your room. We think it was probably meant to go with the other one. It said 'I'm.'"

RJ was silent for a moment. "So the message was supposed to say 'I'm sorry'?"

Tess nodded. "That's what we think."

RJ shrugged. "Well, I think we just need to drop the whole thing. I have no idea who or why anyone would want my bag."

Really? Janice couldn't look at either of her friends. *Because we've got pages and pages of suspects and motives.* Of course, they knew things about the bag RJ didn't know. They now knew about the legend and the time capsule. If someone had expected to find something far more valuable than the $800, just about anyone could fit into the "motive" category.

"Anyway, I just have to quit thinking about it, or I'll make myself crazy," he said. "What's done is done."

Janice knew from watching Lawrence that many men had an uncanny ability to compartmentalize. How in the world did they manage to stuff all the "What ifs" and loose ends into those little mental boxes?

RJ took a step away from them. "I'll keep my eyes open, and I'm sure you will too, but I just can't let all the unanswered questions derail me, you know?"

There was nothing more to say. But the women were derailed, and they were going to stay derailed until they found the answers to those questions.

While everyone was eating, Janice held up the suggestion box and encouraged their guests to write something and sign their names. "You can give us more than one suggestion, of course." No one appeared interested until she blurted, "On Saturday morning at breakfast we'll do a drawing with the suggestions for a fifty-dollar gift card."

Ignoring the quizzical looks of her two partners, she picked up a pot of coffee and began serving their guests.

<hr />

Lunch was busier than they'd seen in weeks, and the primary topic of conversation was the weather. The hopefuls and the sensationalists were equally represented. Janice stared out the window as she filled a water pitcher. The sky was darker than it had been an hour ago. "What do you think, Winnie? Time to build an ark?"

"I'm thinkin' so. You got an alternate plan for the banquet if we gotta get outta here?"

"No. I suppose we'd just have to can—"

"Hey, Janice, your kids are here!" Tess set a tray of empty soup bowls next to the sink.

Janice whipped around, almost dropping the pan of bacon-cheddar muffins she was taking out of Big Red. "My... kids?"

"Yeah, you know... those people who lived with you for eighteen years?"

It had been weeks since Stacy and Stuart had taken their lunch hour at the inn. Why now? The next thought froze her.

Brin. Tess had done a background check, and Brin had passed with flying colors. With LuAnn enthusiastically agreeing with Tess's "keep your suspects closer" philosophy, Janice had no choice but to reluctantly agree. She scanned the room and didn't see Brin. Which meant she was out in the café in plain view.

Though the picture on Brin's phone was a bit fuzzy, it was clear that, as Brin said, she looked so much like her mom they could pass for sisters. Maybe Janice was overreacting, but she couldn't take a chance on Stuart seeing the resemblance. Not yet. What if he started talking to Brin, asking who she was and where she was from? She could almost hear the dominoes falling. He'd talk to Brin, find out who she was and what she knew. Old emotions would be stirred along with new ones—like anger at his mother. He'd be so upset he'd refuse to speak at the banquet. Without a keynote, people would riot, demanding their money back. And then on Monday, Stuart would be so distracted he'd blow the deposition and the Moores wouldn't get their money. Their children would go hungry, and they'd end up on the street living in a cardboard—

"Janice? You okay?" Tess snapped her fingers in front of Janice's face.

"F-fine."

Tess laughed. "You were doing a LuAnn."

"Where's Brin?"

Tess gave her a quizzical look, no doubt reacting to the terror in her voice. "Some kid splashed tomato bisque on her blouse. She went up to change."

Janice flew out the swinging door. Under normal circumstances, the sight of her offspring sitting at a table by the window would have made her smile. She thought of the advice she'd given Noah. *Fake it, woman.* She stretched her mouth into what she hoped closely mimicked a mama-joy smile as she approached the table. "My babies!" They hated that, but at least she was acting in character. "I have to run upstairs for a minute, but I'll be right back to take your order."

And when she said run, she meant run. She couldn't risk taking the elevator and missing Brin. On the way up, she made a quick stop at the supply closet and grabbed a poncho.

The door to Lilac and Sage was open, and Brin was just coming out, retying her apron. "Brin! Can you run an errand for me?"

"Of course. Your slightest wish is my command." Brin grinned. "My first day on the job, and I get to run an errand. Cool."

"Great. Can you run to the store and get jalapeno-stuffed green olives?" She pulled a twenty out of her pocket. "You might have to check a couple of stores."

"No prob." Brin reached for her jacket on the hook next to the door and slipped it on.

"It's raining hard." Janice slipped the poncho over Brin's head before she had a chance to protest. Tugging the hood down over the square-rimmed glasses, she gave a gentle nudge toward the door. "Thank you!"

Crisis averted. The last time Janice had looked, neither local grocery store carried jalapeno-stuffed green olives. Which meant Brin would have to head out of town to Walmart.

Her legs were still wobbly as she rested the edge of a tray on the table her adult children shared. Potato soup for Stuart. Tomato bisque for Stacy. LuAnn had already brought them a basket of muffins—and given Janice orders to sit down with her kids. Janice pulled up a chair. "To what do I owe this honor?"

"Mom," Stuart said, "what's this about a theft?" Janice held her breath as he recounted what he knew. Very little, as it turned out. Several patients had said they'd heard something had been stolen. Not a word about a leather bag.

"People do love to blow things out of proportion." She took a sip of water, trying to appear calm and collected. "One of our guests did have some money stolen, but it was returned very quickly."

"I can't say who, HIPAA laws and all, but someone said you went to Putnam's looking for someone who left a box of..."

Her gaze strayed from her son as two women walked in. Sophisticated. One wore a mid-calf-length tan suede coat trimmed with fur. As she unbuttoned the coat, Janice thought of Emma's description of buttery-soft gloves. This woman's were a rich dark brown with a soft patina. The woman slipped them off, and Janice squinted at her hand. It was much of a coincidence that she'd been staring at the gloves and saw the same stamp Emma had seen. Or was it?

LuAnn ushered the women to a table. When she returned with a coffeepot, Janice tried to catch her eye. When LuAnn glanced her way, Janice tapped the back of her hand and pointed to the two women as inconspicuously as she could, trying to signal LuAnn to look at the women's hands.

"Mom?" Stacy waved a hand in front of Janice's face. "You're acting weird, even for you."

"Hey, we have to communicate with hand signals sometimes." She looked at her son, hoping to find a place of refuge. "How's the talk coming along?"

"All set. I assume you have a Plan B if we get flooding."

She was getting tired of people asking her that. She batted the question away. She could deal with it later. "I have...some thoughts." Most of them panicky. She'd thought of needing to cancel and losing money. She hadn't really considered holding the banquet somewhere on higher ground. She couldn't think about that now. She needed a neutral topic. "How are things at the clinic today?"

"Slow." Stacy broke open a muffin. "We've had a lot of cancellations. People are gearing up for flooding."

"This could get bad. Real bad." Stuart, her stable son, occasionally showed signs of his mother's penchant for drama. "People are lining up for sandbags at that parking lot over on Second, just like last year. But don't worry, I've got the back of my truck piled high."

Janice had listened to the forecast that morning. "I heard there's a good chance the temperature is going to drop low enough that it'll turn to snow by nightfall."

"Here maybe, but it's upriver we have to worry about." As Stuart began a mini meteorological lecture, the door opened again. Brin. Carrying a small white bag. *Goodness gracious goat!*

Janice jumped up, steadied the chair she'd almost tipped, and scurried toward her. Before Brin had a chance to lower her hood, Janice put an arm around her and steered her toward the kitchen. "You're sure they're jalapeno-stuffed?"

"Yep. I remembered seeing them at that little store that sells gourmet oil and vinegar."

So the girl had spent twice as much for something they didn't really need. But Janice had to admire Brin's speed and efficiency. "Thank you. Want to help me stir up some more muffins? One of our guests suggested jalapeno-olive corn muffins. I want to try it."

"Sure. But wouldn't it have worked to just buy jalapenos and olives separately? It'd be a lot cheaper."

Busted. "Why didn't I think of that?" She glanced back at her children as she practically shoved Brin into the kitchen.

LuAnn bustled in right behind them. "It's from an open mic night," she whispered.

"What is?" Janice asked.

"The star stamp." LuAnn wiped her hands on her apron. "They use it for open mic nights at the college."

"Did you ask about the woman in the plaid coat?"

"Yep." LuAnn grinned. "Guess what? She was one of the performers last night."

"What did she do? A magic act where leather bags disappear?"

"She plays the harp. The women didn't know her name, but they knew she was part of a strings group that rehearses tonight." LuAnn held up a hand to Janice for a high five. "We're going to solve this thing *tonight*."

CHAPTER FIFTEEN

"Ithink I found her." Dish towel slung over her shoulder, LuAnn leaned against the counter, looking down at her phone. "Our harp-playing, plaid-coat-wearing, heart box buyer is Belle Archer."

Winnie looked up from wiping down Big Red. "Sounds kinda familiar." Winnie had come back to join them for a reheated soup dinner and to be there to answer the phone and watch the front desk while the Inn Crowd was out.

Janice slid a quart jar of potato soup into the fridge. "Nice name. Wonder if it's real or a stage name. I don't know of any Archers in town."

"You should look her up, Janice. She and I have a couple of mutual friends. You'd probably have a lot more since you've lived here for eons and eons."

"Ah, life was so much easier eons ago..." Janice gave a melodramatic sigh as she pulled out her phone. "But social media was so much harder back in the days of stone tablets." She typed in "Belle Archer." "You're right. We have nineteen mutual friends." She scrolled the list that included Margaret Ashworth, director of the Washington County Historical Society; Paul Townsend, president of Midtown Bank; Robin

Rogers, one of the women on her long list of potential future daughters-in-law; and Maybelline.

According to her profile, Belle had lived in Marietta her whole life. She'd gone to school here and played the harp in several orchestras. There were pictures of concerts, and articles on the music industry she'd thought important enough to share, but nothing personal. What hid behind the smiling face in her profile picture? Hopefully, they would find out soon.

"Thank you for minding the store, Winnie." Tess took off her apron and threw it on a pile of towels and dishcloths to be washed. "We've been leaning on you an awful lot lately."

"You've been payin' me an awful lot lately." Winnie winked. "All for a good cause."

An unexpected mist clouded Janice's vision. Jerry Moore had been off work for three months since a steel beam fell on his shoulder. Hopefully, donations from people like Winnie, and Stuart's expert testimony, would help get the family back on track.

LuAnn stood in the pantry doorway. "Winnie, we need stakeout food."

"Well, let's see, what's good for sittin' under an umbrella in the dark in the middle of a freezin' cold February rain?" She tapped her chin. "Umm...nothin'! You gals are off your rockers. Most people retire so they can relax—sit home by the fire and knit scarves or read books. I bet you three are workin' harder now than you ever did teachin'." With a shake of her head, she opened the freezer door. "I could defrost some tea cakes."

Janice's mouth watered at the thought of the delicacies Winnie had introduced to them as "Kinda like a cookie-cake-biscuit with frosting."

Winnie pulled a plastic box out of the freezer. "How are you ladies coming with your search? And is this stakeout going to put you all in danger?"

"Danger, *shmanger*." LuAnn slipped her notebook into her purse. "What's a little risk and peril when you're on the Lord's side?" She winked at Janice.

Janice caught the hint and hummed the opening note. The three began to harmonize. "'Who is on the Lord's side? Who will serve the King? Who will be His helpers, other lives to bring…'"

"You three! If anyone had told me workin' for you all would be so much fun, I might not have taken a salary."

"Well…" Tess rested a hand on Winnie's shoulder. "If you want to start working for free, let us know."

"It's not *that* much fun!"

The door swung open as Brin walked in. "What are you three laughing so hard about?"

"What are you doing here?" Janice held out a cookie.

"Supper break. There's a pizza buffet at the conference, but I just grabbed a piece and came back. I was hoping I'd catch you." She aimed the remark at Janice. "I heard you talking about losing your caterer, and I just want you to know that I've had a lot of experience cooking for big groups."

"You have?" Janice knew her tone sounded as though she didn't believe Brin. In truth, she didn't. How much experience could she possibly have had in her young life?

Brin nodded. "My mom belongs to a musicians' guild, and every year they hold a couple of huge dinners to raise money for music scholarships. I've been helping with it since I was eight. I've made lasagna, and Cornish hens with chestnut dressing, and last year I was in charge of the dessert." Her chin lifted. "I made a hundred and fifty triple-chocolate mousse cakes all by myself."

"Sounds like we have another pair of hands for the banquet," Tess said.

Janice felt the air seep out of her lungs like a tire that had just run over a nail.

"Um, that's not the only reason I came back." She looked at Winnie and then back at Janice.

Janice nodded, letting her know it was okay to talk in front of Winnie.

Brin twirled a strand of hair around her finger. "I found something today that kind of freaked me out."

Goose bumps formed on the backs of Janice's arms. "What did you find?"

"You know how I said the girl I met online asked me all those questions?" Brin looked at Tess and then LuAnn and back to Janice.

"Yes?" LuAnn answered for all of them.

Brin crossed her arms. Her hands squeezed her biceps. "RJ asked me to take a box of Bibles to one of the rooms and set them on a table in the corner. I did, and there was a file folder on the table with these sticking out of it." She unfolded several papers.

Copies of emails and messages. Janice read the words at the top of one. *From: Nan. Date: January 8 To: Brin. Subject: Time Capsule*

Janice skimmed the pages. Information from Brin about Marietta, the inn, and the leather bag, alternated with questions from Nan about Brin, her mom...and the boy she was in love with twenty years ago. "Do you think Nan is actually here at the conference?"

"Yes. Maybe here at the inn. She must have been lying about having the flu." She exhaled and seemed to deflate with it. "The folder was under a black sweater...with a daisy pin on it."

Tess parked her car on Putnam Street next to the Marietta College Admissions Building.

"We can't get close enough." Janice sighed and ate another cookie. "I was afraid of that. It's been so long since I've been here." Her mind wasn't really engaged in the stakeout. Her thoughts were stuck on a black sweater with a daisy pin.

"Is there a bench over by the McDonough Center?" Tess peered through the windshield at the heavy sky.

"No clue. And if the rain doesn't hold off we'll probably have to scrap the mission. Three old ladies sitting under umbrellas in the dark in a pouring rain would be a little conspicuous."

"What if we go inside?" LuAnn asked. "Couldn't we act like we're just touring the college, admiring the architecture or something?"

Tess shrugged. "If she sees us, our cover is blown. What if we want to casually run into her someplace after this?"

"We could split up." Janice brushed crumbs off her jacket and put on her mittens. "Lu, you should stay hidden. If we find out where she lives, you can be the one to run into her when you're out for a walk."

"Okay." LuAnn pulled her jacket hood low over her forehead. "Let's do this thing."

The dashboard clock read 7:23. Rehearsal was set to end at seven thirty.

Janice zipped her coat up to her chin and pulled her knit hat over her ears as they walked toward the McDonough Center. A young man passed them, carrying a violin case. When they reached the sidewalk to the entrance, LuAnn slid behind a bush. Tess found the park bench she'd been hoping for. Janice walked past her. "I'm going in. If anyone questions me, I'll just ask directions to the restroom."

Once inside, the sounds and smells took her back to her college years. She'd majored in domestic arts and minored in music. For a while, she'd toyed with a dream of becoming a professional concert pianist. And then she'd met Lawrence, fallen in love, gotten her degree and her first teaching job, and found herself swept up in the busyness and fulfillment of being a pastor's wife. She'd willingly traded her dreams for motherhood, teaching, and serving in church, yet she could still hear the words of her concert piano instructor. *"You have such a special touch. When your fingers grace the keys, the audience will be spellbound..."*

"Janice?"

She opened her eyes and fought to clear her vision. "D-Dawson? What are you doing here?" She looked up at a man she hadn't seen in at least thirty years. The fact that he even recognized her was a compliment. Years ago, when Stuart and Stacy were little, she'd joined a small orchestra. Dawson had been their only cello player.

"Playing with a strings group. Lynn and I moved back to Marietta after we retired. I heard about Lawrence. I'm so sorry for your loss. He was a good man."

"Yes." She swallowed. "He was. Thank you."

"Come on in." He took her elbow. "Meet the group. Play for us."

"Oh. I . . . " Couldn't? What she couldn't do was refuse a perfectly good, uncontrived reason to meet Belle Archer. "I'd be honored."

"Wonderful." He opened the door and held up his hand for the music to stop. He swept her through introductions, including the beautiful redhead whose tapered ivory fingers caressed her harp. With a bow and a flourish of his hand, he invited Janice to sit on a polished ebony bench.

Janice rested her fingertips on the keys. And froze. Eyes wide, she looked up at Dawson, who laughed, knowing full well what she was reacting to. "Fazioli?" She let her index finger barely graze the gold letters above the keyboard.

"We have some very generous patrons."

Generous was an understatement. A new Fazioli sold for well over a hundred grand. "Oh my." She let the satin smoothness of the keys, the smell of polished wood, the hush of the room, fall over her. She bowed her head and began to play Beethoven's *Moonlight Sonata*.

By the time she finished, tears blurred her vision. Tears of joy. The room erupted in applause, and the conductor tipped an imaginary cap. "You know how to coax beauty from the strings, ma'am. Thank you for allowing us this pleasure."

Slightly shaken, Janice stood. "The pleasure was all mine." She turned to Dawson. "Thank you. This is a moment that will be etched in my memory forever." Over his shoulder, she watched Belle gathering her music. "What a beautiful harp."

Dawson turned and motioned for her to follow him.

They waited while Belle wrote a note at the top of a page of music. Janice strained to see. Neat script, but tiny, and slanted almost severely to the right.

Unless she had purposely disguised her writing, Belle had not written the message on the sticky note left on the candy box.

Belle looked up. "That was so beautiful. I can't believe you're not playing professionally." She pulled a blue dust cover over her harp.

"Thank you." Janice smiled. After years of playing at Christ Fellowship, where she knew she'd been appreciated but that appreciation wasn't often expressed, the compliment was nice to hear. "I'd love to hear you play sometime." She glanced at Belle's left hand. A small sapphire ring. And a Band-Aid. "Ooh. What happened to your finger?"

"I'm usually so careful. Have to protect these things." She wiggled her fingers. "I was in a hurry, trying to do an errand for my sister between one kid's piano lessons and another's playdate. Got a paper cut."

That would explain the fingerprint. "So you have a family."

"Three children. And a growing extended family." A brief smile softened the lines of her face.

"Oh?" Siblings having children? Or getting married?

"I just recently found out who my grandfather is."

"Really? That's fascinating." Though it was a rabbit trail taking her away from what she really wanted to know, she wanted to hear the story. Especially since there might well be parallels to her own.

"Well...I guess that's the word for it."

Janice gave her a quizzical look. "You don't sound sure."

"Well, it's...confusing. I had this picture of who my family was, my roots. No skeletons, no shady characters or eccentrics, just a normal, stable family. And now..."

"Now you have more *personality* in the family. My late husband was a pastor. One of his favorite ways to describe someone who strained his patience was some version of, 'That person has *so much personality.*'"

Belle laughed. "That's such a nice way of putting it. Your husband was a very wise man. Wait. *Eastman.* My grandfather, the one with all the 'personality,' was just talking about a Pastor Eastman this week."

"Small world. Maybe I know him."

"Oh, I sincerely doubt it. I'm gathering he's never been one to socialize in...good company. Though you may have heard of him."

"What's his name?"

"His real name's Bertrand, but everyone just calls him Axel. Axel Barrett."

"Weird all the way around, I say." Quoting Bonita, Tess peered under the edge of a polka-dot umbrella. "Is she in on this—whatever this is—with Axel? Are they partners in crime, or did he trick her into getting involved in his schemes?"

"Or did *she* trick *him* into getting involved in *her* schemes?" LuAnn opened the car door and collapsed her umbrella. "But you didn't ask her about the candy box?"

Janice shook her head. "There was no way of phrasing it without her knowing we were stalking her. And after she told me about Axel, I was pretty much too flabbergasted to think straight. But I got her number, and we're going to do lunch sometime. To talk about music."

"Right." Tess started the car. "Music."

"Actually, I did get to play for them. They invited me to join."

"Janice, that's so cool. You've been wanting..." Tess left the sentence hanging, unfinished, as a car drove into the parking lot. A red car. A sleek red Porsche sedan.

Belle ran toward the car, holding a file folder over her head to shield herself from the rain, and opened the door on the passenger side. Janice got a glimpse of Maybelline, smiling with a warmth she had never seen on the woman's face. "Follow them!"

Drumming her fingers on the steering wheel, Tess waited until Maybelline backed up and pulled out of the parking lot. "We have to keep our distance," she said in a low voice.

Maybelline turned left on Putnam Street. They followed, five car lengths behind, for three blocks. When she turned right onto Front Street, Tess waited at the corner, counting under her breath. "One…two…three…four…five…go!"

The Porsche pulled to the curb across from Muskingum Park.

"This is where I saw them the other day." LuAnn pressed close to the passenger-side window.

Belle got out, waved, and scurried toward the attorney's office. But instead of going to the main door, she went around to the side.

LuAnn wiped fog off the window. "I bet she lives upstairs."

"With three kids? Goodness." Janice stared at the second story. Smaller than the main level, probably only a two bedroom. If there was a backyard, it was postage-stamp size. Of course, they did live across the street from the park. Across a busy street. She wouldn't trust Larry not to dart into the street to chase a ball or just decide he wanted to play on the swings. "Wonder if the kids' father lives there. And why doesn't she drive herself?"

"One way to find out." LuAnn looked over the back of the seat.

"What's that?"

"You need to do lunch with her tomorrow."

"I have way too much to do tomorrow. You do remember we're hosting a banquet—"

"And if Brin doesn't have an answer before then..."

Janice sighed, then nodded. "I'll do it." She took out Belle's business card and sent an email.

The threats in the texts Brin had received were vague enough to either discount or spark a blaze in an overactive, fearful imagination. Which she had. "Until I get something from Belle, we need to look at our top suspects and drill down on them."

"Drill down?" Tess laughed, turning to look at Janice when she pulled to a stoplight. "What cop show is that from?"

"*White Collar.* Very informative. Anyway, let's plan something for Friday night when the Love Is people come back. It'll be their last night here. Makes sense that we'd throw a little farewell party for them, right?"

"Right."

"Ooh!" Janice strained against the shoulder harness as she leaned forward. "I have an idea! What if we let them do a self-guided tour of the inn?"

"Self-guided?" LuAnn turned, wrinkling her nose. "What's in that blonde head of yours, girl?"

"Not much. But what if we gave them free rein of the whole building, and then we see where they go. Maybe the person who was making the squeaking noises in the middle of the night knows something about the satchel. Maybe they need to get into places that are normally locked. So we open all the closets and the ladder and the secret room."

"I love it!" The car behind them honked when Tess didn't notice that the light had changed to green. "We can draw up a map detailing the ladder and the secret room and the tunnel door. The first ever self-guided tour of the secrets of Wayfarers Inn."

Janice's phone dinged, and she took her mittens off to check it.

"I just got a text from Maybelline."

LuAnn craned her neck to look at her. "She hasn't had time to get home, has she?"

Janice shrugged. "With some phones you can schedule texts. Or maybe Belle told her she talked to me, and she's panicking that we're onto them. Onto what, I don't know, but maybe she's pulled over just around the corner, texting." She read the text.

I believe I have some information about the legend we spoke of. Looking through my copy of Prudence Willard's journal has brought forth some interesting evidence. If you read her entry of July 22, 1863, I believe you will agree. If you do not already have the item in question in your possession, I beseech you to allow me to come and search for it, in the interest of preserving valuable Marietta history. And lives.

July 22, 1863

Ira slept, as did Tabitha in the quilt in the corner. Prudence removed her boots and crept in stockinged feet to the edge of Ira's pallet. Without a sound, she lifted his satchel and pressed it to her chest. Until she returned, hopefully with more information on who he was and what he was doing, Ira wouldn't be able to leave with the satchel.

Heart slamming her ribs, she tiptoed up the uneven steps, down the narrow hallway, out the hidden door, and across the basement. At the top of the stairs, she pressed open the door, and stood, staring, in the pink first glow of dawn, at the back of the massive carved bar, holding her breath. She saw no one, but from the kitchen came the sound of plates being stacked and the smell of coffee. Barely breathing, she climbed to the stairs leading to the third floor.

With a downward push and twist on two spindles, a stair tread lifted. As she shifted the satchel, it opened slightly, and something clanked onto the step, rolled, and tumbled to the next step. Scrambling as soundlessly as she could, she bent and wrapped her hand around it. In her palm lay a gold brooch the size of a silver dollar, the front encrusted with rubies and tiny diamonds. In the thin, shadowy light of a kerosene wall sconce, it glowed red.

The beauty stole her breath for several seconds until she shook her head, stashed it back in the satchel, and shoved the leather bag into the secret compartment she'd had made years earlier. Shoving the satchel inside, she lowered the board back into place and scurried down the basement steps, picked up her boots, and ran.

CHAPTER SIXTEEN

J anice set the suggestion box on the kitchen table and stared at it while waiting for LuAnn, who'd run upstairs to get the sticky note that had been attached to the heart box.

Tess set a bowl of popcorn on the table next to her copy of pages from Prudence Willard's diary. The words of this incredible woman who'd served as a conductor on the Underground Railroad had inspired and encouraged them, taught them about life in the 1800s, and helped them solve several mysteries since they'd uncovered it in the secret sub-basement room in June. Janice fanned the pages of her copy. Her fingers itched to dive into it, but they'd agreed to look at the suggestion cards first.

"What's your gut telling you?" Tess asked. "Who took RJ's bag and why?"

"I seriously have no idea," Janice answered. "We suspect Belle had something to do with the heart box. We're guessing Axel is likely connected in some way. We know Belle and Axel are connected with each other. Noah had dealings—and I use the word deliberately—with Axel."

Tess nodded. "Whoever Nan is, she's either here or she sent copies of her emails to someone who is here. It's doubtful Belle or Axel were at the conference center."

"But Noah was." Janice filled a bowl with popcorn. She rolled her head in a circle, stretching her neck, working out a little of the tension. "And did someone put the emails with Franny's sweater or is she—"

"Don't you be speculating without me." LuAnn pulled the evidence bag containing the sticky note from behind her back with a flourish. "Ready?"

Janice held her breath as she pulled the lid off the oatmeal box and found three index cards. She unfolded the first one. "This is from Noah." She looked at the small printed letters. "Not even close." She turned it so Tess and LuAnn could see, then held it close and read it. "Fresh flowers in the rooms would be nice."

"Wait." Tess leaned in. "Noah said that?"

Janice laughed. "Guess who wants the gift card." She pulled out another card and handed it to LuAnn.

"Noah again. 'Many hotels offer dark-colored washcloths for guests to use for removing makeup. This would keep your towels from getting stained by mascara.'"

LuAnn laughed. "We already do that. Bet he just googled *100 Innkeeper Tips,* and we can expect more from him."

Tess took the last card. "This one is from Cameron." She turned it to face Janice and LuAnn. The words were printed in thick, squared-off letters. "'This would be a wonderful venue for author chats by the fire. I, for one, would love to come back as a guest speaker.'" Tess shook her head. "That man has no lack of confidence. I like the idea. And I really don't think Cameron's guilty of anything but being overly charming."

"We can't discount anyone until we have absolute proof." LuAnn picked up the Suspects list. "Cameron couldn't give a clear answer about why he was late getting to Thorn's—"

The front door chime dinged. Janice, sitting closest to the door, got up and walked out into the café.

A woman stood in front of the door. Midforties, pale and drawn, eyes red and puffy, she looked around as if searching for someone.

"Welcome to Wayfarers Inn. How can I help you?" No need to ask if she had a reservation. Janice knew she didn't.

"I'm looking for Cameron Truman. Is he here?"

"He's at a conference. May I take a message for him?"

"Y-yes." The woman's face crumpled. "T-tell him thank you for saving my son's life."

Janice instinctively reached out, resting her hand on the woman's shoulder, urging her to go on.

"I just found out. The other night...my son was...on the Jeremiah Morrow Bridge." Her eyes seemed to plead for understanding.

Janice knew that bridge. Forty years ago, a boy she and Tess and LuAnn had known well had jumped from Ohio's tallest bridge. She braced herself for what the woman was about to say...and how it related to Cameron.

"He was going to jump. Cameron stopped. Someone called 911, but he was the only one who stopped b-before the police got there. He grabbed him, just at the last...second. He s-saved my Matthew's life, and he's been talking to him every day. I just want him to know how grateful we are." With that, she broke down sobbing, and Janice wrapped her in her arms.

After the woman left, Janice found it hard to focus on her copy of Prudence's journal pages. Her eyes felt raw, her vision slightly blurred. Tess and LuAnn looked at their own copies, isolating entries from the summer of 1863.

"Maybelline was specific about July 22," Janice said. "Let's start there."

Looking down at the artful slant of Prudence's words, Janice felt the same sense of awe she'd experienced the first time she'd touched the fragile, crumbling pages of the journal. They'd found a picture of Prudence and her pet goose Patience, so an image came to mind of a woman with features that hinted of Native American and African blood. A strong, straight-backed woman with determination—and a touch of humor—in her face. In Janice's mind, Prudence was everything she wanted to be. Brave, confident, unwaveringly obedient to God, and able to accomplish the task at hand without fear, no matter the consequences.

The journal ended in December of 1863. They had read it cover to cover but hadn't spent as much time on the pages that went past January 1861, when Abraham Lincoln signed the Emancipation Proclamation and the number of runaways seeking asylum at the inn, then known as the Riverfront House, had dwindled to a trickle.

Janice held the page closer to the light and began to read. "'I looked in the satchel today but didn't find answers, only more questions. Is he who he says he is, or am I walking into a trap? Years ago, Ira's drawings of far-off places filled me with wanderlust and fueled the fire of my longing for freedom. Today, his drawings fill me with fear and sour my stomach. Page after page of pictures of man's cruelty to man. Though I've seen so much over the years, nothing prepared me for what I have seen this week.

"'There are maps. No names of towns or rivers, only symbols and letters that make no sense. Is he gathering intelligence for the North or for the South? Should I believe that he has turned against his slave-holding roots and his entire family and now serves the cause of unification and abolition? Is he telling the truth when he asks me to do this thing I cannot tell my husband about?

"'There are pages written in code, indecipherable, except that I have found the key. Disguised as something precious. I held it in my hand, lifted it to the light. It glowed, red like claret, calling to my longing for beauty and color and trinkets that would have caused a look of reproof from my adoptive mother, but would have brought a smile to Mama's lips. How she loved color. On summer mornings, she plaited flowers into my braids. She made paint, mixing egg white with dried beet root, sweet potato, blueberries, or cinnamon, and painted murals on the walls of our tiny house. Even in Virginia, when life was work, we woke to scenes of home, of the farm we once owned. Our red-painted barn, the apple tree beside the porch, the morning glories that trailed along our fence.

"'Here I go wandering down a path of memories and avoiding the task at hand.'" Janice looked at Tess. "Pru and Lu have a lot in common." She winked at LuAnn.

"Great minds wander." LuAnn pointed at the paper. "Read."

"'I will do this thing and pray God will stop me if I should not. Keep me safe, my Lord. Lead me to the right person. Help me not to be deceived. Let us stop this horrible plot before it can be carried out. Give Thy angels charge over Mr. Lincoln.'"

"Mr. Lincoln?" LuAnn's eyes widened. "How come we didn't catch that before?"

Tess shook her head, a look of bewilderment on her face. "I remember reading that, but I must have been skimming. I thought it was just a general prayer for the president, since the outcome of the war depended on his decisions."

"So Prudence may have helped the Union win the war by prolonging Lincoln's life." Janice set the page on her lap. "We need to research this. Later. What else do we have about the spy?"

Tess pointed to the date on her entry. "Mine is from two days earlier." She turned the page sideways and squinted. Like Janice, she positioned herself closer to a lamp. "There's something written along the side."

Janice turned her page so she could stare at what looked to be a long smudge. "I think there are words, but I can't make it out. If there's anything there, we'd need a magnifying glass to read it."

"Or we need to take a look at the original," LuAnn said.

"Put it on our 'to do' list. It might be important." Tess began to read. "'I thought I was prepared. I thought I could handle it. No one can prepare for what I saw in Portland. Bodies stacked. Prisoners wedged together in boats that appeared ready to capsize. I thought I would go to help, to bind wounds and offer comfort, but my bandages were so inadequate, my words more so. Never have I experienced such desperate helplessness and then, on top of grief, an emotion I was totally unprepared for.'"

Tess cleared her throat and continued reading. "'The Bible promises that God will not suffer us to be tempted above what we are able to bear, but tonight I wonder. I quoted that passage to myself so often in my flight from captivity, especially the part about God providing a way of escape. But yesterday, the temptation to hate was so strong it nearly swallowed me up, until fear took its place, looming so large in my mind I thought surely I would faint. We're told to love our enemies, so I did what seemed right at the time, but now, as I listen to the labored breathing of a man who wears the uniform of my enemy, here in this place where we once hid those escaping oppression, I have to wonder. Did God send a smidgen of love as my escape from hate, or was this all my own misguided choice? Heavenly Father, what have I done?'"

"Wow." Janice squeezed her hands together. "She brought a man who could have been a Confederate spy here, to the secret rooms? Why? Why would Prudence do such a thing?"

Janice was the only one still up when a light knock sounded at the door to the fourth floor. After finding out who it was, she opened the door.

Brin stood in the doorway wearing plaid flannel pajama bottoms and an oversized T-shirt. "Can I talk to you?"

"Of course. Why aren't you sleeping? You all got back late tonight."

Brin yawned. "I am exhausted. They...we...had a prayer meeting after the last session tonight."

Janice pointed to the couch. "Tell me about it."

Brin sprawled on the couch on her belly and propped her chin in her hands. Her wild curls tumbled over her shoulders. It was the first time Janice had seen her without her glasses. Such beautiful eyes.

"Everybody prayed out loud. It was kind of freaky at first."

"Is this new to you?" Janice asked.

"Yeah. In a way. My mom used to be a Christian when she was young and then she wasn't for a long time, and then a few months ago she said she missed Jesus. She said God forgave her for walking away from Him. She quit her band and joined another one and went to Europe with them to sing and tell people about Jesus. It all happened so fast. I didn't like it, so I didn't listen when she tried telling me what she believed, but the conference explained a lot."

Brin sighed and rolled over on her back, hanging her head over the edge of the couch, reminding Janice of Stacy at that age. "But then there's all of the stuff that doesn't make sense. Like how can Jesus be the only way to get to heaven? What about the Native Americans who never heard about him? And why does God allow people to be such jerks to people? How come He flooded the whole earth in Bible times when people were being evil, but He lets people get away with it today? I mean, terrorists who drive cars into crowds where there are children, and creeps who strap bombs to themselves, and racists, and men who take advantage of women, and people who—"

"Whoa. Slow down." Janice held up a hand. "How about if we start with the basics? Like who Jesus is and what He did for us."

Brin rolled over and sat up, legs crossed. "Okay. But first I have to tell you something."

Janice waited while Brin wrapped a long strand of wavy hair around her finger.

"My mom's back in the States. She called from the airport in New York City tonight."

"Oh?"

"Yeah. I told her what's happening here. About RJ's bag getting stolen and about Nan and the creepy messages."

"What did she say?"

"She said there's something in the bag that somebody might want to steal."

Janice leaned forward but didn't interrupt.

"There's a pin in it made of rubies."

"Did she tell you where they hid the satchel?"

"No. Brin tugged at a thread and unraveled the hem of her T-shirt. "I told her about you and how you know the guy in the picture and...she said she's going to come here...tomorrow."

July 22, 1863

Charity galloped with her head high, more spirited yet cooperative than Prudence had seen the stubborn draft horse in years. Prudence patted her side and slowed her to a trot. It would not do to tire her. "Nice and steady. We have important work to do." *I hope.*

As the sky lightened, turning first purple, then awash with thick streaks of orange and gold, she focused on the words she'd memorized, the words she would say to a woman named Mabel Woods, the lies she would give to anyone who might question her.

Lord, go with us. He had thus far. They'd crossed the Ohio on the ferry, which had somehow been spared in the fighting. Crossed into Virginia without being questioned.

Two hours after reaching the Virginia side of the river, Prudence spotted the wooden sign for the newspaper hanging over the door. As she dismounted, three soldiers in gray uniforms, guns resting against their shoulders, rounded a corner. She took a deep breath for courage as she tied Charity's reins to the hitching post.

"What's your business here, ma'am?" One of the soldiers faced her, eyes piercing into her very soul. She turned away quickly, lowering her head and looking at the ground.

"Jus' pos'in' a advertisen' for my mastuh, suh." She pulled the deep drawl from her memories.

She stared at the tips of the soldier's boots in the rutted red clay. Finally, without a word, he moved on. And Prudence allowed herself to breathe again.

A plump woman with dark hair hanging in lush, fat curls around her face sat behind a desk in the office. She greeted Prudence with a smile. "How may I help you?"

Prudence measured her words. She would not speak like a Quaker here. "Might I purchase a copy of the news from the second week of June, please?" It was the question Ira had made her practice.

The woman's eyes widened only slightly, betraying her surprise. She hadn't been expecting a woman. "Come with me." She ushered Prudence into a room with a massive printing press in the middle, then into a small office. On the desk sat a telegraph key mounted to a polished oak board. Mabel closed the door. "Where is Major Fitzhugh?"

"He was wounded. I am an old…friend." Prudence's swallow was audible, at least to her ears. "He said the message is urgent." She held out a folded paper.

Mabel took the paper. "I have a message for him as well. It is not my business to know…" An unexpected smile softened her face. "But I believe this one is personal." She unlocked a drawer and pulled out a rectangular card and handed it to Prudence. An oval tintype of a beautiful young woman was mounted in the middle.

"The message is behind the picture?"

"He will know." Mabel stepped toward the door, signaling that the meeting was over.

"May I ask you a question?"

Mabel nodded.

"What can you tell me about Major Fitzhugh and his... loyalty?"

Mabel's spine stiffened. "You doubt his allegiance to the Union? After all he's been through?"

"No. I'm sorry. I...thank you. I'll be on my way. May God watch over you."

"And you. I gather you are too new at this to know the danger you entered into when you agreed to be a messenger."

Prudence raised her chin, nodded, and walked out.

Danger was not new to her.

CHAPTER SEVENTEEN

Wrung out after an hour of Brin asking questions theologians hadn't been able to answer in two millennia, Janice should have been tired enough to sleep, but too many things clamored for her immediate attention. She made herself a cup of tea and curled in the platform rocker in her room with her copy of Prudence's journal, her laptop, and a magnifying glass.

She found the page with the smudge. Using the magnifying glass, she was able to make out what appeared to say "Pink" followed by several letters she couldn't decipher and then a date. *Sept. 12, 1866.* In a flash of techie genius, she took a picture of the blurred words then enlarged it on her phone. Mixing a bit of imagination, she came up with *Sent letter to A. Pinkerton Re I.F. Sept. 12, 1866.* She wrote it down next to the distorted words.

Allan Pinkerton? *The* Allan Pinkerton, founder of the Pinkerton Detective Agency?

Re. Could mean regarding...So did that mean that Prudence had sent a letter to the famous Chicago detective inquiring about I.F.? 1866 was after the Civil War had ended. Was she enquiring if he was still alive? Maybe she was asking for confirmation on what side of the conflict Ira had been serving.

Did Pinkerton Agency files still exist? Where would they be? In a Chicago Museum, or maybe the Smithsonian? She opened her laptop and typed in *Pinkerton Agency*. What popped up surprised her. The Pinkerton Agency was still in operation, now dealing in corporate risk management. She scanned the agency's timeline. In 1842, Allan Pinkerton immigrated to the US, settled in Chicago, and became a barrel maker. Five years later he joined the police force and, two years after that, became Chicago's first police detective. "Talk about upward mobility."

Janice thought about waking LuAnn, who'd taught history for more than thirty years. When the clock on her laptop told her it was already tomorrow, she decided against it. She continued to read. In the 1850s, the Pinkerton Detective Agency was working alongside local law enforcement, arresting criminals throughout the country. When war broke out between the North and the South, Allan Pinkerton served as head of the Union Intelligence Service, the forerunner of the US Secret Service.

The next entry caught her attention. In 1861, Allan Pinkerton uncovered and stopped a plot to kill Abraham Lincoln.

That was two years before Prudence's mention of a plot, but it seemed likely more attempts would have been made on the life of a president who was adored by some but hated by others.

Janice typed "Pinkerton Agency Files," which led her to a Library of Congress page. The heading read: Pinkerton's National Detective Agency records, 1853-1999.

"Bingo." She scanned the summary. "Correspondence, diaries, essays and other writings, reports, notes, police and prison records, code books, criminal rosters, exhibition texts, legal documents, biographical and genealogical records, procedural guidelines and training manuals, financial records..." The list went on, but what she was really interested in was the first item. Correspondence.

The next paragraph gave an overview. "Documents investigative methods, business principles and practices, and daily business activities. Topics include establishment by Pinkerton of the secret service in 1861 to protect the president and provide military intelligence for the Army of the Potomac, sabotage and espionage in the Washington, DC area during the Civil War..." She was definitely in the right place. If any record of Ira F. still existed, she would find it here.

"Library of Congress registered readers may use the LC Online Catalog." She pushed a button. Her excitement began to fade as she read, "To use this service, you must first obtain a Reader Identification Card, which displays your individual Patron Account Number. When you log in for the first time, you will receive a temporary password either in person or by email."

"I don't have time for this." She snapped her laptop shut. Did she know anyone who would have a Library of Congress ID Card? The public library, most likely. And...the "Maybe it's Maybelline" jingle romped through her head. She was getting punchy from lack of sleep. Maybelline would be a last resort. Who else?

Margaret Ashworth. The Historical Society Director had to have one, right? She tapped on her messaging app and found Margaret. She typed a message and then, with a glance at the time and an "Oh well," she sent it. People who wanted to sleep turned off their notifications at night, so it wasn't her fault if—

Ding. The sound made her jump, and her heart forgot to beat in a regular rhythm.

Glad to know I'm not the only one with insomnia! Yes, I have an LC ID card. How can I help you?

Janice grabbed the journal page. *I am looking for information on an Ira F., who may have been a Civil War spy, most likely for the Union. It appears that Prudence Willard sent a letter of inquiry about him to A. Pinkerton—I assume that is Allan Pinkerton—on September 12, 1866.*

Margaret replied with, *Give me a minute.*

Janice's fingernails ticked against the edge of her keyboard, the staccato rhythm picking up speed with each passing minute.

Ding. She let out a pent-up breath and read the message. *Found a posthumous Commendation of Service for an Ira Robert Fitzhugh. He was employed from 1854 until his death in 1865.*

A sudden rush of sadness surprised Janice. By the time Prudence had sent her inquiry, Ira would have been dead for months. She sent a reply. *Does it give a date of death?*

DOD June 13, 1865. So he lived to see the war end.

And to see the assassination of the president he'd tried to protect.

A long pause followed and then Margaret texted, *Entering Prudence's name.*

Too restless to sit, Janice got up and began pacing from her chair to her desk to the window. The clouds had receded, and moonlight bathed the barren garden behind the inn. Eerie yet peaceful…until headlights painted a swath of light on the trees behind the inn, much the way they had when Thorn had come to her rescue, but not as close. A car driving by on Ohio Street? The lights stopped moving, then went out. If the car had parked, where would it be? Not next to the building where Thorn had parked. Across the street but aimed at the inn?

Janice slipped into her robe, cinched it, then went out into their common area. The only windows on the fourth floor that faced the river were in Tess's and LuAnn's rooms. If she wanted to see out, she'd either have to go down to the first floor or wake one of her friends.

LuAnn's door was open several inches, but Tess was the lighter sleeper. She stood in front of Tess's door, hand raised. Was it worth risking Tess being irritated with her?

Yes. She knocked and waited, then knocked louder.

"Come on in," Tess called, sounding like she was still half asleep.

None of them locked their doors. Janice walked in and straight to the window in Tess's sitting room. Without disturbing the curtain, she peered through a slit between the two panels.

An old pickup truck, its color indistinguishable in the dark, sat facing the inn.

"What's going on?" Tess walked groggily in. "Turn on the light."

"No!"

"Wow. Okay. What's down there, and why are you up?" Tess joined her at the window.

"That truck." Janice pointed. "It just parked there. Why is it facing this way, and why in the middle of the night?" She positioned the camera lens of her phone in the space between the curtain panels. Just before clicking the button she remembered to shut off her flash. "Probably won't get much in the dark, but it's worth a try."

Tess touched her arm. "We can wait a few minutes and watch when it leaves. It has to pass under a streetlight, no matter which way it goes."

As they waited, Janice told Tess what she discovered about the blurred message written on the side of the journal page and then repeated what she'd learned from Margaret.

Tess took a fleece throw from the back of a chair and wrapped it around her shoulders. "That's sad. Prudence saved him, and then he died two years later."

"But maybe, because of him and Prudence, Lincoln lived long enough to ensure the union would be restored."

Tess put her hand over her heart. "Our Prudence saved the nation from annihilation. Did Margaret find anything about a letter from Pru to Pinkerton?"

"I don't know. I was getting restless waiting for her answers, so I started pacing, and that's when I saw the headlights." She got down on her hands and knees and slowly lifted a corner of the curtain. "They can't see us in the dark, can they?" With a larger viewing area, she could see the silhouette of a figure in the driver's seat but couldn't make out any details. "I'm pretty sure it's just one person. No clue if it's a man or a woman."

The car sat there for another five minutes and then the engine came on.

Janice held her breath. Beside her, she felt Tess tense.

The pickup turned to leave and passed under a streetlight. From four stories up, they got a good view of the catfish on top of the cab.

"Wow," Tess said. "That should narrow it down a bit."

Once again, Tess's dry humor broke the tension. Janice breathed again and said one word.

"Axel."

After explaining to Tess how she knew whose pickup that was, Janice brought her laptop into Tess's room. Tess motioned toward her recliner. Janice sat and Tess leaned on the back of the chair, looking over her shoulder as Janice found the last messages left by Margaret.

After several "Are you there? Where did you go?" messages, Margaret had said she was going to bed. Janice scrolled up.

I found several letters. Margaret had inserted screen shots.

November 8, 1863

Dear Mr. Pinkerton,

I understand the sensitive nature of this correspondence, so I will use the utmost care. I believe you will know the reason I am contacting you without my needing to ask. Please let me know if you have any information about the whereabouts and well-being of our mutual friend. I wish to advise him of a delivery that arrived for him in July.

Sincerely,
Jennie Fitzhugh

A photograph of a handwritten message under the heading Illinois Telegraph Company and dated September 20, 1865 followed.

To: Jennie Fitzhugh

Continued sympathy and prayers for you and children. Red heirloom unaccounted for. Still investigating.

It was signed "Allan J. Pinkerton."

"Red heirloom?" Tess pulled a footstool next to Janice's chair. "Is that referring to the 'something of value' in the satchel?

"I know what that something is." Janice told her what she'd learned from Brin.

"Whoa. Wonder what it's worth. That explains... a lot."

Janice took a quick inhale as she looked at the date of the last letter. September 12, 1866.

Dear Mr. Pinkerton,

Three years ago, I had opportunity to meet an associate of yours, a Mr. Ira Fitzhugh. He left some things with me for safekeeping and has not returned for them. I am hoping you can get a message to him for me. Please tell him that his belongings are here. As I may not be available to assist him, let him know I hope for a lovely moonlit night. He can use the same entrance he used at his first visit. The items in question are nineteen paces up. A right turn at the fourth and fifth bars will allow access.

Yours,

The Eagle

"Who is the Eagle?" Tess tightened the blanket around her shoulders.

"I don't know, but this letter was written the same day Prudence said a letter was sent to Allen Pinkerton." Janice typed an answer to Margaret. *Hope this isn't waking you. So sorry I disappeared for a bit. We had a little disruption here. Thank you so much for your time. This information is so helpful. I will be sure to let you know if we learn more.*

Tess yawned. "I suppose we should try to get some—"

Ding. A new message appeared.

So glad you're still awake. I almost called the police. The last thing I found has me so jumpy, I had convinced myself you were in trouble. Maybelline has been asking what I know about a Civil War satchel supposedly lost or hidden in your building. I had heard this mentioned decades ago, but it was all so vague. After reading about Mr. Fitzhugh and the cryptic message from "The Eagle," I expanded my search to old newspaper articles. What do you think of this?

The Clarke Courier
Berryville, Va
December 8, 1889

More than twenty years have passed since Mr. Clarence Fitzhugh's mother received a telegram informing her of her husband's death "in service to his country." Clarence was only three years old at the time and has only a dim memory of his father being "a very tall man with a scar on his forehead." What Clarence remembers vividly is his mother, who passed away two years ago, sobbing about the family being destitute because, "Your father took my dowry to Chicago."

Years later Clarence learned some of the rest of the story. His father, Ira Fitzhugh, was in the employ of the Pinkerton Detective Agency when the War began. Desiring to protect his family's wealth, he took a pouch filled with gold coins and jewelry, including a diamond pendant reportedly worn by Clarence's great-grandmother at Queen Victoria's coronation, and a ruby brooch passed down from Ann Hughes Fitzhugh, wife of Captain William Fitzhugh, a close confidant of General George Washington. The diamond pendant returned to the family but, for unknown reasons, the ruby brooch was never found.

The mystery still haunts the Fitzhugh family. Was Clarence's father buried with the priceless brooch? Was it stolen? Does it now sit in the jewel box of some young woman who knows nothing about its origin?

The brooch is described as a round gold pin about the circumference of a hen's egg with a circle of rubies and several small diamonds. The pin is inscribed with the initials AHF. A substantial reward is being offered by the Fitzhugh family. Anyone with information or inquiries may contact the *Courier*.

CHAPTER EIGHTEEN

Belle agreed to meet Janice for lunch at Tampico. The atmosphere of the Mexican restaurant, with its bright green back wall and chairs painted red, blue, and purple, was casual, the ambience light and open. Unthreatening.

Janice arrived early and sat with a cup of water and waited, rehearsing her words. She'd decided to just come out and ask Belle about the heart box. They were running out of time for slowly coaxing information and, after last night, the importance of finding out why the candy box had been left for RJ had faded in importance. Now that they knew—almost beyond the shadow of a doubt—what was in the satchel, their focus had to be on what was going to happen next.

Someone was after it, and that someone was most likely Axel Barrett.

She thought of his truck parked in front of their building. He'd sat there watching...for what? The right time to break in? A chill shot through her, and she suddenly knew what she had to do. Without another thought, she picked up her phone and dialed the non-emergency number for the Marietta Police Department and told them everything.

"So the stolen money was returned, and the owner doesn't want to press charges?" the woman on the other end asked.

"Yes."

"And you believe Axel Barrett has plans to steal an item of jewelry from the inn, but you're not sure if the item even exists?"

"Y-yes."

"You saw Axel Barrett's truck outside your establishment at approximately midnight, but he didn't get out of the car?"

"Yes."

By the time she hung up, she felt ridiculous for calling. The woman had promised that they would keep an eye on the property, whatever that meant. Janice closed her eyes and put her hand over her face.

"Hi!" Interrupting Janice's humiliation, Belle bustled toward her, three children in tow. "Sorry I'm late. I had to bring the crew."

"No problem." Janice smiled at three little cherubs with mischief in their eyes.

Belle pushed a high chair up to the table while introducing Zach, Molly, and Patrick.

"Nice to meet all of you." Janice looked at six-year-old Patrick. "I have a grandson who—"

"Hey, Mrs. Eastman, how's it going?" Kip, a young man Thorn was mentoring, walked toward her with a to-go bag.

"It's going well, Kip. How've you been?"

"Life's good. Hey, I heard there's more creepy stuff going on at the inn. A mystery thief, huh? How much stuff did he take?"

Was there anyone in Marietta who didn't know some distorted version of the story? "News sure does get blown out of proportion around here."

"Yeah, well, hope you catch whoever did it." He waved and walked away.

"Thief? Inn? Do tell." Belle stuffed a pile of mittens into her purse.

"Two friends and I own Wayfarers Inn."

"Really? Then you've met— Never mind." Belle's smile wobbled for a split second but recovered quickly. "Did that guy, Johnny, get his heart box?"

"Yes, he did." Was this a dumb time to play dumb? "How did you know about that?"

"I left it there."

Janice shaped her mouth into an expression of surprise. "The candy was from you?"

Belle laughed. "No. No, I do not need a man in my life right now. I left it at the inn for a friend."

"Oh really?"

"Yep. One of my sorority sisters mailed the note and a fifty-dollar bill and asked me—" Her hand slid over her mouth. "And that would be why they call me Loose Lips. Why do so many people want me to keep secrets? I can't keep track of all of them. I wasn't supposed to say anything. It's part of some big, elaborate surprise a friend of hers is doing for her boyfriend. I was supposed to drop it off an hour later and actually take it inside, but Patrick's throat was hurting, and I just had to get him home." She held up her bandaged ring finger.

"That's when I did this. Things happen when you're in a hurry."

"What's your sorority sister's name?" If Belle lived up to her nickname, maybe Janice could get a bit more information.

Belle giggled. "I don't know."

"You don't know her name?" Janice felt the ridges forming between her eyebrows.

"She just signed it 'Sis.' We do that. I sign all our round robin letters 'Sister Belle.'"

"But there was no name?"

"No. And there are fourteen of us, so who knows?" Belle took a container of raisins out of her purse, opened it, and handed it to Molly.

"Did you save the letter or the envelope?"

"No." Belle shrugged. "I'm kind of a minimalist. Don't you just hate paper clutter?"

This paper clutter I wouldn't have minded. "Did you recognize the writing?"

"It was typed." Belle stopped Zach from throwing a crayon at Patrick. "Except the note, and I didn't recognize that writing. Guess whoever it was really wanted it to be a surprise."

Their server approached. After they ordered, Belle delved into the topic of music, asking Janice questions about playing with Dawson "back in the day," and the history of the baby grand at Janice's church—all while handing crayons to the children and trying to keep them quiet. There was no artful way to turn the conversation back to Nan.

When the children were somewhat quietly munching on tacos, Janice tried another path. "I saw Maybelline Rector pick you up last night."

"Yes. She's been such a dear. I don't know what I'd do with-out her living so close. My ex lost his job, so that means the checks aren't coming in, so it'll be a while before I can get my car fixed and—"

A shriek came from Molly, followed by a flurry of "I'm sor-rys" from Patrick as the contents of Belle's large soda splashed onto Molly's face and flooded the table, soaking Janice as well as the two-year-old.

And that was the end of their lunch.

Janice drove home with more questions than she'd had when she'd left the inn. Lunch was winding down when she slipped in the back door, her ivory pants and pale blue blouse soaked with Dr Pepper. She filled LuAnn in on what she'd learned and told her to tell Tess, then went upstairs to shower.

By the time she came down, the café was empty, and Tess and LuAnn were rearranging the kitchen.

"Ready?" LuAnn took hold of one end of a folding table, and Tess grabbed the other. They shoved it into a corner of the kitchen.

"Banquet Central," Janice announced. This would be the place to stash and organize dishes, linens, decorations, and nonperishable food.

Tess opened a box of silver plastic flatware. "So that's all she said about the box?"

"Yep. One of her sorority sisters sent the sticky note along with a fifty. She was supposed to deliver it later and bring it inside."

LuAnn took a plastic fork from the box in Tess's hand and hefted it. "Looks real enough. Got a little weight to it." Turning to Janice she said, "Guess you don't have to finish dusting those glasses for fingerprints."

Janice checked flatware off the master list on the counter. "I'm pretty sure she was clueless about anything else."

"So it's just a coincidence she's Maybelline's neighbor?" LuAnn untied her apron. "Sorry. Not buying it."

"Maybe Belle is an innocent who was just used." Tess stacked navy-blue linen-like paper tablecloths on the table. "But maybe Maybelline is not so innocent."

Janice couldn't help it. Without missing a beat, she broke into the "Maybe it's Maybelline" jingle.

Tess, Winnie, and LuAnn burst out laughing.

"The official Valentine Villain theme song," LuAnn said.

The front desk phone rang, and Janice ran to get it. "Wayfarers Inn. This is Janice, how may I help you?"

"Janice." A hushed and gravelly voice answered. "This is Irene."

"Irene? Can you speak up a bit? I'm having a hard time hearing you."

"No." Still a whisper, but more emphatic. "I can't talk any louder. Something big's going to go down any minute here."

"At your house?"

"No. At the MURM. I'm hiding out in the back room."

"You're *what?*" Never in her life had she met an octogenarian with as much spunk as Irene Bickerton Martin.

"Just get here. Come around to the back. I opened a window so you can hear. But be quick. They're going to feel the draft any minute, and then I'm busted."

They made it to the Marietta Underground Railroad Museum on foot in six minutes. Winded and wheezing, they scurried through the narrow space between the museum and the building next to it to find the open window.

They heard a vehicle pull up and park beside the museum. The women hunkered down behind the building's air-conditioning unit.

They heard someone get out, slam the door with far more force than any vehicle deserved, and head to the front of the building.

Tess slunk to the window, crouching to keep her head below the sill, and motioned for LuAnn and Janice to follow. They waited, hearing nothing but traffic noises and the rumble of thunder. And then...laughter. But not the nice kind.

"Well, well, if it isn't the man himself." Maybelline's voice, thick with derision. The women looked at each other in astonishment. Maybelline?

"Don't start, May. I'm here. What do you want?"

Janice recognized the voice. "Axel," she whispered to the other two.

"You need to stop this." Maybelline's voice was tight with emotion. "Think about the girls, and Belle's children could get hurt..."

"Don't pull the kid card on me. I'm the one that loves kids, remember. This is all for them, can't you see that?" Axel's voice was harsh, gravelly.

"I want out. I was only interested in the historical significance. I didn't know it was going to be sold. You conveniently left that part out."

"Convenient." Axel's voice faded, as if he was walking away. "Like the money I just gave you from my last job? Hard as I try, that's all I ever was to you, wasn't I? A convenient—what in the... *Irene*? What in the world are you—"

"Don't hit me! I...where am I? Daddy, is that you?"

"The woman deserves an Oscar," Tess muttered, pulling out her phone. "I'm calling 9—"

"No time. We have to help her." Janice took a deep breath. "Let's go." She led Tess and LuAnn around the building but stopped at the massive old front door. "All we have to do is walk in and let them know someone's here." Straightening her shoulders, she hefted the door open.

Maybelline stood with her hands latched on Axel's bicep. "Don't hurt her."

"Why would I hurt—" Axel looked toward them. His face transformed instantly into a grin. "Ladies, welcome to the Marietta Underground Railroad Museum. Irene here is a little disoriented and we're help—"·

"Oh fishfeathers! Unhand me, Axel Barrett." Irene's cottony head popped up, reaching just above Axel's elbow. "The only one disoriented here is you." She tightened her wool scarf with a yank. "Ladies, would you mind walking me to my car?"

⚜

Brad Grimes paced around Thelma and Irene's kitchen table for the third time. "You can't mess with men like that, Aunt Irene!"

"I'm tougher that I look, kid." This from the little woman who sat at the table swallowed up by a quilt until not much more than her head showed. She reminded Janice of a turtle preparing to duck back into its shell.

"I know that." Brad slowed his pacing and lowered his voice. "But I'm pretty sure Axel Barrett has hurt some pretty tough people in his life."

LuAnn motioned toward a chair, and Brad sat with a resigned sigh.

Janice took a sip of tea. "Start at the beginning. Tell us why you were there and everything you heard before Axel got there."

"Well, I went in because I wanted to ask Maybelline what she knew about the legend of the satchel. I'd heard something about it years and years ago, but now that everyone's talking about it, I thought I'd get it from the horse's mouth." Irene set her cup down as she laughed. "Her mouth is a little like a horse's, isn't it?"

"Irene!" Thelma stood in the doorway, blinking as though she'd just awakened. "Even if it's true, that's a rude thing to say."

Irene's lined face crinkled with mirth. "Anyway, when I got there, Maybelline didn't hear me come in. She was on the phone, and didn't even look up. So I figured, why not go snooping?"

"Irene!" Again, a scolding from Thelma, who was making her way to the chair at the opposite end of the table.

"Well, the woman hoards things that should be seen by the public. She has a whole file cabinet of stuff about the Civil War that should be on display at the River Museum, or she should donate it to the Sons of Union Veterans of the Civil War. Bradley, you know that's true. You went to the dedication of the historical marker for Camp Putnam and you heard—"

"Irene." Brad rested his hand on her thin shoulder. "What did you hear at the MURM that made you call LuAnn and her friends?"

"Like I said, Maybelline was on the phone. I heard her say, 'Axel, just get over here. This has to end now. You're putting our granddaughters and our great-grandchildren at risk.'"

Chapter Nineteen

"N ot used to seeing you up before the others." Winnie smiled as Janice walked into the kitchen with the oatmeal box. "Any more suggestions?"

"Three. Another one from Noah. He thinks we should add breath mints to our goody baskets."

Winnie laughed. "That boy just wants the gift card."

"Yep." Janice poured herself a cup of coffee. "The other two were from the Porters. Sammy gave us a recipe for chocolate-zucchini muffins, and Sam suggested we have surveillance cameras put on the utility poles out front. I'm guessing he has his ear to the ground, and he's heard something."

"Makes me feel good you've got a police officer here at night," Winnie said. "You tell him anything?"

"No. The Marietta Police will have to handle anything that happens here." *And only when something actually happens.* She hadn't told anyone about her phone call to the police yet. Janice rubbed the spot that was tightening on the back of her neck. "I think you're right, we should talk to Sam."

LuAnn walked in. "Morning." She glanced at the box on the table. "Any new suggestions?"

"Nothing that helps." Janice slid the box across the counter. "Evidently the gift card isn't enough motivation to anyone but

Noah. And now that we're pretty sure Axel is the one we need to be worried about and, at least in my mind, Cameron is no longer a suspect, and we've seen Noah's printing, this whole handwriting thing is just…" She didn't bother finishing the sentence. LuAnn would understand her frustration.

LuAnn's brows shot up. "I have an idea. How about a guest book? We pass it around and don't give anyone the option of not signing." She was halfway to the door before she said, "I think I can find a blank book somewhere."

Janice laughed. LuAnn had a supply of unused notebooks that would last until she was in her nineties. She was back in ten minutes with a beautiful teal leather book in hand.

When everyone was seated for breakfast, LuAnn handed their new guest book to Natalie. "We'd love it if you would each take a moment while you're eating to write something in our guest book. Just a line or two and your name and where you're from. Your thoughts will mean a lot to us and to future guests."

Janice poured Natalie's coffee, peering over the woman's shoulder as she took the silver pen and wrote, "Quaint and beautiful. Great place to gather with friends and wind down in the evening. Hope to be back someday." Her letters slanted to the right at a forty-five-degree angle. She wrote quickly—one of the things they were watching for. Anyone who seemed slow and deliberate would be under immediate suspicion. She passed the pen and book to Cameron.

"Nothing but glowing things to say." Cameron asked the rest of them to join him in a round of applause for their hosts.

"Thank you." Janice gave a slight bow. "You have all been such wonderful guests." *Except, maybe, for those of you who might still be planning on stealing from the inn.* "We know that you have your last conference session in the morning, and so this is your last night with us. We've arranged a little surprise for all of you. We have, on occasion, given tours of the inn, letting our guests in on all of its secrets." She watched eyes for signs of interest. Noah's eyebrows rose. Natalie seemed transfixed. RJ looked up but kept eating. "Tonight, just for you, we are offering our first-ever self-guided tour. You will have access to the entire building, including the secret rooms and passages used by Underground Railroad conductors. We'll give you each a map. Of course, it's up to you if you want to open your rooms to others. We hope it's something you'll all enjoy."

Another round of applause and more than one "Wow!"

Cameron raised his coffee mug. "That's awesome. Can't wait."

No one seemed uninterested, so maybe they'd get the whole group involved. Janice poured orange juice and watched as RJ's strong, even hand filled multiple lines.

Noah was next. He printed in a cramped, uneven line. *Nice place. Good people.* As they already knew, it was nothing like the message on the sticky note.

Janice and Tess fussed over their guests, filling coffee cups and juice glasses, as they took turns writing. Franny wrote more than anyone else. Neat, pretty words with little artsy flourishes between letters.

They met in the kitchen after everyone had signed. Tess turned up both hands. "Nothing. We got nothing."

"Brin didn't write anything," LuAnn observed. She walked out and came back with Brin. "We'll let you get back to breakfast, but we have a favor to ask, along with the other things you're already doing for the banquet. I almost forgot about place cards. How is your penmanship?"

"You mean cursive?" Brin asked.

"Yes."

"I wish I could, but I can't."

Tess halted, Big Red's door half open. LuAnn turned off the water and stared at Brin. "You can't, as in you won't have time?" Janice asked.

"No. I would absolutely make time if I could do it, but I went to this avant-garde, progressive school that didn't teach cursive. I wish I'd learned it. Do you think it's too late to— What? Why are you guys looking at me like that?"

Her only answer was relieved laughter.

⌒⟡⌒

Alone in the laundry room, Janice hugged a load of towels fresh out of the dryer. The heat seeped into her tired body, but it couldn't touch her tired soul. Oddly, she was too exhausted to be anxious. She was alone in the inn. Tess had gone to watch her grand-triplets and wouldn't be home until six. LuAnn was getting her hair cut. The Sams were meeting friends and wouldn't be back until late. The Love Is crowd was having a celebratory dinner at The Galley and would return any minute. Usually, she hated being down here alone, but right now she was actually enjoying the quiet with only the hum of the dryer to play backup to her thoughts.

She should be happy. Banquet details were under control. In spite of all of their arguments against it, Winnie had announced after breakfast that she was staying home to handle the cooking. She wasn't all that close to the niece who was getting married anyway. At least that's what she claimed. All she'd been looking forward to was a chance to dress up, and she could do that right here. So they had a respectable cooking and serving team.

She should be happy.

Maybe it was just the weather. Thunder rattled the basement windows. An hour ago, the Washington County Alert System had sent out a text declaring a flood watch. Janice looked down at the platform Thorn built to raise the washers and dryers off the floor. If the Ohio flooded like it had this time last year, the platform could turn into a raft. *Lord, please send snow instead!*

If the river overflowed its banks again they'd be in trouble.

Fear had been her go-to emotion for as long as she could remember. Claustrophobia, arachnophobia…she'd once looked at a list of phobias and put a check by twenty-eight of them. Fear of bugs, cancer, roller coasters, clowns, zombies, public speaking, death, being alone, the dark, deep water, mice, frogs, bees… Little by little she'd begun to conquer her fears. Here she was in the basement alone, after all.

The last towel she pulled out was still slightly damp in the middle. She threw it back in and pulled out her phone. Leaning against the dryer, she dialed Stacy's number. She needed some six-year-old giggles.

Larry answered. "Hi, Nana! Guess what? I learned a silly song at school. Uncle Stuart's here and I sang it for him. You wanna hear—"

Janice gasped and dropped her phone as the dryer stopped and the room turned pitch black.

Silence. As thick and stifling as the darkness that engulfed her, and then the rain began in earnest, slamming against the window above her. Janice dropped to her knees, reaching for her phone as she fought for breath. A skittering sound from behind the washer. A mouse? *Oh gracious* . . . Her pulse hammered her eardrums. And then a scraping sound. Familiar. She held her breath, waiting for footsteps coming from the small end room where the entrance to the tunnel was concealed by a built-in stool. A stool that scraped the floor when pulled out of place. Was someone coming or going?

The footsteps came. She crouched in the corner, strangely grateful for the cover of the darkness that usually terrified her. Across the basement, running steps. Soft-soled shoes. Up the stairs to the first floor. The door at the top of the stairs squeaked open, then closed. She let out her breath and calmed her voice.

"Larry, honey, I would love to hear your song. But can I talk to your Uncle Stuart for a minute please?" She waited while Larry yelled for his uncle.

"Mom?"

Stuart's voice startled her, and she almost dropped the phone again. She wiped her sweaty, trembling hand on her jeans. "Hi, honey. Are you busy right now?"

"What's wrong? You sound upset."

"I'm in the basement. The p-power went out. S-someone's here."

"Someone?" She heard his breathing quicken. "Someone who isn't supposed to be there?"

"I th-think so."

"I'm in the car. On my way. Sit tight. I'll stay on the phone. Tell me what happened."

She told him about the scraping sound and the foot-steps.

"You're sure it wasn't Lu or Tess or one of your staff?"

"They would have said something."

"I suppose. Did you call to them?"

"And take the chance it wasn't them? No. You may call it wimpy, my son, but I call it smart."

"Hey, I read my talk to Stace. She thinks it's a little too clini-cal, imagine that. So we figured out some places where I could make it 'resonate' better, as she put it. I think it's pretty good. And don't worry, I'm as prepared for the deposition as anyone could be. I think it's going to go well. I'm just hoping it doesn't get postponed because of flooding. I just want to get it over with. And I can't imagine how much the Moores want to get this behind them."

Sweet boy. He was rambling to get her mind off whoever lurked upstairs. "Sh-should we call the police?"

"Wait until I get there. If it looks like something's suspicious, we'll call. Maybe it's nothing. Maybe lightning hit a transformer."

She rose on shaky legs and looked out the window. "The street lights are still lit."

"Okay, well, could be the old wiring. Maybe what you heard was just the rain. Stay where you are. I'll check out the other floors and let you know when it's safe to come up."

Not a chance. She wasn't going to hover here in the dark while her son put himself in mortal danger. "I'm going to check the circuit box." She took one step out of the laundry room. *And I'm texting Thorn and Sam.*

"No. Leave that to me," Stuart commanded.

She dimmed the light on her phone, slipped out of her shoes, and tiptoed across the basement, jumping at every crack of thunder until she reached the gray metal box. She looped one finger under the opener and pulled slowly, soundlessly. She raised her phone, aiming the light onto the panel. The main breaker hadn't been flipped. She scanned the rows of black switches. Not a single spot of red. "No one's touched the circuit box," she whispered into the phone.

A loud, irritated sigh met her ear. "I'm here now. I'm going to check the perimeter, then come in the back door. I'm going to hang up now. Stay in the basement."

She stayed. Just long enough to send a text. *Power out at inn. Storm? Heard footsteps. Help.* She sent it to Sam and Thorn.

She crept up the stairs. The chime on the front door dinged as she eased open the basement door. Friend or foe?

Laughter. Cameron's booming laugh made her exhale, long and loud, and gave her the courage to open the door the rest of the way.

"This is creepy." That was RJ.

"I think it's kinda cool," Brin said.

Janice joined them as they all pulled out phones. "The power just went out." The door opened again, and Franny and Natalie entered.

"What happened?" Franny asked. She directed her question at RJ, who moved closer to her. No comforting arm, but Janice imagined just his nearness spoke volumes. Franny didn't move away.

Cameron took off his rain-spotted coat. "It was sleeting a few minutes ago, but it's starting to pour now. Sounds like we're really going to get hit with something. Think it's safe to stay here? Do you have battery backups for your sump pumps?"

"Yes, we do." Though, in reality, a sump pump wouldn't do diddly-squat if the river rose too high. She didn't need to terrify her guests. It was up to her to play the role of consummate host—while she watched her guests like a hawk. "If one of you wouldn't mind putting a few more logs on the fire, we can all get cozy. Lu and Tess will be back any minute. We've got a gas stove, so we'll make some hot chocolate and just turn this into an adventure."

"Can we still do the tour?" Brin's eyes glowed in the filmy light of her phone screen.

"Oh, let's!" Natalie, in a break from her usual poise, clapped her hands together.

"Sure. Stuart will check the . . ." Her voice faltered. Stuart was here and so was Brin. Her swallow was probably loud enough for everyone to hear. "If the power doesn't come on soon, we'll hold our first annual Wayfarers Inn Treasure Hunt in the dark."

Once again, the door opened. Stuart, drenching wet. As the others migrated to the parlor, Stuart motioned for Janice to follow him into the kitchen. Before the swinging door had completely closed behind them, he whispered. "I'm calling the police. Someone who knew what they were doing cut the meter seal and stole the whole bloomin' thing."

July 22, 1863

Prudence crept through the tunnel, the smell of must and mud stinging her nostrils. The sense of unease increased as she stood in the small end room, fingertips digging into the edge of the door. An inner tug stopped her from opening it.

Voices. And then a sob. Tabitha.

Prudence eased the door open just a crack.

"…be more careful, Miss. Following you was like chasin' an albino rabbit on a full moon night."

"What…will thee do with him?"

"Oh, don't you worry. We'll take good care of him. Thanks for patchin' him up."

"Will thee send him to a prison camp?"

The man laughed. "Oh no, ma'am, we've got other plans."

Tabitha gasped. "Please…"

Prudence pressed her hand to her mouth. Who were they? If she knew they were Union soldiers, she would run out, explain who he was and what he was doing. But what if they were Confederate? As the voices grew louder, she opened the door the width of her hand and peered down the long, dark hallway.

A lantern flickered past the opening, giving just enough light to show a checkered shirt and suspenders. The men were not in uniform.

CHAPTER TWENTY

I'm with your mom on this, Stu." Tess ladled hot chocolate into a carafe in the light of three battery-powered hurricane lamps they'd set on the kitchen table. "Let's see how the tour plays out." She and LuAnn had walked into a standoff, with Janice agreeing they needed to call the police but wanting to wait another hour, and Stuart telling her she was being ridiculous.

Stuart ruffled his hair. "Look, I know you all love your mysteries, but this one is getting out of hand. There is no way under the sun I'm going to allow you to go ahead with this tour idea."

"Stu..." Janice's voice was just above a whisper. The time for secrets, for trying to protect her son, was gone. They had only a matter of hours until Nan was going to do something to Brin or her mother. "I—"

"I'm going out to look at the meter again." He walked into the café.

With a shrug, Janice sucked in a breath, exhaled a prayer, and turned to her two best friends. Would they ever be able to forgive her, to understand her reasons for holding out on them? "Lu, Tess, I need to tell you something before Stuart comes back. I need you to listen to the whole thing and then—"

235

The door swung open, and Stuart strode in, his face frighteningly pale. "Mom, who is that girl with the big glasses and curly hair?"

LuAnn stepped out of the pantry with a bag of marshmallows in hand. "She works for us, temporarily anyway. That's Brin. Brin Mc—"

The front door chimed, and a squeal from the parlor overshadowed Janice's attempt to silence LuAnn with a look. Stuart opened the kitchen door and swayed as if he'd been blasted with a gale force wind. Janice reached out to steady him as Brin bounded through the door, pulling behind her a woman who appeared to be in her midthirties. Mahogany hair with hints of red fell in a riot of curls around her shoulders.

"Hey, everyone!" Brin yelled. "I want you all to meet my—"

"Neo?" The woman looked at Stuart, blinking as if to clear the picture.

Stuart took a step back, staring at the woman who was, though older, almost a mirror image of Brin. "Zelda?"

"Mom?" Brin let the door close behind her as she gaped at the two people staring at each other, stunned, wide-eyed, and transfixed.

Janice sank against the counter.

"Tess," LuAnn whispered. "Let's go serve our guests."

"O-kay." Confusion laced Tess's voice, but she picked up a carafe of hot chocolate and a plate of stakeout cookies and followed LuAnn.

"Mom?" Brin waved her hand in front of her mother's face. "What's going on? Do you know him? Ooooh! It's him, isn't it? But..." She turned questioning eyes on Janice.

"He's my son." Janice blinked back tears. "So I guess...that makes me your grandmother."

"*What?*" Stuart and Zelda whirled in unison to face her as their one-word questions overlapped.

"Ma! What in the world?" Stuart's face flushed. "No! She's not. We...*no!*"

Zelda, whose face was a complementary shade of red, shook her head vehemently. "Stuart is not...We never...*No.*"

Heat rose from Janice's collarbones to the top of her head. She turned to Brin. "I...you said...I just assumed..."

Brin's laugh sliced through the awkwardness. "It's my fault. I guess I can see how you could have thought that. But I showed you the picture. Didn't you recognize...Oh. He's the one you were protecting." Her gaze conveyed disappointment.

"You knew she was Zel's daughter and you didn't tell me?" Stuart added his dismay to Brin's. The condemnation in the room was palpable. "Why would you do that?"

"Why would you not tell me you had a history with this building? Why would you not tell me you'd been in lo—" Janice snapped her mouth shut and closed her eyes.

A rap at the door jolted her, and she opened it to see Sam, looking worried and confused, standing in front of Thorn, who had his back to Sam, clearly observing their guests. It looked like a practiced military stance to guard each other's backs.

Janice pulled them out of the kitchen and to the basement door. In as few words as possible, she filled them in.

"I'm calling the local authorities," Sam said. Thorn nodded, and she didn't argue. "But go ahead with what you had planned. Someone tampered with the electric box. At the very least, that's a misdemeanor. We need to catch this guy." Sam pulled a phone out of his shirt pocket.

As he made the call, Thorn went to the basement to "check things out." Janice walked back into the kitchen.

"...youth concert in Paris and we played just a block from the venue at this adorable coffee house. We shared the gospel every night, and so many kids gave their hearts to Jesus. It was so amazing. You would have loved it." Zelda's short-nailed fingertips grazed the back of Stuart's hand.

"Wish I could have been there." Twenty years' worth of loss and regret surrounded Stuart's words. "Zel...Why...?"

Wayward curls trailed over her face as Zelda looked down at the table, then glanced at her daughter. "Two months after I went back to Boston, I was with some friends at a party. All I was drinking was root beer, but I walked away from my drink and someone slipped something in it...I woke up in a strange room, and well..."

Silence hung for several seconds in the room lit by candlelight as the full impact of what she had not said registered in Janice's mind, and, she could tell by the look on her son's face, Stuart's.

"Oh, Zel." Stuart looked from her to Brin. "I'm so sorry."

"I..." Zelda wiped her eyes. "So many times I wanted to call you. I didn't answer the phone for a year because I was afraid of hearing your voice. My mom said you sounded so sad every time you called." She dug a tissue out of her pocket. "The day we were supposed to meet, I cried all day."

"Why didn't you tell me?" The agony in Stuart's voice wrenched Janice's heart.

"How many times over that summer did we talk about our life plans? You had it all mapped out. College, med school... I was supposed to work to support you and then we would buy a house and start our family. We were so young, so starry-eyed. We thought life would play out just the way we planned it..." She looked around the room as if seeing the changes for the first time. "...right here." Her bottom lip quivered as she took a deep breath. "But it didn't."

"But we could have found a way. I would have been there—"

"I know you would have. That's *why* I didn't tell you. But look, you're a successful doctor." She reached out and pulled Brin into a hug. "And I have a beautiful daughter. God has been good to both of us."

Before Stuart had a chance to argue or agree, Tess and LuAnn walked in. Their gazes circled the table and landed on Janice.

With an apologetic smile as prelude, Janice said, "We need to talk. Maybe we should hand out maps and flashlights and let them start the tour while we're talking."

"Mom." Stuart stared at Zelda, as if asking permission for whatever he was about to say. "Unless someone has already found it and moved it, we know where the spy bag is."

Janice nodded. "I know. But we're going to go ahead with the tour."

Stuart tapped folded hands on the table. Another gesture of impatience. "Somebody, quite possibly somebody in this building right now, cut off the power. Who knows what they intend to do now that we're all sitting ducks in the dark? Zel and I will see if the bag is still where we left it, and then no one can steal it."

"But then we won't know who cut the power. And RJ needs to know who stole his bag." For peace of mind if nothing else. He needed to know whom he could trust. Janice hated being at odds with her son, especially when he was right about them being sitting ducks. But with Thorn and Sam in the building and the police on the way, she felt secure. Relatively, anyway.

Janice looked at Stuart. "I'll hand out the maps while you tell Lu and Tess whatever you want to tell them about twenty years ago, and then I'll come back in and apologize for everything I knew and didn't tell you all and why, and then we all need to spread out and watch where everyone searches and...wait a minute. I have an idea. Stu and..." It suddenly dawned on her that she hadn't actually been introduced to Brin's mother. She held out her hand. "Nice to meet you, Zelda. I'm Stuart's mom, Janice."

"So nice to meet you." Zelda grasped her hand with a firm squeeze.

"If you two will come with me, I think we might be able to set a trap for our culprit."

They took the stairs to the fourth floor. Janice wondered what looks were being exchanged behind her as they hurried up the steps.

"I can't believe you all actually renovated this building," Zelda said. "I've thought about it so often…what it could be if someone just gave it some TLC. And a whole lot of money, I imagine."

Janice laughed. "A whole lot." They reached the fourth floor. "Wait here." Janice walked ahead and into her room. On the floor of her closet she found what she was looking for. She brought it out and handed it to Stuart, who started laughing.

"This just might work." He held out the handmade cardboard box with wires trailing out of it.

Zelda bent close to examine it, then shrugged. "What is it?"

"It's a motion sensor alarm I made in college to scare my buddies away from stealing my soda."

"Ah." Zelda nodded. "So if we put it under the step…"

"Yep." Stuart put his arm around Janice's shoulders. "My mom, the thief catcher. Can you keep people from coming up the stairs?"

"I can do that." She put her arm around his waist. They walked out, and she locked the door. The fourth floor would not be open to their guests. "I'll leave you to it then."

On the first floor, the scene in the parlor stopped her, and she stared with an irrational sense of tranquility at their guests gathered in front of a roaring fire. Candles glinted from the mantel.

On the love seat, RJ sat with his arm around Franny as she showed him a daisy necklace from her collection. Natalie stood, silhouetted by the flames, refilling cups from the carafe. Noah had returned and stood next to the fireplace, mopping his face with a towel. Cameron had his head bent over a word search book.

She took in the whole, peaceful picture. And then it hit her. That one tiny detail she'd missed.

One of their guests was ambidextrous.

CHAPTER TWENTY-ONE

When Stuart and Zelda returned, Janice told Brin to let them write detailed instructions on where to find the satchel in a text to Nan. As LuAnn handed out the maps, and Tess gave instructions, Brin waited with the other guests, unobtrusively waiting for a signal from Janice.

They'd given everyone the opportunity to leave their room doors open if they wanted them included on the tour. "So if it's not locked, feel free to snoop." Tess swept out her hand in a gesture meant to include the entire building. "We'll be in the café if you have any questions."

Janice nodded to Brin, and the group of six dispersed throughout the inn, flashlights glowing.

Thorn and Sam, who'd left Sammy with their friends, joined them for coffee in the café. Sam was in contact with the police. An accident on the bridge held them up, taking priority over their non-emergency call. Sam was now officially in charge.

In the room lit only by the red glow from two Exit signs and several candles, they chatted about rain and flood predictions until a faint sound interrupted their deliberately casual conversation.

Squeak. Squeak. Squeak.

Stuart looked at Zelda. Zelda smiled, a touch of nostalgia making her eyes glisten. Stuart nodded to Sam, who slid his chair back. They waited. Silence, followed by more squeaks, each growing louder.

Tess drummed her fingers on the table. LuAnn tapped her silver pen. Janice leaned toward Sam. "What will happen to the—"

Beep! Beep! Beep!

Sam leaped out of his chair. Moving like a man half his age, he ran toward the stairs.

Running steps crossed the balcony above them. RJ and Franny flew down the stairs. "What's going on?" The incessant beeping continued.

Janice put her finger over her mouth. "Come sit down." She got up and offered Franny her chair. RJ grabbed one from a nearby table and set it next to Franny.

"We've caught the Valentine Villain," Tess whispered.

The beeping finally stopped and they all breathed a collective sigh. But the silence wasn't comforting. It just offered a quieter form of fear.

Sam descended the steps. He ran his hand through thick, graying hair. "Sorry. They were too fast for me. I checked the second and third floors. All the doors are open, but I didn't see anyone. But they didn't take it."

Stuart leaned forward. "It's still there?"

"Just like you described it."

Janice lifted her hands, palm out. "Let's let everyone settle down for the night before we—"

Noah opened the basement door. "Pretty cool. That room down there was actually to hide slaves?"

"Sure was." LuAnn motioned for him to join them. Noah pulled a chair next to Franny. "We found a journal of a woman who was an Underground Railroad conductor in the 1850s."

"Cool. So Mr. Barrett owned it like a whole century after that, huh?"

Janice swiveled to face Noah as Tess and Janice looked at him in surprise. "Axel owned this building?"

"Yeah. Back in the 1960s. Can you believe he's that old?" Noah picked up a cookie from the plate on the table.

Tess took a chair. Anyone who didn't know her would think that the way she crossed her legs and kept time to some silent beat meant she was relaxed, but Janice knew better. "Really? I thought we knew the history of the place pretty well. What was it back then?"

"A chop shop." Noah's eyes lit with more energy than they'd seen in him yet. "Yeah, it was a big operation. That loading door, they'd drive stolen cars in and truckloads of parts out through there. Pretty big operation it sounds like. Axel got busted and spent like a long time locked up."

Which meant he would know the layout of the inn like the back of his hand.

Cameron and Brin came through the basement door and pulled chairs close to the others. "What are the hash marks on the bricks in the tunnel for?" Cameron asked. Apparently, the sound of the alarm had not reached the basement.

"Our best guess is that it's a record of the number of slaves who passed through there," LuAnn said.

Natalie was the next one to come upstairs. "What are all those little rooms for?"

"They were either used for hotel staff or to house runaway slaves. Or both," Tess said.

"I can't imagine what it must have been like for them," Franny said. "I have a good friend whose great-great-something grandfather was a slave in North Carolina. Her mom has his freedom papers framed and hanging in the living room next to a picture of him."

Natalie nodded. "The tunnel, and that ladder...imagine bounty hunters chasing you and not even knowing for sure if the place you were hiding in was safe."

"She was the only one gutsy enough to climb the ladder." Cameron bowed to Natalie. "I spent two months on a sub in the navy. It took away my fondness for tight spaces."

After half an hour of questions about the history of the inn, their guests trailed off to bed, flashlights in hand.

Stuart set his phone down. "They'll be here to work on it within an hour. Didn't sound like replacing the meter would take too long." Sam had taken pictures, and the police had given the go-ahead to have the meter replaced.

"Good." Janice scrolled on her phone as she wracked her brain for a name that had slid through the many cracks in her gray matter.

"Now?" Stuart's eyes pleaded with Janice the way they once had when she'd told him he couldn't go swimming until after his supper digested. Her son had no more patience than his six-year-old nephew.

Janice set her phone down. It made no difference if she could prove who had the *intention* of stealing something. Because of her silly plan to catch them with the alarm, the culprit hadn't gotten away with it. Her brilliant idea of catching the perp red-handed had bombed. It was time to focus on the treasure—another link to Prudence—that had been hiding in the inn since 1863, maybe seen only by the two people sitting across the table from her. She smiled at her son. "Now."

Pointing flashlights, Stuart and Zelda led the way to the stairway between the second and third floors. Tess, LuAnn, Janice, Brin, and Sam crowded in behind them.

"We found this by accident," Stuart whispered, winking at Zelda.

"That step was cracked." Zelda pointed to a spot two stairs above the one she stood on. "I tripped on it and grabbed these spindles when I fell." She placed her hands on two rails and turned them simultaneously to the left. A single familiar squeak echoed in the stairway. And the stair tread popped up.

Janice, and everyone else in the crowded space, gasped. "How is it possible that wasn't found during our renovations?"

"It won't open any other way. You have to know what you're looking for...or have a serendipitous accident." Stuart smiled at Zelda and lifted the tread.

Inside lay a leather bag much like RJ's, covered in dust and cobwebs.

———— ❦ ————

Tess and LuAnn brought lanterns from the living room, and they gathered around the harvest table. At Sam's request, LuAnn produced a box of food-prep latex gloves for Stuart and Zelda.

Zelda pulled out a folded piece of notebook paper, opened it, blushed, and set it aside. Stuart did the same with a second folded paper. And an identical blush. "We wrote these."

Janice stared in wonder at her son's face. Glowing. That was the only word to describe it. She had never seen that sparkle in his eyes. All these years, all of the women she'd tried to set him up with…now it was clear. No one could compare with his first love.

"These are the drawings." Stuart slid out a stack of papers pressed between two pieces of thick leather and bound by strips of cowhide. With the careful, skilled hands of a doctor, he untied the bow and lifted the top piece of leather.

The first picture caused a wave of sharp inhales. An ink drawing of a battlefield. In the background, smoke rose from a cannon. In the foreground, so many bodies. The next page was similar. And the next. And then Stuart lifted a drawing that caused only Tess, LuAnn, and Janice to gasp.

"Prudence!"

Eyes closed, hands folded in prayer, she sat on the dirt floor, Bible on her lap, a hurricane lamp beside her. Behind her, a wall of bricks. The uneven, hand-formed bricks of the secret basement room. Slanted at the top of the page was sketched a single eagle feather and the words, "I bore you on the Eagle's wings and brought you unto myself." In the bottom corner, the initials IRF.

"Ira Fitzhugh," LuAnn whispered.

Stuart and Zelda took turns pulling items out of the bag, growing concern on both faces. A gold pocket watch, a moth-eaten handkerchief, several coins, and a roll of Confederate bills along with things they had added—the class ring Stuart claimed he'd lost, a wide, beaded barrette, and a red-and-white checkered cloth napkin. A tintype photograph of a woman fell out of its cardboard frame when Stuart lifted it. On the back of the picture was inked "Clarence b. July 1863."

Zelda felt the bottom of the satchel, then turned it upside down. "The velvet bag…the ruby pin isn't here."

Sam took notes as he leafed through the Clues and Suspects list. "If you had to make a guess, based on everything you've seen and heard, who do you think is after the brooch?"

"Axel." Tess and LuAnn answered together.

Janice chewed on her bottom lip. The last thing she wanted to do was accuse one of their guests, but she'd kept enough from her best friends. She took a deep breath. "Natalie."

"What?" Tess looked at her like she'd sprouted horns. "What motive would she have?"

"I don't know. But I discovered something about her tonight that we've all missed." Janice paused, second-guessing her conclusion, but decided to continue. "This morning she wrote with her right hand, but tonight she was pouring hot chocolate with her left hand."

Tess's brow rose. "When I waitressed back in the day we had to learn to pour coffee with both hands."

"The one dressed in all black?" Stuart looked at her like another horn had popped out the top of her skull. "She sure doesn't look like a thief."

Thorn laughed. "What does a thief look like, Stu?"

Sam stroked the white stubble on his chin. "If this Axel guy has a record, I'd put money on it being him, but we need to check out every lead."

If only she could think of— "Capitol City Tactical!" She hadn't meant to say it out loud. She tapped the name into her phone. "Natalie taught Urban Escape and Evasion classes. Listen to this: 'The focus is on learning skills such as advanced lock picking, forced entry methods, and disabling security systems.'"

"Hmm." Sam's one-shoulder shrug was the only concession to her idea.

The desk phone rang, and Janice went to answer it. She manufactured a semblance of a smile. "Wayfarers Inn. This is Janice. How may I help you?"

"Hello?" A familiar but ragged-sounding voice. "Who is this?" Was it anger or tears that made the woman's voice so hoarse?

"Maybelline? Is that you? This is Janice."

"Janice. I'm at the MURM. I need to con—"

An ear-splitting *bang* smothered her voice, and the phone went dead.

Janice gripped the edge of the front desk and turned to the group. "Somebody shot Maybelline!"

July 22, 1863

Prudence waited interminable minutes after the upstairs door closed, the only sound the muffled cry of her friend. Finally, she opened the door and walked out. The basement was empty, so she slipped behind the hidden door, walked past the ladder, pausing to look up and listen, then silently opened the door to the secret room.

On her knees, skirt puddled around her, Tabitha sobbed. A single candle flickered next to the rumpled pallet.

"Tabitha. Who were they?"

Tabitha stared at her, eyes wild. "Did thee know his wife is expecting a baby any day now? And now he won't—"

Prudence gripped Tabitha's shoulders. "Who were they? Who took him?"

"I don't know. They had a photograph of Ira. Ruth, the woman who offered to take him in Susannah's wagon, identified him. He didn't seem scared, but no one said anything. I don't know if they were rescuing him or capturing him. Two men carried him out, and the other two were searching for something."

The satchel. They wouldn't have found it. Did that mean she'd interfered with the transfer of information that would help the North, or kept Union secrets out of the hands of Confederate soldiers? Prudence sank to the pallet, her hand sliding under the pillow, and finding a pencil. She shoved the pillow aside.

On the muslin sheet, outlined in black... an eagle feather. *The eagle feather means safety.*

With tears, she looked down at Tabitha. "He's okay. Thank God. He's safe."

CHAPTER TWENTY-TWO

Two white police cruisers sat in front of the Marietta Underground Railroad Museum when Tess pulled her car up behind Sam and Stuart. The rain had stopped, but the wind was high. Tree branches swayed in front of street lamps, casting ghostly shadows.

Stuart jumped out and ran across the street. Sam walked over to their car and tapped on the window. "Wait here." He strode across the street to talk to Chief Mayfield and another officer. An ambulance slid in behind the squad cars, and two EMTs ran into the building, bags in hand.

"That's a good sign, right?" Tess craned her neck to watch the EMTs enter the building. "They're not going in with a stretcher."

"Or a body bag," Janice added.

"Janice!" LuAnn reached back from the passenger seat to swat her arm but missed.

"Do you think Axel did it?" Tess turned from the driver's seat. "If she was ready to confess everything, and he knew it..."

Janice nodded. "He stole the ruby pin, escaped down the ladder and out the tunnel, and came here. Maybe Maybelline told him she was going to confess, or maybe he just didn't want to share his part of the take."

"Too many CSI episodes, girl." LuAnn rolled the window down about two inches. "Shh...I can hear them."

"...can't ever catch...we'll get prints...be our chance." Chief Mayfield's voice drifted in and out with the wind.

"Are they talking about Axel? Or Maybelline?" Janice added a layer of mystery to her voice on the last word. "She's got the perfect cover. She's been a pillar in the community forever and—" She stopped talking as Belle walked out the front door and went straight to Chief Mayfield.

Belle's words, much softer than Mayfield's, were almost impossible to pick out. "...told her not to...dangerous...stubborn..." She nodded, looked across the street, and began walking toward them.

Tess opened the window the rest of the way. Belle leaned down. "Thank you for calling the police. I hate to think how long she would have lain there if you hadn't. I'm just glad she was talking to someone when it happened. Although it probably wouldn't have happened at all if she hadn't been talking to you."

Janice imagined Axel lurking in the corner of the museum, the ruby pin in his pocket. Maybe he was about to show it to Maybelline, his partner in crime, when he heard her starting to confess.

Belle smiled, an odd reaction, but Janice had seen it before in response to stressful situations. "I bought her one of those alert buttons to wear around her neck, but she refuses to wear it. I hate it when she comes here at night. Anything can happen."

"How bad is she?" LuAnn asked.

"Just a scrape. Not the first time it's happened."

"What?" Three voices asked in unison with equal incredulity.

Tess opened her mouth, closed it, then finally found her voice. "She's been shot at before?"

"Shot at? What?" Belle matched their expressions.

Janice slunk back, hiding her humiliation. Was she wrong once again? "I heard a shot, and the phone went dead."

Belle's surprise morphed into a laugh. "You thought she'd been shot? Oh, no. It was that stupid door. It weighs like eight hundred pounds, and it can slam shut and practically kill a person. She was talking to you on the phone and carrying a pile of books in her other arm, so she couldn't catch it. It smacked her shoulder pretty hard but only left a scrape."

Silence filled the car as the truth set in. Then LuAnn's giggle began to fill the silence. "I'm s-sorry. It's just…" She sobered, but the gleam didn't leave her eyes. "Janice said she called to confess something. Do you know what it was?"

"I don't know anything about a confession. She said she was calling to continue a conversation that got cut off earlier."

Con…tinue. Not con…fess. Janice splayed her fingers across her face. Laugh or cry? The two were so very close these days.

"Anyway, thanks." Belle stuck her hands in the pockets of her plaid coat. "It's comforting to know Grandma has so many good friends."

"Grandma?" Janice and Tess asked. LuAnn wasn't far behind.

"Oh...you didn't know? Maybelline is my grandmother. I actually just found out not too long ago."

Janice had a feeling she knew how Alice felt as she began sliding down the rabbit hole to Wonderland.

"Axel Barrett and Maybelline Rector are my mom's parents. It was all a big scandal back in the day, of course, so Maybelline gave up my mom for adoption to her cousin, who I always thought was my grandma."

As the only one in the car who had grown up in Marietta, Janice was probably the only one who fully understood what a huge scandal that would have been "back in the day." She couldn't wrap her brain around it. *Axel and Maybelline?* What could possibly have drawn them together?

They said goodbye to Belle and headed back to the inn, where the perpetrator was probably sleeping soundly now that another Janice blunder had given him—or her—enough time to easily stash the goods.

The power was still out when Brad dropped them off, but a Washington Electric truck was parked next to the inn. A single battery lantern remained lit on the desk next to a note that read: *Janice—Hope it's okay that Mom stays with me. Brin*

Janice yawned. "Let's call it a ridiculous day." She looked down at her shoes. "Sorry I messed everything up."

"What do you mean?" Tess appeared genuinely surprised at her remorse. What a sweet friend. "This has been an awesome day."

LuAnn nodded. "We made memories today, and tomorrow we're going to make a ton more. We're going to host the most fabulous banquet Marietta has ever seen. But we can't do it all without sleep." She nodded for Janice to lead the way.

It was kind of them to make her feel like she hadn't led them down the rabbit hole once again, but a sense of failure made her legs feel like lead as she trudged up the stairs.

"Do you think we're safe?" she whispered. She didn't want to be the kind of woman who needed a man around to feel protected, but the truth was that for almost forty years she'd had a man around. "We don't know when Sam will get back."

"I don't think we're in any real danger," Tess answered.

The key word being *real.* Meaning they were probably in some degree of danger.

"We've got Cameron. And RJ," LuAnn added. "I've got all of their cell numbers on my phone."

She was right. Assuming they were right about crossing both men off the suspects list.

With a tired nod, Janice resigned herself to a night of fitful sleep. "I'm taking two melatonin, a hot bath, and—" The power came on, revealing that half the lights in the inn were on. "Praise the Lord for elec—"

On the floor in front of Lily and Lace, a spark of luminous red gleamed in the light of the hallway sconces. Janice moved to one side, and the crimson glow grew brighter. She bent and touched it, then gasped. She picked up the object and set it in the palm of her hand, then motioned for Tess and LuAnn to turn around and go back downstairs.

Under the bright light over the harvest table, she opened her hand. A round-cut ruby, the diameter of a pencil eraser, gleamed on her palm.

⸙

Zelda, sitting at the harvest table in a terry cloth robe over flannel pajamas, nuzzled her face in Huck's fur. After Sam had returned and looked at the evidence, they'd awakened Zelda to look at the ruby. Thankfully, they'd managed not to disturb Brin. Zelda stared at the gem twinkling in Sam's hand. "There were twelve of them in a circle."

"Twelve?" LuAnn almost dropped the plate of stakeout cookies she'd brought to the table. "All that big?" She sank into a chair next to Sam, whose eyes appeared ready to pop out.

"I remember because I thought it would make a cool watch, with a ruby for each number. The pin was about this big." Making a circle with her fingers, Zelda left an opening the size of a golf ball. "There was another circle of tiny diamonds inside the rubies, and the rest was gold. It looked like initials etched in the center, but we couldn't tell what they were. Some kind of fancy script. It was like a locket. When you opened it, there was a circle of letters and another circle of numbers inside that. Neo—*Stuart*—said it looked like a spy decoder ring he had when he was a kid. I've looked up pictures since then, and I'm sure he was right. It was pretty common for telegraph messages to be sent in code. The recipient would use a decoder disk to decipher the message." She pulled her hair back and tamed it in a hair band. "I cannot believe we were dumb enough to leave it here. It could have been in a museum."

"You were in love," Tess said, patting Zelda's arm. "Love makes your brain fuzzy. And you were very young."

A sudden flash of memory hit Janice from out of nowhere. They'd taken a rare family vacation to Washington DC the week after Stuart graduated from high school. As they walked through the Hall of Geology, Gems, and Minerals at the Smithsonian, their tour guide talked about how gems were formed, where they were found, and occasionally told them the current worth of the stones on display. When he'd pointed to a single ruby, maybe twice the size of the one now resting in Sam's hand and mentioned a figure with a lot of zeroes, Stuart had stopped abruptly, almost causing a pileup in their tour group. "*How* much?" he'd asked. The guide repeated the dollar amount. "And what if it was, like, half that size?" Stuart asked. The guide had laughed. "Like, half as much, I suppose."

She remembered now worrying about Stuart on that trip. Moodier than usual, he'd barely said a word, and she hadn't, until this moment, connected it with their visit to the Smithsonian.

"What now?" Sam set the gem in Zelda's hand. "Call Chief Mayfield and have him issue a search warrant for Axel Barrett's place? Or... I hate to bother your guests, but I'm wondering if there's some validity to your earlier observation, Janice, considering where you found this."

"If it was her, and that's a big if, wouldn't she have found a way to get it off the premises by now? She'd assume there was a possibility we'd search all the rooms. She probably left when . . . " LuAnn left the statement dangling between them.

"When I took us on another wild-goose chase." Janice watched cream circling like a coiling snake in her cup.

"Maybe she's already gone." Tess picked up a cookie but set it down again. "I guess we should find out before she gets too far."

"I don't have the right to search your guests' rooms, but you all do. Do you want to be up front—just knock on the door, and I'll question her while you look—or should we take a different approach?"

They all startled at footsteps. A sleepy-eyed Brin shuffled down the stairs. "What's going on? I woke up, and Mom was gone."

Zelda filled her in on what had happened over the last hour, and then Janice told Sam about Brin's contact with the mysterious Nan.

"Did you bring your phone down?" Janice asked. "Sam should see the messages."

Brin pulled her phone out of the pocket of her plaid pajama bottoms and began explaining how Nan had made contact with her.

Sam scanned the messages. After reading the last one he looked up. "This constitutes a threat. I'm calling Mayfield." He turned to the Inn Crowd as he picked up his phone. "I need everything you have on Natalie. Credit card number, reservation information, anything you remember about her coming and going, even seemingly irrelevant comments."

"Natalie?" Brin gaped at Sam. "You think she's Nan?"

Janice stood. "I'll go get her credit card info." She walked toward the kitchen door, exhaustion dragging at her. This had all seemed like a fun adventure until it came down to actually confronting one of their guests about a crime.

"Wait!" Brin yelled, her gaze riveted to a page in LuAnn's notebook. "It's not Natalie. It's Noah! Look!" She held up LuAnn's notebook and pointed to the page with "Noah" at the top. "Look." She tapped a line with his full name. "Look at his initials."

Noah Allen Nichols.

NAN.

CHAPTER TWENTY-THREE

Janice watched Noah, shrinking into a chair in the corner of the parlor as Chief Mayfield peppered him with questions. She fought the maternal desire to swoop in and save him from this humiliation. Whatever his reasons for taking the brooch, and probably RJ's bag, she felt nothing but pity for him.

Chief Mayfield had called for backup. Officer Randy Lewis looked around until he saw Mayfield, then shrugged out of his wet jacket. "County just issued an updated flood watch. Looks like you may have to evacuate, Mrs. Eastman."

Randy Lewis had been one of the troublemakers in her Sunday school class years ago. Now he was the one warning them of trouble. Janice took his jacket and said she'd bring him coffee.

Zelda had called Stuart. They sat, all six of them yawning and sipping coffee, in the café at two in the morning, watching the interrogation. Sam sat next to Noah and seemed to talk only to Chief Mayfield. Mayfield, who wasn't known for his quiet demeanor, was managing to speak so low they couldn't hear much of what he was saying. He straddled a café chair facing Noah, who kept his eyes down and shook his head to every question.

"It would be so much easier for him if he'd just confess," Stuart whispered.

After about half an hour, in which time Noah never once nodded a yes, and only looked up once, to hand over his phone, Chief Mayfield rose slowly from the chair, turned, and he and Sam walked toward the gawkers in the café.

"I don't think he's our guy." Mayfield took a chair. Noah had apparently been told not to move. The poor guy sat staring at them, a pleading look in his eyes. "He's got an old record for petty theft, but I think he's telling the truth on this one. He said he was in the basement talking on the phone to a friend at the time you think the brooch was stolen. It checks out."

"What about the money?" Janice asked. "He gave Axel a huge wad of cash."

"Well..." Sam glanced up at the balcony. "It appears our guy has a serious crush on one of your other guests, who asked him to give the money to Axel."

"Franny?" The name came out of Janice's mouth on a squeak.

"No." Mayfield followed Sam's gaze to the door at the top of the stairs. "Natalie Hemmingway."

LuAnn shook her head. "This feels so deceptive. What do we do, knock on her door and ask if she wants to join us for three a.m. tea?" In spite of clear misgivings, she stood to lead the way up the stairs. Chief Mayfield instructed her to stand to the left of the door when she knocked, then he and Randy followed at her heels.

Huck jumped off Zelda's lap and ran to the front door.

"Huck!" Janice jumped up, suddenly remembering Huck standing over the ladder, looking down at Larry. "We have to guard the ladder. She might try to escape."

Stuart leaped out of his chair and ran to the basement door. "Stay here," Stuart called over his shoulder.

"Fat chance," Janice answered under her breath. She waited for him to descend the basement stairs and then followed. Taking quick steps, she crossed the span of concrete and slid through the camouflaged door at the end of a row of cabinets.

Lit by flashlight, Stuart glowered at her when she edged in front of him and stared up into the shaft. The trap door in the kitchen was closed and locked. "We unlocked all of the trap doors. That means . . ." She looked at Stuart. "We need to open all the trap doors so we can see all the way up. She might sneak into RJ's room or"—she swallowed hard—"mine, and climb out the window."

"Ma. That's a little dramatic. Let's—"

Don't you dramatic me, boy. Without another thought, she grabbed hold of the ladder. *Don't look up.* She climbed until she could see the next door. She hadn't stopped to think she'd have to let go of the ladder to open the doors.

A wave of dizziness slammed into her, and she wrapped her left hand around the top rung. Slowly, she eased her right leg up to the next rung, using her head and her right hand to ease the door up, careful not to let it bang against the wall. She eased the trap door until it rested against the wall, and fastened the leather loop to the hook on the wall. She stood in front of the hidden "closet" door in the kitchen. She could simply open the door and walk out into the kitchen. But she wouldn't.

One more floor of rungs. Quieter than before, she eased up to the trap door in the hidden closet in Lily and Lace. With moves that would do a ninja proud, she inched the door against the wall.

Voices. Chief Mayfield wasn't easing into it. "Where did you put it?"

"I don't know what you're talking about," Natalie answered.

Janice's pulse skipped two beats. One step. Two. *Breathe.* Three. Something brushed against the backs of her fingers. Clamping her eyes shut, she willed herself not to scream. And then it brushed again. Something swaying. With a shaky breath, she stretched out her fingers. And touched something soft.

A velvet pouch.

<hr/>

Natalie occupied the same chair Noah had sat in an hour earlier. By now, word had spread through the inn, and all of their guests were up.

"RJ." Sam walked toward the café and motioned for him. "Ladies." He nodded toward Tess, LuAnn, and Janice. "Brin and Noah too. You all need to hear this."

Randy took his jacket from the hook next to the door. "I'm going to pay an early-morning visit to Mr. Barrett." He put on his cap and nodded. With a half smile he said, "Won't be the first time."

Janice let out a sigh of relief as LuAnn came toward her. "So it was Axel."

Janice followed Tess and LuAnn into the parlor where Sam and Stuart were arranging chairs.

Natalie looked at RJ, eyes red-rimmed, cheeks pink. "I'm sorry," she whispered.

I'm sorry. The words on the conversation hearts. Janice's own heart went out to Natalie.

The young woman turned to Brin. "When I read the email you sent asking about registering for the conference, your story intrigued me. I'm a gamer. Have you heard of Birdwatcher?"

Brin nodded. To her mother she said, "It's a real-life spy game. Birdwatcher is a code word for spy. I played it once."

A wistful expression crossed Natalie's face. "My grandpa and I are big fans, and he's from Marietta, so I told him about what your mom had found. I had no idea he knew so much about this building. As it turned out, he used to own it."

Janice shook her head to clear it. "Axel Barrett is your grandfather?"

Head down, Natalie nodded.

"But he's..." Tess made the same kind of quick nod, head-clearing move. "So you're Belle's..."

"Sister. But she had nothing to do with this. I asked her to leave the box of candy because I wanted to get RJ away from the inn. I'd seen a ton of pictures of him with his bag, and I figured I could use it as a decoy or maybe put it in place of the real one if I found it or…make you think someone else was after the real one. Belle didn't even know I was the one asking. She said she thought it was from one of her sorority sisters. I asked her not to tell anyone we were related." Natalie covered her face.

"But wait a minute," Janice said. "I remember that RJ said that only one person here knew that his name was Johnny, and that was Franny. How did you know?"

"I was in charge of reservations and registration, remember?" Natalie gave her a sad smile. "RJ had to use his full name on some of the forms he filled out for the venue. I figured if I called him Johnny, it might mean something special to him. Being in charge of reservations is also the way I could make sure he was in Woodsmoke and Pine, and I was right below him in Lily and Lace."

After a few minutes of slow breathing she said, "When I told my grandpa about the bag, he started joking around, talking about how we could steal it. He drew out a floor plan and showed me all of the ways we could get in. I…" She took a shuddering breath. "I told him things I've learned about breaking locks and sneaking around without being heard. It was all in fun for the longest time, and then I realized he was serious. He was really going to break in and take it. He was going to meet me here that first night, and it wasn't until the next morning at breakfast that I heard you all chased someone away from the inn.

"My grandma got scared and told me not to come here, to stay away from him, because if anyone found out we'd been talking about it I could get arrested as an accomplice. But I had to stop him. If he stole it and got caught, he'd go to prison for years." She looked at RJ. "He's a felon."

"Noah." Natalie looked at the man who would not look at her. "I'm sorry I got you involved. I couldn't leave the conference that day. I thought I'd convinced my grandpa to take Belle and the kids up to a cabin north of Cincinnati for the weekend. I offered to pay. I tried telling him it would be smarter to look for the satchel when there weren't any guests here. I almost had him convinced but..." She turned back to Brin. "He was afraid you would find it first."

She aimed a sad smile at Brin, who appeared to be in shock. "A kid I used to babysit turned Natalie Ann into 'Nan.'" She shrugged. "I'm sorry." This time she turned to Tess, LuAnn, and Janice, who stood together. "I never intended to keep it. I just had to keep him from finding it. But then I couldn't find it. I tried turning the spindles on the stairs, I even tried sawing one of them a little, just to see if I could make something happen, but I didn't want to deface the inn, so I gave up on that. It wasn't until I got the text from Brin that told me how to open the stair that I found the bag."

Chief Mayfield stood. "Can one of you get her coat? Let's take a little trip down to the station, Ms. Hemmingway."

Moments later, as Mayfield took her by the elbow, Natalie's gaze swept the room. "This is such a beautiful place, and you've all been so kind." She shook her head. "I'm so, so sorry." Tears mingled with raindrops as she was led out the door. "P-pray for me?"

"You know we will," Janice said.

Sam put a hand on Janice's shoulder. "Good work, Janice. Did you notice, she wears her watch on her right arm? Pretty sure you nailed it—she's probably quite capable of writing with either hand. We wouldn't have caught her without your sharp eye."

On any other day, she would have basked in the compliment. Now, as she watched the figures heading through the rain, it landed flat.

Beyond the squad car, the river lapped at the door to the tunnel.

Stuart stood behind Janice. "Cancel the banquet, Mom. We need to get out of here while we can."

CHAPTER TWENTY-FOUR

A rms folded across blue sparkles and the string of pearls Zelda had loaned her, Janice leaned against the counter in the church kitchen, looking through the pass window, staring at a miracle. Eyes misting from thirty years of memories, she breathed a long, relieved sigh. They'd pulled it off. The usually stark, cold fellowship hall shimmered with tiny white lights and votive candles. Translucent navy fabric camouflaged the white walls, rippling from fans, set on low, behind them. White icicle lights hung around the perimeter, their light reflected in the silver stars dangling from the ceiling. Wooden silhouettes of trees covered in miniature lights lined one wall. Round tables, covered in dark blue linen and set with white china rimmed in silver, were occupied by smiling, satisfied guests.

"Anything else we can do?" Franny peeked into the kitchen, followed closely by RJ.

Winnie shook her head. "We're good until dessert. Y'all go enjoy yourselves."

Tears sprang to Janice's eyes. "You've already done so much. If you hadn't stayed..." She grabbed a napkin, not wanting anything to ruin the makeup Zelda had so expertly applied.

"Hey." RJ put his arm across Franny's shoulders. "I was looking for an excuse to ask this sweet one out again. We've got some talking to do."

Janice smiled at them. "I hope you don't usually have to hang stars from the ceiling to get a girl to pay attention to you."

Franny batted her eyelashes. "He pretty much just hangs the stars no matter where he is."

Cameron walked in, wearing a Wayfarers Inn cobbler's apron. As he set a tray of empty salad plates next to the dishwasher, Janice thanked him again for all the chopping and stirring he'd done to help produce the delectable smells that wafted through the dining room.

Cameron grinned. "Wouldn't have missed this for the world."

"Go eat your salad before they're done with the main course." Janice pointed to an empty space at a table marked with place cards printed by Brin. She followed him out and stood against the wall next to Tess. LuAnn walked over to them, and the three clasped hands in a circle.

"Thank You, Lord," Tess whispered. A simple prayer that encompassed everything.

LuAnn went to join Brad, and Tess took the seat next to Cameron. Only Noah was missing. He'd gone home this morning with a fifty-dollar gift certificate, compliments of Wayfarers Inn.

Chief Mayfield entered the basement wearing a tux, his wife on his arm. He walked over to Janice. "Sorry we're late. It's been a long day."

"Natalie?" She couldn't formulate a longer question.

"She'll be charged with tampering with power company property. Not sure how the theft charges will play out. She hadn't taken the brooch out of the building, and a sympathetic judge may take her intent into account. I'm guessing you three will be asked to testify. And you should know that Axel Barrett said he'd come to the inn that night you saw his pickup to break in, but he kept thinking of your husband and all the time he'd spent with him, and he couldn't go through with it."

Janice nodded, showed them to their seats, then stood against the wall, surveying the miracle of Marietta Moonlight. A mile away, the river had crested. Water lapped over the road in front of the inn. Six inches of water covered the basement. Thorn and Kip were busy pumping it out. It would require work, but the inn would be up and running again in no time.

Janice looked out at the filled tables.

Sam and Sammy sat close, shoulders touching. He passed her the salt, making eye contact as he did. The lines around her eyes crinkled as she took it from him. Affection radiated from both of them. The molecules in the air around them seemed to pulsate with an energy born of shared admiration.

Turning away from the doe-eyed couple, her gaze landed on Brad and LuAnn. Like the sterling silver salt shakers on every table, the two made a striking pair.

Stuart walked in, got a drink of water, and put his arm around her. "What do you think, Ma?"

She followed the laser line of his attention to the woman with the mahogany curls. "She's amazing." Janice looked up at her son. All these years of praying for twitterpation and trying to make it happen for him, and here he'd known the girl of his adventurous dreams all along. "She's perfect."

"All is well," Stuart whispered. After another squeeze of his mother's shoulders, he set the glass down and walked toward the podium. The room quieted. Stuart looked at Zelda, and Janice knew he was unaware of anyone else in the room. He held out his hand, and she joined him, guitar strap over a simple, flowing batik-print dress. She played a chord, and the two began to sing a song the band Petra had made popular back in the nineties...a song they'd sung together when they'd met for picnics in the inn Janice now called home.

"'Love is patient, love is kind...'" Their voices blended in harmony. "'No eyes of envy, true love is blind...'"

We raised a good boy, Lawrence. He's found a girl...without my help. And I think, just maybe, we're going to have a grown-up, curly-haired, very chatty granddaughter pretty soon. She tuned back in to the song.

"'Despite all wrong, true love still stands...'"

Dear Reader,

I hope you've enjoyed your time with the Inn Crowd. It was fun for me to spend time with Janice, Tess, and LuAnn again.

Looking back on this past year—from the time I started writing *Family Secrets* until I finished *Moonlit Shadows*, I can easily tear up when I think of all the ways "Love is" has played out in my life.

The research trip to Marietta I'd eagerly planned almost didn't happen. Three weeks before we were scheduled to leave, Bill, my husband, and nine other men were diagnosed with toxoplasmosis—an illness contracted from eating venison at a men's retreat. Though we were told the illness was self-limiting, it meant fatigue and occasional fevers. But my sweet man was insistent on continuing with the trip. We cancelled our camping plans and booked a hotel. Once in Ohio, he accompanied me on some excursions and, at other times, he slept while I wandered the cobblestone streets of beautiful Marietta alone. It meant so much that he was willing to be there with me, supporting my dreams. *Love is kind. It is not self-seeking.*

When my edits for *Moonlit Shadows* came back, I knew I was in for some long hours at the computer. On most days, I'd lose track of time until I'd sense I was being watched. There stood my sweet man in the doorway, not interrupting my train of thought, just waiting to ask, "What can I fix you for lunch?" *Love never fails.*

Through the writing of both of these books, I've had a group of amazing women interceding for me—and for *you*. So grateful for these faithful prayer warriors and encouragers. *Love always perseveres.*

Love always hopes...which brings me to my hope for you...that you are daily on the giving and receiving ends of all that LOVE IS.

Love is patient, love is kind. It does not envy, it does not boast, it is not proud. It does not dishonor others, it is not self-seeking, it is not easily angered, it keeps no record of wrongs. Love does not delight in evil but rejoices with the truth. It always protects, always trusts, always hopes, always perseveres.
Love never fails. —1 Corinthians 13:4-8 NIV

Love,
Becky

ABOUT THE AUTHOR

Wisconsin author Becky Melby and her husband have four married sons and fifteen grandchildren. When not writing, reading, or spoiling grandkids, Becky may be found plotting and brainstorming on the back of their Honda Gold Wing or traveling the country with their camper. Connect with Becky at: beckymelby.com or on her Facebook Author Page at: facebook.com/Becky-Melby-Author-Page-147542291976020.

Civil War Hospital Ships and POW Camps

Though the Battle of Buffington Island actually took place, the makeshift steamboat hospital on which Prudence served is fictitious. Many such boats were pressed into service during the Civil War as the Union Army used ships to move wounded soldiers from Southern battlefields to Northern hospitals.

In 1862, the privately run United States Sanitary Commission began outfitting steamboats with hospital equipment and supplies and providing surgeons to staff them at no cost to the government. By May of that year, seven ships worked on the York and James Rivers, transporting casualties from General McClellan's army of one hundred thousand men during a series of major battles.

Several women were assigned to each of these hospital transports. Many African American women—some escaped slaves—served as nursing personnel in both paid and volunteer capacities. The women took charge of the patients' comfort and welfare—feeding, dressing wounds, and ensuring that all had clean beds and clothing.

Eventually, dozens of hospital ships working on a fixed schedule were able to transport some twenty thousand wounded per month from Virginia to hospitals in New York, Missouri, Ohio, and Kentucky.

Prudence's fear of what would happen to Ira if he were sent to Camp Chase prison camp in Columbus is based on historical fact. The number of prisoners housed at Camp Chase at one time in 1863 was more than eight thousand men. Living conditions were harsh. As in any military conflict, the primary goal of Northern officials was to feed and equip the men serving in their own army. This left little food and medical supplies for prisoners. The large number of men in close quarters also led to outbreaks of disease. During the winter of 1863–1864, hundreds of prisoners died in a smallpox epidemic. In November 1864, Union and Confederate authorities agreed upon a prisoner exchange hoping to alleviate the suffering of sick prisoners held by both sides. A total of ten thousand prisoners were exchanged.

During the course of the Civil War, more than two thousand Confederate prisoners died at Camp Chase.

SOMETHING DELICIOUS FROM OUR WAYFARERS INN FRIENDS

Winnie's Stakeout Cookies
(Old-Fashioned Southern Tea Cakes)

Ingredients:

¼ cup unsalted butter, room temperature

¼ cup butter-flavored shortening

1 cup granulated sugar

1 egg, room temperature

lemon zest (1 small lemon)

½ vanilla bean, scraped

2 cups flour

2 teaspoons baking powder

½ teaspoon salt

¼ teaspoon nutmeg

¼ cup buttermilk

Instructions:

In a large bowl, cream together butter and shortening. Mix in sugar until well combined.

Mix in egg. Mix in lemon zest and vanilla bean paste. Set aside.

In medium bowl, sift together flour, baking powder, salt, and nutmeg. Mix dry ingredients into wet ingredients, alternating with the buttermilk. Turn dough onto a smooth surface and knead until dough is soft. Shape into a disk and cover with plastic wrap. Refrigerate for 1 hour (or freeze for 30 minutes).

Preheat oven to 350 degrees Fahrenheit. Line a large baking sheet with parchment paper. Set aside.

Remove dough from fridge and plastic wrap. Knead dough to soften it. Roll dough to ¼-inch thick. (Winnie rolls them on parchment paper to prevent sticking.) Use a round cookie cutter to cut out circle shapes.

Place cookies on prepared pan about 2 inches apart. (Dough should be cold when put in oven. Refrigerate again if necessary.) Bake for 8-10 minutes until bottoms are lightly golden. (Do not overbake! They will not get golden on the tops and will continue to cook as they cool.) Remove from pan and place on cooling rack to finish cooling. Once cooled, store in airtight container.

Read on for a sneak peek of another exciting book
in the Secrets of Wayfarers Inn series!

PICTURE THIS
by Kathleen Y'Barbo

*Fear and loss walk hand-in-hand down a path that leads to a
place of reckoning. Someday the Lord will have us give explanation for what we held so tightly to ourselves. For some, the things
of this world are what we do not hasten to give up. Others hold
these same things loosely with an open palm and yet still do not
trust God completely. It is that group to which I too often belong.
What cannot be taken from me is what I must seek. And yet
there is fear. Always that small worrisome thought that harm
will come to those I love. For the devil can harm me in any way
he likes, but when he thinks to come for my husband and son,
that is another matter entirely. And that is where fear and loss,
and the fear of loss, hold me captive.*

—*from Prudence's diary*
June 1, 1860

May 1, 1860

Prudence and Jason Willard strolled down the path that ran alongside the Muskingum River toward Marietta with little Moses toddling along between them. At nearly one year of age, the child was already sturdy and well-built as a boy nearly twice his age, and he had been walking for more than a month.

Moses also favored his papa in determination. Today that trait showed itself in his demand to be allowed to walk rather than be carried. Each time Prudence hauled him into her arms, he wiggled out.

"Walk," he had learned to say almost as easily as he had learned the word *no*. At first she had encouraged the little one's independence. Today, she wished perhaps she had not.

Not a day went by that Prudence did not wonder why the Lord gave her such a willful child. Of course, the thought was always quickly followed by another: because he is far too much like his mama.

Thus they were making slow progress down a path that offered more dangers than tripping over a root or stepping into soft ground. For much as Prudence worried about those things in light of her husband's injured leg, she also worried about what went on in the slave state of Virginia just across the river.

There had been talk of war for far too long for it to pass as rumor. Prudence cast a glance across the river and marveled once again at the land so like the place where she stood and yet so unlike it. Here she was free. There she would not be.

At the sound of something rumbling, Prudence stopped to reach for Moses. Of course he made a fuss, but this time she ignored him.

"The child is too big for thee to carry him on such an uneven path," Jason protested as Prudence lifted their son onto her hip. "Best I do it."

Indeed her husband spoke the truth, but she knew quite well that Jason's injuries would pain him even more were he to be the one to carry Moses. "Truly he is not a burden," she responded as she inclined her head to place a kiss on the boy's chubby cheek. "Does thee hear that?"

Jason paused to lift his ear toward the sky. "I do, and it appears to be coming from the north, or perhaps just east of due north." He shook his head. "A curious sound, it is."

The rumbling got louder, and a strange whistling sound now accompanied the noise. "What is it, Husband?" she whispered.

He nodded toward the sky, seemingly unable to speak. "There," he finally managed.

Prudence followed the direction of his wide-eyed stare to look up at the deep blue spring sky. A fast-moving object streaked across the northern horizon leaving a trail of fire and wisps of white in its wake.

The ground shook beneath their feet, and Moses began to whimper. She reached for Jason with her free hand. "Has war finally come?"

The café area of the inn was a favorite gathering spot for many in the town of Marietta, Ohio, but especially for LuAnn Sherrill, Tess Wallace, and Janice Eastman. The trio were retired teachers, best friends, and the owners of the beautifully restored historic Wayfarers Inn. With its homey ambiance, its wide variety of yummy soups as well as teas and coffees, it was a natural gathering place for those who enjoyed a delicious lunch, a relaxing atmosphere, and views of the river.

Today two of the three innkeepers were enjoying coffee after lunch and discussing an idea that had been in the making for a while: their very first Marietta First Friday event. While First Friday had become a tradition in Marietta, this was the first time the inn had been included in the monthly celebration of food, family fun, and the arts. All along the downtown streets, shop owners would be throwing open their doors after hours to offer their wares as well as to showcase art or food that would be added for the occasion.

LuAnn turned the page in her notebook to review her checklist. As the one who provided organization and her own dash of perfection in everything she did at the inn, she had been tasked with preparing for tonight's festivities. There were lists, spreadsheets, and a lengthy file on her computer dedicated to the event.

Still she felt there were details that had escaped her. But then LuAnn often felt that way—thus the notebook and the checklists that kept her on track.

"It's our debut. Everything must be perfect," she told Tess.

Tess nudged her and offered a grin. "With you in charge, it's guaranteed. Besides, it's just barely past lunchtime. You have hours to go yet."

"Nothing is guaranteed," LuAnn said as she suppressed a shudder. "Especially since Grant keeps changing his mind about which photographs he wants to let us hang for the event. Doesn't he realize that one change affects everything else?"

At Brad Grimes's insistence, LuAnn had examined his younger brother Grant's collection of photographs and deemed them absolutely amazing. Since the event combined food and art, showcasing Grant's photos was the perfect choice. Now the photos hung all around the first floor of the inn awaiting purchase by First Friday shoppers.

Tess grinned. "He has turned out to be as much of a perfectionist as you are."

"I'm not so much a perfectionist as just someone who likes things a certain way." Even as she said the words, LuAnn knew how silly her protest must sound, so she added a smile. "Okay maybe I do have a teeny tiny problem, but I'm working on it."

"No you're not, but that's okay." Tess laughed and reached across the table to pat LuAnn's arm. "I wouldn't have you change a thing, my friend. Thanks to you the inn is running like clockwork and looks absolutely gorgeous."

"It does look gorgeous, doesn't it?" LuAnn allowed her eyes to travel around the room as she took note of every detail.

Each table in the café had been decorated with small photographs in silver frames marked with discreet price stickers on the back, while the larger pieces had been hung on the walls in the parlor and along the stairwell that led to the second floor. Each beautiful work of art hanging in the inn had a small card with the photographer's name on it, as well as the price.

LuAnn straightened the card on the table in front of her. The photograph on this table was a shot of the inn taken a few weeks after its grand opening. Captured at sunset, the golden colors of the sky highlighted the old building and provided for a beautiful scene.

"He really has a great eye, doesn't he?"

"He's brilliant," Tess said. "But then I knew that after he did that set of portraits of the triplets. He even managed to get Henry to smile. The man is a genius."

LuAnn glanced down at her watch, and her heart lurched. "It absolutely cannot be half past one." She stood and checked the time on the clock behind the desk. Indeed, that was the time.

"We did start lunch late," Tess said as she rose and picked up their coffee mugs. "I'll take care of these. You go do whatever you need to do."

Tess wandered toward the kitchen, passing the reception desk on her way. There, a pair of black-and-white images of the river from last year's Sternwheel Festival competed with an enlarged portrait of the trio of retired teachers and best friends who comprised the Inn Crowd, seated on the tailgate of her son's antique red pickup truck.

Taken just before last year's Marietta Fourth of July parade, the photo showed Janice smiling from the center with LuAnn and Tess on either side. The quilt that was currently draped over the inn's second floor railing added color to the scene. In Janice's lap was a sign indicating the names of the owners of the inn.

Robin, their employee who not only helped in the kitchen but also assisted in running the inn, popped out of the office to offer a smile. "That one is my favorite," she said.

"That was a very good day." Tess said as LuAnn walked up to join them. "Hot as blazes, even for the Fourth of July parade, but a good day all the same. Except for the part where the FBI showed up," she added with a shrug.

"I don't think I've heard this story," Robin said. "Why would the FBI show up at the inn?"

"Oh, you know," Tess said with a wave of her hand. "These things happen. Suffice it to say that it all worked out just fine in the end." She caught LuAnn's eye. "Just like this will. All is well. Stop worrying, Lu."

"I'm not worrying," LuAnn insisted as she hurried to straighten a frame that seemed to be tilting too far to the right. "Although I wish it was a little warmer today. Wouldn't it be nice to direct some of our visitors out to the patio under the stars? We could put candles on each table and offer mugs of coffee and hot chocolate."

Tess shook her head. "We can still do that. Just not in March, my friend."

LuAnn smiled. "Well, true. Unless we decide not to, we should still be participating in First Fridays once the weather is warm. Oh, I have such great plans for that area of the inn. Still,

I worry about getting the flow just right. I mean, it is so lovely here in the inn, and just as lovely out back but—"

"What is LuAnn worrying about now?" Janice called from the second floor as she walked down the stairs toward them. "Did the caterer cancel again?"

LuAnn froze. "What do you mean, *again?*" She lifted her gaze toward Janice. "Did the caterer cancel? I certainly heard nothing about this."

She studied Tess's neutral expression and then turned to look up at Janice. Surely she was teasing. Still, with Winnie out of town for the weekend and every guest room in the inn filled, having a last-minute cancellation of the delicious snacks she had planned to serve would mean certain disaster.

They were already in unfamiliar territory without their beloved Winnie manning the vintage stove they called Big Red and churning out her fabulous foods. Still, Janice had done a fabulous job of mustering the troops from her years teaching domestic arts.

With her supervising and Robin acting as Janice's second-in-command, their team was turning out lunchtime soups for the café that were every bit as delicious as Winnie's. Of course, none of them would dare admit that to their intrepid chef when she returned.

LuAnn gave thanks once again for Winnie's determination to make two types of desserts and put them in the freezer in anticipation of tonight's event. Their cook had also made loaves of her fabulous sourdough bread to go along with the spreads Janice's team had made. With the dough rising in the kitchen, LuAnn had high hopes of convincing guests tonight that the amazing Winnie was still in the kitchen cooking, despite the fact they were using a caterer for the remainder of the food.

And speaking of caterers...

LuAnn returned her attention to Tess. "Please tell me you are just having a little fun with me. Not that it's fun, mind you, because there are a lot of last-minute details that still need to be handled. Please tell me the caterer is not one of them."

Robin slipped past them to reach for the mugs in Tess's hand. "I'll just go wash these and check to see how well the bread is rising," she said as she hurried to disappear into the kitchen.

Once Robin was gone, Tess rested her palms on LuAnn's shoulders and offered a comforting look. "Lu," she said gently, "everything is fine. Just relax."

"Tess," LuAnn said as she let out a long breath. "This is me. Since when have you known me to relax when we are facing something of this magnitude? This is our very first time to participate in First Friday."

"So you have said."

"It has to be—"

"Perfect." Tess rolled her eyes. "Yes, I know. The food is fine. No one will know that Winnie prepared the appetizers ahead of time, and the rest of the food will be just as good. Trust in your team, Lu. They know what to do. The evening will be fine."

"I know, but still. I wish Winnie was here. Then we wouldn't have to depend on a caterer."

"Well, she isn't, and that can't be helped. She'll be here next time, and you can plan something wonderful that can be eaten out on the new patio. It will be great. In the meantime...oh!" Tess nodded toward the window. "See, look there. The food truck is parked right out front. I'm sure they're just checking to be sure they have the correct address." Tess dropped her hands. "I'll just go say hello."

"Hold on," LuAnn said as Tess hurried toward the inn's front door. "I don't remember anything about a food truck."

Janice slipped her arm around LuAnn's waist and offered a hug. "It's fine. The first caterer had a previous engagement. He recommended the food truck. We called, and there it is right out front. Not only are they early, but Yelp also says their lettuce cups are the best in town." She shrugged. "So it's fine."

Yelp? Since when did Janice know about Yelp?

What in the world was a lettuce cup?

And why in the world hadn't anyone thought to tell her about something as important as a change in catering? Just one thing wrong with the food, and the entire evening could be ruined.

LuAnn released the breath she hadn't realized she'd been holding. Hadn't she read in her new Bible study *Praise Before Panic* just that morning about having faith? About allowing God to have His way with her, including letting Him have control of her worries and her lists?

It was so like her to give Him advice and let Him know what worked best for each situation. However, she was learning. "Pause and praise before panic," she whispered as she took hold of this morning's fresh teaching. "Pause and praise before panic."

The reason she hadn't been told was becoming unfortunately obvious. Had she known, she would have panicked. But not today. Not the new LuAnn. She allowed a smile.

"Yes," she said calmly as she opened her notebook and put a check beside the notation regarding food for this evening. "Thank You, Lord. It is fine. Perfectly fine. A food truck with excellent lettuce cups, it is."

The sound of tires squealing caused her to jump. Her pen clattered to the floor. A moment later Tess walked back in. "Well that was odd."

A Note from the Editors

We hope you enjoy Secrets of Wayfarers Inn, created by the Books and Inspirational Media Division of Guideposts, a nonprofit organization that touches millions of lives every day through products and services that inspire, encourage, help you grow in your faith, and celebrate God's love in every aspect of your daily life.

Thank you for making a difference with your purchase of this book, which helps fund our many outreach programs to military personnel, prisons, hospitals, nursing homes, and educational institutions. To learn more, visit Guideposts Foundation.org.

We also maintain many useful and uplifting online resources. Visit Guideposts.org to read true stories of hope and inspiration, access OurPrayer network, sign up for free newsletters, download free e-books, join our Facebook community, and follow our stimulating blogs.

To learn about other Guideposts publications, including the best-selling devotional *Daily Guideposts*, go to ShopGuideposts .org, call (800) 932-2145, or write to Guideposts, PO Box 5815, Harlan, Iowa 51593.

Sign up for the
Guideposts Fiction Newsletter
and stay up-to-date on
the books you love!

You'll get sneak peeks of new releases, recommendations from
other Guideposts readers, and special offers just for you . . .
and it's FREE!

Just go to Guideposts.org/Newsletters
today to sign up.

Guideposts®   Visit Guideposts.org/Shop
or call (800) 932-2145

Find more inspiring fiction in these best-loved Guideposts series!

Tearoom Mysteries Series
Mix one stately Victorian home, a charming lakeside town in Maine, and two adventurous cousins with a passion for tea and hospitality. Add a large scoop of intriguing mystery and sprinkle generously with faith, family, and friends, and you have the recipe for *Tearoom Mysteries*.

Sugarcreek Amish Mysteries
Be intrigued by the suspense and joyful "aha" moments in these delightful stories. Each book in the series brings together two women of vastly different backgrounds and traditions, who realize there's much more to the "simple life" than meets the eye.

Mysteries of Martha's Vineyard
What does Priscilla Latham Grant, a Kansas farm girl know about hidden treasure and rising tides, maritime history and local isle lore? Not much—but to save her lighthouse and family reputation, she better learn quickly!

Mysteries of Silver Peak
Escape to the historic mining town of Silver Peak, Colorado, and discover how one woman's love of antiques helps her solve mysteries buried deep in the town's checkered past.

To learn more about these books, visit Guideposts.org/Shop